Palo Alto City Library

The individual borrower is responsible for all library material borrowed on his or her card.

Charges as determined by the CITY OF PALO ALTO will be assessed for each overdue item.

Damaged or non-returned property will be billed to the individual borrower by the CITY OF PALO ALTO.

P.O. Box 10250, Palo Alto, CA 94303

A Dying Art

A Dying Art

Nageeba Davis

BERKLEY PRIME CRIME, NEW YORK

To Paul, my best friend.

A DYING ART

A Berkley Prime Crime Book
Published by The Berkley Publishing Group,
a division of Penguin Putnam Inc.,
375 Hudson Street, New York, New York 10014.

The Penguin Putnam Inc. World Wide Web site address is
www.penguinputnam.com

First edition: July 2001

Library of Congress Cataloging-in-Publication Data

Davis, Nageeba.
 A dying art / Nageeba Davis.
  p.   cm.
 ISBN 0-425-17951-6 (alk. paper)
 I. Title.
PS3554.A93744   D9   2001
813'.6—dc21   00-048580

PRINTED IN THE UNITED STATES OF AMERICA

10   9   8   7   6   5   4   3   2   1

Chapter One

I t was one rotten day.
I'm talking beyond rotten. It started out badly and sped rapidly downhill. I burned my toast twice in the chipped enamel toaster with the broken pop-up. I tripped over the base of the six-foot halogen lamp and stubbed my toe on the back of the couch, the same toe that was already missing a nail. Out of ten toes, what are the odds? And that was before eight o'clock. A.M., that is. I didn't care if the sky was blue and the birds were singing. The way my life was going, I fully expected to run out of deodorant, find a hole in the seat of my shorts, back my bald tires over a rusty nail, and plow into someone's fender while using the rearview mirror to put on my mascara. But I didn't expect to find a dead person.

Who does?

Who would think a quick visit to the toilet could set off a whole slew of incidents that would eventually lead me right here, wilting on my front porch step and staring up into a pair of flaring nostrils?

"What made you decide to check the septic tank?" This was Mr. Nostrils talking.

"I've told you already. I told your partner and I told that guy over there." I pointed to the man with the shaggy mane of hair standing with a group of policemen huddled in the middle of my yard.

"Bear with me, Mrs. . . ." He thumbed through the papers on his clipboard.

"Kean. Maggie Kean," I repeated for the umpteenth time that morning.

"Uh, yes, that's right."

Thanks, buddy, glad you believed me."

"Mrs. Kean, I'm—"

"It's Ms."

"Huh?"

"It's *Ms*. Kean." I'm not usually a stickler for all that feminist protocol stuff, but when some guy starts throwing his weight around, it's nice to toss in a little political correctness, just to be a royal pain. All that deference to the right word irritates every man I've ever met, every man except those sensitive types who already dance on the edge of Milquetoast and order tapioca for dessert. I'd gone over this story so many times I wanted to strangle this fat, bumbling idiot who was sucking up all the oxygen within a five-mile radius through nasal passages the size of sewer pipes.

"Ms. Kean," Vacuum Nose repeated, patiently exaggerating the *Ms.,* "I'm just trying to make sure I have all the facts. Anything you remember, even the smallest detail, something that may seem insignificant now can make or break a case."

I took a deep breath, counted to ten, and let it out slowly. I wasn't trying to be uncooperative, not intentionally at least, but how many times could I say that I didn't know anything? Putting a hand up to shield my eyes from the sun, I looked around my patch of yard now covered in blue uniforms, badges, yellow tape, and an ambulance, its red emergency light still flashing. I felt frustrated; like a fresh deli sandwich left open on a picnic blanket, I was defenseless against the swarm of red ants circling past the potato salad and heading my way. There wasn't a thing I could do.

"There aren't any other details, Officer . . ." I said, squinting to read his name tag. I'd like to blame the sun for my squinting, but the truth is, I'm blind without my glasses. "Mailer."

"I'm sure it seems like you covered everything, Ms. Kean, but I'd like to go over your story one more time just to make sure I have it all down." He touched my arm gently. "Look, why don't you sit back and try to relax a little. Then just start from the beginning."

Okay, I know the guy appeared to be solicitous and he sounded nauseatingly sincere, but I wasn't buying his act. I mean, I wasn't exactly a novice at this sort of thing. Not that I see dead people or decomposing body parts on a daily basis, but I do like a good mystery and I grew up watching reruns of *Columbo* and *Perry Mason*. The bumbling, overly concerned, "you can trust me" expression is just a well-honed disguise cops use to break down a witness's defenses, and I wasn't about to fall for that old trick. These guys ask you the same questions over and over, looking for holes or discrepancies in your story. Then they scratch their heads, rub their five o'clock shadows, and shuffle away, leaving you with sweaty palms and dripping armpits. And just when you start to breathe a little easier, they turn back, point a long bony finger at your chest, and single out the small misstep that lands your butt in jail. For life. That's assuming you're guilty, of course.

"Why don't you read me your notes and I'll stop you if I remember anything new," I suggested helpfully.

"Ms. Kean, I realize this is unpleasant, but . . ."

This was more than unpleasant, Vacuum Nose.

"And I'm sure this has been a frightening experience for you."

No kidding, Einstein.

"But I have to follow police procedures. If you could try and help me a little here, this will be over before you know it. Let's start with why you decided to get your septic tank pumped today."

I shrugged. "I heard there were a lot of attractive eligible men on the service crew and I thought I might be able to scare up a date for Saturday night." Okay, I admit to being a little obnoxious when I've been scared out of my wits. Officer Mailer started to snort and grunt like a bull facing a cocky matador. Evidently he didn't like my answer. I leaned back on the palms of my hands, trying to put as much distance as I could between the two of us, seriously contemplating the chances of a quick getaway.

"I'll take it from here, Tom." Officer Mailer stiffened at the deep voice and reluctantly turned away, but not before boring two nasty holes in me with his beady little eyes. So much for the concerned approach.

"I take it you're pretty shook up."

The voice belonged to the shaggy-haired guy, the only one who wasn't wearing a uniform. He stood in front of me, placing one cowboy boot on the bottom step, a black shadow swooping in like a modern-day Zorro.

"Not really. What's a body or two floating around in a septic tank?"

Zorro chuckled. "Tell me, are you always this difficult?"

"You caught me on a good day."

He leaned forward. "Look, I know this isn't easy, but we've got a dead body on our hands. A particularly gruesome murder, to be exact. The faster we get some information, the faster we can clear out of here and let you get back to normal. But in the meantime, we need your cooperation."

I gave him what I hoped was a good bland poker face.

He sighed. Waving me over with his hand, he sat down next to me on the porch step, rubbed his palms over his face, and dragged his fingers through his unruly mop of hair, a mop of wavy hair that was simply too sinful to waste on a guy. Especially a cop.

"I know this is the last thing you want to hear, but you'll have to tell the story again . . . and probably again after that. Do it now and everything will be a lot easier for all of us." Coffee and cigarette smells clung to him. "Otherwise, I'm going to have to drag you down to the station, where people aren't quite as friendly."

"Is this where we play good cop/bad cop?"

He gave me a grim smile. "Honey, this is as good as it gets. I'm being a real sweetheart right now. Much more of this and we're going to play 'Lock the Bad Lady Up.' *Capisce?*"

"Oh, God, you're Italian."

He lifted his left eyebrow until it disappeared under

a lock of hair that had fallen over his forehead. Okay, so I was fixated on the man's hair.

"You've got a problem with that?"

"Not a problem exactly. My ex-husband is Italian and I just believe that one Italian in your life is more than the average Joe should have to put up with." I tossed my head in a casual gesture of indifference. "But then again, there isn't much you can do about your heritage. You're pretty much stuck with what you get."

"You make it sound like a curse."

"More like a disability . . . a handicap that keeps you from functioning like a normal person."

The edges of his mouth twitched. "A normal person like you, I assume?"

I shrugged. "Not to brag, but that would be a big step forward for you, or any Italian, actually."

The twitch turned into a full-blown grin. And it was a humdinger. This guy with the unknown name had full lips and straight, sparkling teeth.

"Did your husband—"

"*Ex*-husband."

"Sorry. Your *ex*-husband. Did he ever mention your lousy habit of changing the subject?"

"Maybe once or twice."

Zorro shook his head. "I've got to congratulate you, lady. You've got a great way of scooting under, around, and over a subject."

"Thanks."

"But as much as I've enjoyed this little chat, my patience is running a bit thin here." He stared straight into my eyes, no blinking. "What you saw frightened you badly, more than badly. Believe me, I understand that. But unfortunately, I don't have time to baby-sit you while your nerves rattle around inside. Do us both a favor. Start the story and finish the story in one straight line with no detours."

Fine. I was no idiot. This guy was getting irritated and I knew all about Italian tempers from personal experience. Besides, he did have a crime to solve and apparently I was the biggest clue they had at this point. Leaning forward, I wrapped my arms around my knees and started rocking a bit. My Italian inquisitor probably thought I was more than a little wacko, but at that point I didn't much care.

"There isn't much to add to what I've already said. My toilet had been acting up—"

"When did this happen?"

I turned to him. "You really want to hear everything?"

"Every last gory detail."

"Yesterday morning. It started yesterday morning when I woke up and went to use the bathroom. I noticed that the toilet was bubbling a little and wouldn't flush very well. It didn't surprise me because I'd been hearing sounds lately, gurgling sounds in the bathroom pipes . . . you know, the shower, the faucet, so I already knew there were problems. Anyway, I tried using the plunger, but that didn't do anything, so I poured a bunch of Drano down the toilet. I guess it was too much to ask that it would work miracles, like it does in the commercials." I dropped my chin onto my knees and stared out into the yard. "But I guess the problem turned out to be much bigger than a pipe clogged with hair."

"So you called Waste Management."

I nodded. "Yeah. He got here late yesterday afternoon."

"Who got here?"

I pointed to the man standing next to the juniper bushes talking to a cop. "That guy over there wearing the green-and-white-striped uniform with *Waste Management, Inc.* written in bold letters on the back of his shirt." A nail that hadn't been hammered all the way into the step was gouging a hole in the back of my thigh and I shifted my bottom a couple of inches to ease the pressure. "If that was your idea of a tough question, then I've got a feeling this case will be showing up on television one day on *Unsolved Mysteries.*"

He ignored my sarcasm and went on. "Did he have a partner or did he come alone?"

"Alone, as far as I know."

"What happened next?"

"Not much. I took him upstairs, showed him the bathroom. He tinkered around a little and then asked me to show him where the septic tank was buried. So I did."

He noticed my hesitation. "It's better if you just say it all at once."

Maybe he was right. Surely he had more experience with dead people than I did.

"Then the guy, the one in the striped shirt, dug a hole about a foot down or so until he hit concrete. Then he widened the hole until he could lift the entire lid off the tank. Afterward, he stuck this long accordionlike tubing down into the tank. It looked like the stuff that's used on the back of a gas clothes dryer." I took a deep breath and pushed on. "Then he flipped a switch on. And nothing happened."

"Nothing?"

"Nope. Something wasn't working. I don't know what it was, but he had to switch trucks. He said he'd come back tomorrow, which was today, with a new truck or motor or whatever and pump it out for me. So he put the lid back. He came back early this morning, stuck the tubing into the tank again, and started up the pump."

I shuddered. Suddenly, without warning, everything came rushing back. Horrible pictures flooded my brain. I could see the dark head gently drifting in the putrid cesspool like a buoy in the ocean, but with less bounce. The face, bloated and puffy, was a deep blue color, almost purple. The skin was papery thin and wrinkled, the way it gets after an hour in a hot bath. And the features were distorted. Distorted but not unrecognizable, because there was no doubt in my mind who it was. It was my neighbor. The very esteemed, the very grand, and the extremely wealthy Mrs. Elizabeth Boyer was floating in my sewage.

There was no way to miss that hair of hers, tied up in its usual tight bun, tight enough to stay put even if someone comes along and drowns you. It's the kind of thing Elizabeth wouldn't overlook. Surely she didn't expect to be tossed into a tank full of unspeakable debris, but it was just that sort of surprise event she insisted on being prepared for. A few strands had escaped the rubber band and the scarf tied around her head like a turban, a limp knot secured on the left side in what was originally a bow, but otherwise, her hair had held up pretty well under a spur-of-the-moment murder.

I recognized more than her hair. She was on her back, drifting along as though she was waiting for someone to open the lid and let the sunshine in. The eyebrows were still arched and the nose still small and petite. Her chin, the one she pointed in the air whenever she marched across the lawn separating our two houses to briskly register her opinion on something I had or had not done, still jutted out like the true patrician she was. Or used to be.

"Is that when you saw the body?"

I shook my head. "No. I was standing away from the truck a few feet. I've got a slight germ phobia and I really wasn't anxious to get too close. Besides, the smell was enough to knock you off your feet." Poor Elizabeth. Someone really *had* swept her off her feet. Oh, God. Bad jokes bubbled up at a furious pace and I was helpless to stop them. I bit my tongue and clenched my teeth to keep them from spilling out. I was pretty certain cops frowned on morbid humor at the scene of a crime, especially from the main witness.

"Go on."

I got myself under control and continued. "I just stood there watching the machine sucking stuff out of the tank, like a giant motorized turkey baster. It went on for a little while until I heard this big *whomp!* and everything seemed to stop. The sucking went dead, except for this kind of muffled whine, and it was obvious that something wasn't working right. I just figured it was the same problem he had yesterday. But the guy tugged on the hose a little like he was trying to jar something loose, and when that didn't seem to work, he reeled the hose into the side of the tank while he squatted down and looked into the hole. Then he jerked back and fell on his butt like a rattlesnake had bitten him. I started to ask what was wrong, but he dropped the hose, crawled over to my flower garden, and heaved up his guts."

"What did you do?"

"I didn't know what to do. Something gross was obviously in the tank and I wasn't in a big hurry to see what it was. But while that guy was over there on his knees losing his lunch, I guess my natural curiosity overcame my aversion to raw sewage." I held up my hands in a classic gesture of defeat. "I can't explain why I did it. It's like when you're a kid and someone pukes in class and you start yelling, 'That's disgusting!' but at the same time you're racing over to get a good look at the mess." Zorro didn't look too surprised. I guess nothing surprises cops.

"Anyway, I held my nose and walked over to the hole and sort of leaned over the edge, and there was Elizabeth looking straight at me, at least it seemed that way with that tubing stuck to her cheek." I tugged at the hem of my shorts. "So I ran to the phone and called the police, and Officer Mailer arrived with a whole battalion of cars, with you included . . . who are you anyway?"

"Sam Villari."

"What's your job?"

"Homicide detective."

"Well, Detective Villari, I've told you the story from start to finish, just like you requested. No detours or side trips, just like a good little witness. Now I'd like to leave."

He held up his hand to stop me. "There are a couple more questions I'd like to ask before I let you go." Villari cleared his throat. "Can you positively identify the body as Mrs. Boyer?"

"It's definitely her. Believe me, I'd know that chin anywhere."

"Sounds like you had trouble with her."

"And you sound like a bad imitation of a psychiatrist stating the obvious," I replied, restless with this whole procedure. I was tired of answering questions as though I was a suspect. It wasn't my fault I had plumbing problems, although admittedly, they were bigger ones than I had originally suspected. "Not really. She was just your average, everyday meddling neighbor."

"That bad, huh?"

I looked over to see if he was commiserating or pumping me for information. Unfortunately, his face didn't give anything away. I shook my head. "Elizabeth was a hybrid . . . a cross between Joan Collins and Aunt Bea. She could dissect, critique, and rearrange my life while she poured me coffee and patted my hand." Oh, God, I could feel the rush of tears bottling up behind my eyes while my nose started to run. I hate any kind of womanly emotion like the sudden spurt of tears that threatened to burst forth, especially when I was doing my damnedest to buck up and maintain control. My revulsion for tears probably springs from my upbringing. My brother, Andy, couldn't stand to see any woman cry, and when we were growing up he'd haul off and punch me if my eyes even started to mist. He thought it was unmanly to cry, and since I was the nearest thing he had to a brother, he expected me to feel the same way.

Villari gently touched my hand. "You really cared about her, didn't you?"

I pinched the bridge of my nose in a vain attempt to stop sniffling. "She was lonely . . . probably like a lot of older people. Her husband died ten or fifteen years ago," I said, waving in the general direction of her house, which was mostly obscured by the pine trees and scrub oak that covered the property, "and obviously left her a boatload of money. Apparently it didn't change her disposition too much because she was always popping in over here to boss me around or complain about one thing or another. But mostly, she was interested in my art-work."

"Your artwork?"

"Yeah, I sculpt."

"You sculpt?"

"Why are you repeating everything I say?"

"Sorry. I haven't run into too many artists. I guess I expected more of a bohemian sort of look. You know, lots of color, flowing scarves, that sort of thing." Villari looked embarrassed. "Maybe a knitted hat or a pair of leather sandals," he added lamely.

"And I don't quite match the image?" It was amusing to watch this big hunk of a man squirm, although I could understand how he felt. Wearing my usual outfit of baggy shorts and oversized T-shirt, I looked more like a scruffy tomboy than anything else, a look I'd fought on and off for years. At different times in my life, I took a stab at being, or at least looking more, well, *womanly*. First, I tried to develop a more sophisticated image, thinking it would start to feel right if I let it hang there long enough. But during this more mature, more adult period, my blouses caved in where they were supposed to expand and my feet hurt like hell in stilettos, so I returned to sneakers before I ended up toppling down a flight of stairs and breaking an ankle.

But I refused to give up. If I couldn't do sophisti-cated, I would try for Zen-like composure. Searching for a calm, tranquil demeanor, I waded through a slew of philosophy books, meditating and chanting mantras so often I sounded like a hive of worker bees. Then one morning, a white-haired old lady, barely tall enough to see over the dashboard of the boat-size Cadillac she was driving, cut me off in the fast lane of the freeway going forty-five miles per hour. I tossed serenity out the window and flattened it with my back tires. Road rage stops for no one.

And still I persevered. Reaching for the provocative image, I exposed a little cleavage, a little thigh, and developed a lash-batting coyness to rein in the opposite sex. That lasted even less time than the tranquil phase. I didn't have enough cleavage to push in, up, or out, and my legs were too hairy, despite the new razor my stepmother dropped in my Christmas stocking every year. Besides, there's only so much cuteness I can stand before the need to retch threatens to empty my stomach.

So I'm stuck with me, a very average five-foot-five with a mess of curly brown hair that looks like a swimsuit cap with wire springs glued on top. My chest is fair to flat and my legs are lean enough but could definitely use a shave on a more regular basis, something more consistent than my hit-or-miss regimen, and some lotion action. Everyone says my eyes, green, are my best feature, which is lucky for me because I don't do anything more than swipe on a little mascara to spruce them up. My nose is pretty nondescript. It's not cute or perky or turned up or down, it's not big or small or hooked or anything more than functional. All in all, I possess enough looks to keep a man from gagging, and if I'm lucky, catch a date now and then.

"I didn't mean that in a bad way."

Yeah, sure. "Look, it's no problem. It isn't my real job. I mean I don't support myself by sculpting, at least not yet, although it's always been a dream of mine. In real life, I'm a teacher."

He lifted his brow skeptically.

"It's true. I teach art at the elementary school down the road." I held up my hand to stop him from sticking his foot in his mouth a second time. "I know, I know. I don't look like a teacher either. The only thing I do look like is a third baseman on a weekend softball team—a position I do play, by the way—with extraordinarily bad taste in clothes."

A small, slightly lopsided grin hovered over Villari's lips, vanishing quickly as he remembered why he was sitting next to me in the first place.

"I got the impression that Elizabeth thought I was . . ." I hesitated.

"Was what?"

"Talented." I could feel the heat burn my cheeks. Despite the way my big mouth shoots off now and then, I'm actually pretty modest when it comes to talking about my sculpture. The truth is, sometimes I can't shake the feeling that I'm only kidding myself, that one day I'll wake up and find I'm just goofing around with a chunk of clay.

"Not to be rude, but why would that matter to her?"

I had asked myself the same question a million times. "She never really told me for sure."

"But you have an idea."

I nodded. "I got the feeling that she wanted to support me somehow. Maybe it was my imagination, or"—I looked at Villari—"or my deepest hope, but she was awfully critical of my work and kept pushing and prodding me to change this or that. She seemed to take it very seriously. And when something was done to her satisfaction, she acted proud, like it was her work, too."

Villari seemed to be deep in thought. "Did you ever meet any members of her family?"

"You mean those 'two spoiled brats that aren't smart enough to spell *Boyer* and don't have enough backbone to carry the name'?"

"I suppose those were her words?"

"Yep. She thought the two grandkids were useless."

"What do you think?"

"Cassandra is practically a stranger to me. She doesn't spend much time being neighborly. Aside from watching her zip in and out of her grandmother's driveway in her little red BMW, I hardly see her."

"And her brother?"

"He's a jerk. It was the one thing Elizabeth and I agreed on."

"Why's that?"

"Find out for yourself. He's marching his skinny little ass over here right now."

Chapter Two

William Boyer was one of those guys who just begged to be made fun of, and I've no doubt his school years were a nightmare. Despite my feelings, which ranged from extreme dislike to total revulsion, I felt little twinges of sadness for his life growing up. I could see him as a little boy, his pasty white face staring arrogantly from behind black horn-rimmed glasses, his spindly body stiffly encased in a perfectly starched white shirt and pressed pleated pants. It wasn't just the way he looked that made you want to flatten his sharp little nose, it was his attitude—his superior, patronizing demeanor—that would attract bullies like maggots to rotted meat. He was so obnoxious I'm sure he garnered very little sympathy, despite having lost both parents in a grisly automobile accident, a head-on collision with a drunk driver one New Year's Eve.

I never knew him as a child, but I doubt he had changed much over the years. Although Elizabeth Boyer seldom talked of her grandson, she had dropped little bits of information over the years, even if the information was delivered tonelessly, with little warmth or affection. Apparently he was a loner and had very few friends, none of whom she ever named. I'm not sure she could have named them if she'd wanted to. He seemed to live life on the sidelines while sneering at those getting dirty in the middle of the game. Elizabeth, insisting I use her first name, called William her greatest failure.

"I don't know," she mused aloud one day while staring out my studio window, "whether William was always so distant or whether it was just the trauma of losing his mother and father at the same time. Somehow he associates me with their death and sometimes I believe he hates me, as though I killed his parents." She shuddered, wrapping her arms around herself. "It was a horrible time, one that I try to push into the back of my mind as much as possible. But then, it never goes away, does it?"

I laid my sketchpad down on my lap and hooked my ankles on the legs of the stool. "I don't think you ever forget something like that. When my mother died, my father took her photograph off the mantel. It was a picture of her crouching in the garden with all these colorful flowers surrounding her. Flowers she was in the middle of planting. He had snapped the shot without her realizing it, and I still remember her complaining about how awful she looked. But it was his favorite picture." I paused. It was still hard to talk about her death without sliding into a cavern of sadness. "Anyway, my dad took the picture and commissioned an artist to paint a large portrait. He hung it in his office across from his desk so he could see it every day as he worked. At first I thought it was really sweet, but after a few years I began to think it was morbid, that he ought to take it down and get on with his life."

Elizabeth turned slowly from the window. "And now what do you think?"

"That it was his way of grieving. He never stopped loving her, but he wanted something to look at, something to talk to as he mourned. Eventually, the pain began to ease a little. Years later, after I left home, he remarried. She's a very nice lady."

"And the portrait?"

"It's still in his office. I'm not sure, but I think he still talks to her. He probably can't wait for my mom to meet Sherri, the woman he married."

She sighed. "I'm afraid that will never happen to William. He seems incapable of putting anything behind him, and quite frankly, women don't seem to find him very attractive or appealing."

Then she stared right at me and snookered me. "Of course, if someone who knew his background and understood what he's been through, if someone like that spent some time with him . . ."

Dear God, tell me what I thought was happening wasn't really happening.

"Uh, Elizabeth, I think Will would prefer to find his own dates. He doesn't seem like the type to enjoy being set up. Matchmaking seldom works, you know." I was starting to babble, but that was because a heavy dose of panic was constricting my chest.

"My dear child, William doesn't have the first idea of what is good for him. Never has. He spends his days in that dreary office downtown, hating every minute of it, and hating me for securing the job for him. But what choice did I have? The boy never applied himself in school, made terrible grades, where else could he go?"

I drew a few firm strokes and fleshed out the woman's leg, smudging the charcoal lines with the side of my palm as I went along. "No offense, but Will has never been very friendly toward me. I don't think he likes me."

Elizabeth turned from the window and came to stand next to me. "The calves need more definition, Maggie."

As much as it annoyed me to admit, she was right. As usual. I added a few short lines, tensed up the slender muscle, and arched the foot.

She paced the floor behind me. "Maggie, Will hates everyone, me especially. Quite frankly, I'm not all that wild about him or his sister, but it is my job to do the best I can, and I think a woman is called for in this instance." She stopped and placed a hand on my shoulder. "Please say you'll try it one night, something casual like dinner, and if it doesn't work out, I promise to let the matter drop."

So I capitulated like the spineless excuse of a woman that I was.

Of course, it came as no surprise that dinner was a total disaster.

And now, watching that bony little twerp navigating his way across my lawn, I wanted to reach out and pummel his nose just like the bullies of his youth because I couldn't stand to see his mousy little face sully the memory of a woman who lovingly badgered me every day of my life. A woman now zipped into a body bag.

I stood up before he reached the porch.

"Hello, Will."

He sent a venomous glare my way and then spoke

directly to Villari, who was now standing next to me. "Just what the hell are you doing about my grandmother's death? We have a murder here and the two of you are sitting on the steps gabbing like teenagers."

"I'm well aware of what we have here, Mr. Boyer."

"Then shouldn't you be testing for fingerprints and whatever else one does in a murder case?" he retorted, curling his lip at me. "Something other than wasting time with a wannabe artist?" His insolent gaze swept up and down my body like I was a piece of rotting fruit. "My grandmother may have wasted her time with this woman," he spat, "but I see no reason for the rest of us, especially the police, to do the same."

Apparently he didn't enjoy our date any more than I did.

"I realize this is difficult for you," Villari began, "but hostility will get us nowhere."

"And exactly where do you see this little chat with Ms. Kean taking us?"

Villari was doing a masterful job of keeping his temper in check. I glanced at his profile and, judging by the clenched jaw and protruding vein in his temple, realized he was one step away from tossing William in the septic tank himself.

"Mr. Boyer, the police are doing everything possible right now," he explained in a very calm, well-modulated voice. "Your grandmother is being taken to the medical examiner's office, where an autopsy will be performed. In the meantime, we are scouring the grounds and interviewing neighbors for information, which is why I was talking to Ms. Kean here before you interrupted. A police investigation must seem interminably slow to the victim's family and I apologize for that. But being methodical and thorough is a necessity."

"You sound like a cop speaking to a class of third-graders on Career Day. My grandmother just died, she was *murdered,* for God's sake, and I want to see my tax dollars going to something other than a dozen donuts and a cup of hot coffee."

"Then I suggest you go back home and write the mayor, Mr. Boyer, and get the hell out of my way."

I didn't think it was possible for William to blanch, not with that bleached-out, pasty skin of his. But sure enough, the little color he did have drained from his face, leaving a chalky-white complexion that was even less attractive than before.

"You have no right to talk to me that way," he sputtered. "I want to speak to your captain and I want to speak to him now."

Villari stepped down until he was standing eye to eye with Will. The Shaggy Mane not only topped six feet, an easy five-inch advantage, but his lean, athletic body was powerful enough to squash Will like the annoying gnat he was, without breaking a sweat.

"If you want to talk to my captain, look him up in the phone book. In the meantime, crawl back into that hole you emerged from until I'm ready to question you." He leaned forward. "And trust me, Mr. Boyer, I will be questioning you very soon," he said menacingly. Villari stared a minute longer and then looked up and over. At me.

"Don't leave town, Ms. Kean. I'm sure we'll be talking again." He put two fingers against his brow and sent me a lazy salute before turning and walking away.

"Why would he want to talk with you, Maggie?"

I stayed on the porch. Without Villari's height advantage, I was as close to Will as I wanted to be. The little weasel gave me the creeps.

"Gee, hard to imagine. Do you think it could have anything to do with a dead body that showed up in my yard?"

"You always were such a smart-ass. I never could understand what Grandmother saw in you."

"And I never could understand how you could be carrying her genes." The little runt had a big mouth and nothing to back it up. His nasty demeanor didn't intimidate me, but it angered me enough to throw diplomacy to the wind. Marching down the steps, I stopped in front of Will and poked my finger in his chest. "Listen, you little twerp. Why don't you cooperate with the police so they can find out who did this to your grandmother? Try dropping the haughty attitude for a change. You might discover that people don't find you nearly as repulsive as they do now."

"I don't give a damn what people think about me," he snarled, grabbing my arm as I stepped around him.

I stopped. "Sure you do. Otherwise you wouldn't work so hard at trying to make them hate you."

He tightened his grip. "You're going to psychoanalyze me?" he asked incredulously.

"I don't have the time or the interest, Will. Right now I have a friend to mourn." Emotions I couldn't read flitted across his face. I stared straight into his eyes without flinching until he released my arm. I headed across the yard, taking a wide turn around the septic tank, which was still open and surrounded by cops who had apparently grown accustomed to the stench. The gravel driveway crunched under my feet as I passed a few feet behind Detective Villari. He was talking to the serviceman, the same one who had found my neighbor this morning.

"Didn't notice anything," I heard him say. Villari jotted a few notes down and asked something I couldn't hear. The guy in the striped shirt shook his head.

"Nope. It was my first appointment."

Not wanting to hear any more, I hurried past and followed the sidewalk toward what I called my backyard. There was only a crooked line of shrubbery, scrub oak mostly, separating the front section of my property, where my house stood, from that of my neighbor. The back of the property was wide open. Elizabeth Boyer had requested that it be kept that way. All the previous occupants agreed, as I did, and the land was left alone, unmarred by rock, brick, or barbed-wire fences. It was left as nature intended, wild and spacious, overflowing with ponderosa pines and blue spruce trees. I liked having a private forest behind my house and took walks there whenever I could get away. I was headed there now, looking forward to the cool shade and fresh pine scent, when my stomach lurched at the sound of a familiar screech. It was the slam of very expensive brakes and the pings of little rocks ricocheting off the underbelly of a fancy BMW as it fishtailed on the gravel road. I didn't have to look back to know the car was red.

"Maggie!"

"As if Will wasn't bad enough, Queen Bee just arrived," I muttered, picking up speed until I was practically jogging toward the back forest. The last thing I wanted was a scene. Cassandra Boyer was the antithesis of her brother. She inherited all the looks in the family and all the dramatic flair. If she wanted something, she went after it, even if it meant parking her car in the midst of thirty or more cops milling around a taped-off crime scene. Cassandra ignored the whole bunch of them to pursue me with a vengeance.

"Maggie! Maggie! Wait up!"

Power-walking now, I ignored her calls. I figured I'd be safe just beyond the row of pines that stood up ahead like three undecorated Christmas trees. Just a few steps past the trees was a sharp incline that would protect me like a shroud against unwanted visitors, especially those with spiked heels. Cassie, a nickname I used just to provoke her, would never venture far enough to actually touch a tree or follow a trail. Imagine the damage to freshly painted nails and silk stockings.

"Maggie! Stop! I've got to talk to you!"

On any other day, I would have kept walking, but today there were extenuating circumstances. I reluctantly turned around and waited for Cassie to pick her way across the uneven ground. She looked funny hopping along the ground like a barefoot kid stepping on stickers, but I bit the inside of my cheek to keep from laughing. Knowing Cassie, she would take it the wrong way and call me "uncouth" or "common" for laughing on the day of her grandmother's death.

"How can you go off for a walk when Grandmother just passed away?" Typical Cassie. Instantly on the attack, ready to dig her polished talons into my neck and squeeze.

"I've talked to the police until I'm blue in the face. I didn't see any reason to stick around."

"Of course there's a reason. This is a horrible situation that needs to be taken care of as quickly and quietly as possible."

I shoved my hands into my pockets and nudged a small rock with the toe of my tennis shoe. "And what exactly does that have to do with me?"

She gasped and brought her hand up to her chest as though I'd just triggered a minor heart attack with my stupidity. "This has everything to do with you. This unfortunate situation occurred at your house, on your land, and we need to discuss how to keep it from turning into a media circus. Those reporters would just love to latch onto a story like this and blow it completely out of proportion." She took one look at my face and realized she'd gone too far. "Please, don't misunderstand me. This is completely dreadful and I've been an absolute mess ever since that awful policeman showed up at my door with the news. Of course, I will miss Grandmother so, she was such a dear lady," she whimpered, actually managing to squeeze out a tear, "but I know she would be just horrified to have her picture plastered all over the newspapers during this horrible incident."

Where do these people come from? "Do whatever you need to do. I'm going for a walk."

"Aren't you listening? You can't just ignore this and let things 'fall as they may.' It's imperative that we speak with William, have a meeting with just the three of us, and discuss how we should present this to the media before the Boyer name gets dragged through the rumor mill and ugly accusations are made."

"I know I'm going to regret asking this, but what are you talking about?"

She lifted one thin, pale shoulder. "People are always

ready to tear down the wealthy, even if they have to make up lies to do so."

"Call me dense, but I still don't understand what you and Will and I need to talk about. The facts are there for any journalist to report, or at least the facts we know so far, and I don't see what you can do about it."

"Ah, Maggie dear, you are so naive."

I sighed. I could hear a lecture coming on, detailing the tremendous problems the wealthy must endure, problems that none of us common folk could possibly understand, blah-blah-blah. It was becoming clearer and clearer why Elizabeth visited me so often. It wasn't to see me. It was to get away from them.

"Maggie, I know you think I'm exaggerating, but the truth is, people will make up reasons to explain why and how Grandmother died. They'll say she squandered all the Boyer money and committed suicide, or that she had an affair with a married man and the jilted wife killed her, or even that Will and I hired someone to get rid of her in order to get our hands on the trust money."

I didn't think her last statement seemed so farfetched. "Look, Cassie, I'm not going to talk to any reporters for the simple reason that I don't have anything to say beyond the fact that I found her. Well, technically, the serviceman did. But that's all I know. If people make up stories, I don't know how we can stop them, and truthfully, I'm not sure I want to. How do I know that you and Will *didn't* hire someone?"

"My God, Maggie, I was simply giving you hypotheticals about why we should present a united front to the media. How could you possibly accuse us of a such a thing?"

I propped my hands on my hips and stared at her in

disbelief. "You're kidding, right? You don't see anything odd about two siblings whose only concern on the day their grandmother is found murdered is to antagonize the police, circle the wagons, and hide from the media? What are you afraid of—that your country-club membership will be withdrawn or that the maître d' at L'Orangerie will forget the name of your favorite wine?" I swallowed my disgust. "Reality is harsh, Cassie. I found Elizabeth floating in a pool of raw sewage and I don't have the patience to stand here and listen to you whine about how this affects your standing in the community." I leaned forward. "Catch a clue here. Us common folk couldn't care less about your current public-relations crisis."

She didn't even flinch. "You're simply being unreasonable and I don't have time to fight with you right now. There is too much to be done. I must find William. If you can't join with us during our time of need, perhaps I can ask that we not associate with each other any more than necessary."

It was the best news I'd had all day.

Chapter Three

Underneath a green canopy of slightly wet elm trees, a small somber crowd gathered to pay their last respects to Elizabeth Boyer. The earthy smell of damp soil soaked the air as the sun finally cracked the sleet-gray clouds and wiggled through the branches, dappling the ground like the back of an Appaloosa. The mahogany coffin, meticulously waxed to a glossy sheen, was gently lowered into the ground, into a black cavern where the spit and polish would make no difference.

Standing there, I imagined Elizabeth rising up out of her grave. I watched her lean against the rough bark of the ancient elm that draped its branches over the rectangular patch of newly turned sod. Drawing her knees to her chest, she hugged her legs and stared out across the sloping hills as quiet breezes ruffled the leaves overhead. Small bunches of wildflowers, tucked under the white crosses and smooth arches, splashed color against the seamless green grass. I saw Elizabeth smile then, high up on her private knoll, content with the vastness, the openness, the unlimited rolling land. *Draw it, Maggie. Put it on paper. Don't skimp on the details. You have a tendency to do that, you know, to take the lazy way out. Well, don't. Not this time. Not on my grave. Do it right.*

Even in death, she was bossy. I almost laughed out loud. Here I was, standing at a burial service, the eulogy droning in the background, and I was talking to a ghost. Or rather, the ghost was talking to me, telling me what to do, insisting on it no less. It was so typical. Even in death, Elizabeth wanted it done her way.

"Are you okay?"

His deep voice startled me out of my one-sided conversation with the dead. One-sided because Elizabeth was doing all the talking.

"I didn't expect to see you here," I said, turning around. I hadn't realized that the service had ended. "Is it normal for a detective to show up at the funeral of the deceased?"

Villari shrugged. "Sometimes. Not always."

"Are you always this forthcoming with information?" I asked as we walked away from the burial site.

He smiled. "Sometimes. Not always."

It was a wonderful smile. His lips were slightly crooked, which made the smile even more male, more endearing. His eyes crinkled at the corners and he had beautiful white teeth, his full lips edged with one tiny little dimple, a small parenthesis etched in his left cheek.

"So why did you decide to come today?"

"To check out the guest list. Sometimes a burial is like a quick synopsis. It gives you a glimpse of the overall picture and the players involved."

"You think the murderer is here?" I whipped around

and eagerly scanned the area as though I expected to see someone milling through the crowd, carrying a sign with the words MURDERER HERE, EAGER TO BE ARRESTED scrawled across it.

"It's happened before."

"So now what? We can't just walk up and start asking people if they killed Elizabeth Boyer."

"First off, *we* don't do anything. This is nothing to fool around with and I've got enough to do without worrying about an amateur sleuth getting in my way and possibly destroying evidence."

"But if I can help find her killer, why wouldn't you use me? I know these people," I insisted. "They were Elizabeth's friends and neighbors. And mine. It's a close-knit community and they don't trust easily. They'll be more willing to talk to me than a detective who, quite frankly, could use a little work on his people skills."

He ignored my comment. "The medical examiner has determined that the time of death was between twelve and twenty-four hours before she was found. Anyone who had anything to do with Mrs. Boyer will need to be questioned." His black eyes bored into mine. "That includes everyone from the milkman to you."

"Are you saying I'm a suspect?"

"It's a bit coincidental that you experienced septic problems right around the time of her death."

"My toilet backs up and I'm a suspect?"

He shrugged. "It doesn't help your case any. A septic tank is not a common place to dump a dead body. Ms. Boyer was bludgeoned in the back of the head with a heavy object and then thrown into the tank."

For once in my life I kept quiet. I had a pretty good idea where this was going.

"Normally, murderers try to dispose of their victims quickly and quietly. The bottom of a river is a popular choice. All it takes is a couple of stones anchored to the body, a quick toss off the bridge before driving off, and the whole drop is neat and clean, completed in less than a couple of minutes."

Digging through his blazer, Villari pulled out a pack of cigarettes. He shook one out, offered the pack to me, and when I said no, shoved the crumpled package back into his pocket. He stuck the cigarette between his lips, struck a match, and lit it. Inhaling deeply, he shook the match and dropped it on the ground.

"Now, a septic tank takes a little more work," he continued, blowing out smoke, "because first, you've got to know where it's located. Then there's the digging and lifting the lid, which involves significant time and makes a lot of noise when you drag it across the casing, since it weighs more than a bag of groceries. Not to mention the smell. All in all, it's a messy conclusion to a murder and it provides ample opportunities for eyewitnesses."

"So that let's me off the hook, right?"

"Nope. That puts you squarely *on* the hook. You know where the tank is. The digging was already done for you the day before you supposedly found the body, and the lid had been loosened. That side of your house is secluded from any neighbors except for the deceased, and even there, small trees and scrub-oak bushes block full vision. So the risk of being seen is minimal. And noise isn't a problem with the houses set so far apart. For you, it's the perfect drop-off."

I couldn't believe this. Villari was drawing a straight line from plumbing trouble to prime murder suspect.

"There are other things," he added, as though he could read my mind. "There are no signs of a struggle and no unfamiliar footprints. The only prints we uncovered were those of yours and Elizabeth's . . . and the service guy who fixed your tank."

"So why aren't you handcuffing me?"

"Details. The concrete lid. The fact that you cared about the lady. The lack of motive."

"It seems like you're right back where you started, Detective Villari."

"Maybe."

My temper was beginning to simmer. "I'm leaving now. This discussion is pointless. You have nothing but speculation, and because you have nothing you're taking the easy way out and pointing a finger at me. I don't appreciate all the spoken and unspoken innuendos and raised eyebrows. I didn't do anything wrong. It's no wonder people don't want to get involved anymore, not if this is what happens." I turned to go, paused, then swung around to face Villari again. "Think about this. If my tank was such a great 'drop-off' as you called it, why didn't I just leave her there? She'd be chalked up as a missing old lady and simply become another statistic."

Villari took his time answering. Taking a long pull from his cigarette, he tilted his head back and blew the smoke toward the sky. He nodded. "Good point. However, that scenario has a flip side. What if you were simply trying to minimize your risk? If the police started looking for Mrs. Boyer and the trail led to your house, which it would since she spent so much time there, it wouldn't be long before the police discovered the freshly turned earth and became suspicious." He shook his head.

"No, it would make much more sense to 'discover' the body and play the innocent neighbor."

"You're confusing me, Villari. Either arrest me or let me go. I don't want to play cat and mouse with you."

He grinned. "You do come out swinging when you feel cornered."

"If that means you expected me to curl up in a fetal position and whimper, you're right. I'll fight back tooth and nail. But . . ." I couldn't finish because I spotted Will stalking across the grass toward us, followed several feet behind by Cassie, who was desperately trying to keep from tripping in her ridiculously high heels, which sank into the ground like mini-aerators.

Will cut between the two of us and turned to face me, his back to the detective. "The meeting has been scheduled for two-thirty this afternoon," he snapped out like a drill sergeant.

"What meeting?"

"Mr. Prestwood didn't call you?"

Completely baffled, I turned to Cassie, who was scowling at her ruined stilettos as she reached our cozy little group. "Would you please explain what's going on?"

"Will called Mr. Prestwood last night to set up a meeting to discuss Grandmother's estate."

"Nothing like a little greed to get things moving," I murmured.

"Mr. Prestwood was more than happy to meet with us," Cassie huffed self-righteously. "But he told Will that you should be there, too."

"Why?"

"That's exactly what we want to know," Will said, taking over. "I tried to get Mr. Prestwood to explain further, but he refused to do so. In any event, the will is going to be read this afternoon at the house, in Grandmother's office. We expect you there."

I took a deep breath. These people had a way of getting under my skin, and not pleasantly so. Villari stepped from behind Will and stood next to him, waiting for my answer. His expression was unreadable, but I felt sure this latest development fed his suspicions even further.

"First of all, I have no idea why I need to be there. Second of all, I don't enjoy being summoned like some kind of servant, but because your grandmother is being represented, I'll be there, in spite of your lousy manners." A glint of humor sparked in Villari's eyes, but I didn't stick around long enough to find out what was so funny. I glared at Will and Cassie and stomped off in a dramatic show of anger.

The next two hours loomed ahead like an eternity. Reaching my Jeep, I slipped off my pumps and tossed them in the backseat, hiked my straight black skirt up to my thighs, and climbed in. I turned the key and listened to the motor spit and sputter before the engine caught. Angry at the world, I distractedly shifted gears and jerked out into the road, narrowly missing an oncoming car. The red-faced driver laid heavily on the horn, threw finger messages, and startled me back to reality, which was fortunate because I'm not the best of drivers even under perfect conditions. My brother nicknamed me "Space Queen" when I was first learning to drive because I tended to drift off into daydreams in the middle of heavy traffic, scaring the pants off of him and probably every other nearby motorist. Things hadn't changed too much.

I headed toward the mountains. Colorado was heaven

on earth after a summer rain. The smell of sodden earth
permeated the air like damp straw and I breathed deeply
through the open window. Water droplets hung like rain-
bow prisms from the ends of pine needles. Lush green
foliage blanketed the mountains and salmon-colored
rock formations jutted toward the sky. The road threaded
its way up the mountain, winding slowly through the
pass and dropping down into shallow valleys where
grassy plains freckled with purple, orange, and yellow
blossoms shivered in the light breeze. The sun reached
through the clouds, drawing and erasing varying patterns
of light and shadow. Peace filtered the air.

Gravel spewed up against the Jeep as I pulled over
and parked on the shoulder of the road. I shuffled
through the dewy grass until I found a boulder to sit on.
Ignoring the dampness that seeped through my skirt, I
gazed across the land that always soothed me like a
lover's caress. But now confusion clouded the landscape. Elizabeth Boyer, a woman who had snuck in and
haphazardly broke through my defenses and filled an
emptiness within me I hadn't known about, had been
killed. She had surreptitiously slipped in and become my
caretaker, watching over me and refusing to let my stiff
pride scare her off. In a very real sense, she had become
a mother to me. When my biological mother died, I grew
very independent, a lone wolf, in a sense, insisting that
I did not need anyone. It was the only way I knew to
keep from hurting that badly ever again. But my
propped-up defenses crumbled the day I met my deceiv-
ingly petite and fragile neighbor. Long before I realized
it, I needed her.

And now I needed her worse than ever.

Instead, I was saddled with her two spoiled grand-

kids, breathing fire down my back like two angry drag-
ons. I'd always avoided those two in the past, but now
our lives were intertwined in a Gordian knot I didn't
have a clue how to untie. There was no doubt that Elizabeth came to my house to get away from those two.
After spending just a few minutes with them, I was
amazed that she didn't knock on my door every day at
the crack of dawn.

Maybe it shouldn't have surprised me that Elizabeth
put me in the will in some small way, but it had never
crossed my mind. Of course I knew she was very
wealthy; it wasn't something you could ignore. Not that
she flaunted her wealth. She never had to. It was in the
way she carried herself, the way she stood tall and
straight as though she did not have to kowtow to anyone.
She wore understated, but very elegant, very expensive
clothes. She and I were a study in contrasts. While I
wore black leggings and a long sweatshirt with the DEN-
VER BRONCOS emblazoned across the front, she wore
cashmere slacks of subdued colors and a silk blouse with
a solid gold choker. I used to panic when she walked
into my studio, worried she would sit on a ball of clay
or rub her sleeve against a charcoal sketch and ruin her
clothes. But whenever I suggested she wear something
more casual, she looked at me like I was crazy. Clothes
were to be worn, she said, not hidden under plastic bags
hanging uselessly in the closet. Finally, I gave up worrying, realizing even stains would look exactly right on
her.

The only visible concession she made to her artistic
side was the scarves. Villari was right about the bohemian look. Certainly my neighbor was never mistaken
for a gypsy, but she did tie vividly colored ribbons and

bows in her hair or around her neck to spice up an otherwise sedate outfit. She glided into my studio wearing
brilliant stripes, polka dots, and paisley designs tied
about her waist or slipped under the lapels of a blazer.
Somewhere, somehow, she wrapped herself in a swatch
of color that quickly became her signature.

Shaking off the memories, I dragged myself back to
the car. The meeting started in forty-five minutes, just
enough time to drive leisurely back down the pass and
arrive at the Boyers' house a comfortable ten minutes
late. No doubt my tardiness would infuriate Will and
Cassie and brighten my day.

"I should have known you'd take this lightly and sashay
in here whenever you felt like it."

"Get a grip, Will. I've never sashayed anywhere in
my life. I hardly think arriving fifteen minutes late is
cause for a lecture. What are you going to do, ground
me?" Admittedly, I was later than I originally planned
because sudden hunger pangs had me pulling into a
drive-through frozen yogurt store, but Will and Cassie's
anger was worth the extra few minutes. Those two were
chomping at the bit for the inheritance money Elizabeth
had promised them. I was surprised they hadn't vaulted
across the desk where Mr. Prestwood now stood and torn
the will from his hands.

I stuck out my hand and introduced myself to the
silver-haired gentleman.

Tall and lean, with a pencil-thin mustache arching
over his upper lip like an older Clark Gable, Mr. Prestwood graciously stood and reached across the desktop
to clasp my hand.

"It is very nice to meet you, Ms. Kean," he said, his voice deep and gravelly with just a hint of a British accent. "Elizabeth spoke of you often."

I smiled. "She was a wonderful lady."

"Yes, she was. I will miss her tremendously." He cleared his throat and looked sternly around the room like a disappointed parent. "I'm sure we all will."

Will nodded somberly and Cassie dabbed at nonexistent tears. I wanted to run from this phony display of affection, but before I could leave, Mr. Prestwood waved his hands at the chairs circling the desk.

"Why don't we all take a seat and begin." Mr. Prestwood picked up a file and walked around the desk. He glanced at Will. "I appreciate the offer," he explained, "but I don't feel it's quite appropriate to use Elizabeth's desk at this time. I'm sure we'll all feel more comfortable taking a seat here." He turned in his chair and looked toward the back of the room. "Mr. Villari, will you be joining us?"

I spun around in shock. Detective Villari stood silhouetted in the sunlight streaming through the large window. Lounging against the floor-to-ceiling bookshelves, his arms were crossed and his right foot hooked over his left ankle. Given his posture, I expected a toothpick in his mouth and a felt hat slung low over his forehead.

"What are you doing here?"

"Police business."

I turned to Mr. Prestwood. "Is this normal procedure? Do detectives usually attend the reading of a will?"

"There's nothing normal about murder, Ms. Kean," Villari said from behind. He walked toward me, pulled out a chair, and with a flick of his hand invited me to sit down. I ignored him and moved to another chair across from Mr. Prestwood.

"Unless someone objects"—Villari addressed the group, a hint of mockery in his tone—"I will stay to hear the will." He glanced at me. "Do you object, Ms. Kean?"

"The only thing I object to is the feeling that you're lurking around every corner."

"Are you afraid I might pounce?" he murmured.

Mr. Prestwood cleared his throat before I could answer. I shot Villari an irritated look, but he simply lifted an eyebrow, apparently amused by the exchange.

"Could we get on with this?" Will said impatiently.

"Why the big hurry, Will?" I asked. "Expecting to make a large bank deposit this afternoon?"

He huffed like the Big Bad Wolf and then sputtered, "Not at all. I'm simply trying to expedite matters to make it easier for everyone involved."

"Remind me not to name you in my Living Will. I'd hate to think of you 'expediting' matters and accidentally yanking the plug while I was still breathing, just to make it easier on everyone."

Will pursed his lips and regarded me angrily, but evidently decided not to say anything more. Mr. Prestwood cleared his throat again and ruffled his papers to get everyone's attention, staring pointedly at me.

"Sorry," I mumbled.

He nodded solemnly and reached for the glasses in his top pocket, but not before I saw a glint of laughter in his eyes. "Before I begin, let me say that Mrs. Boyer's will is very clear and concise. She was especially aware of the problems that inherited wealth could cause if the wishes of the deceased were not laid out very clearly.

Elizabeth was careful to review her will every year at exactly the same time. Except for the codicil which added Ms. Kean's name, everything has remained essentially the same over the last ten years." Prestwood slipped on his glasses and shook his head. "Elizabeth was a very predictable creature in some ways. As a matter of fact, I was quite surprised when she called to set up a meeting for next week."

"She wasn't due to discuss her will?" Villari asked.

Prestwood frowned. "Actually, she wasn't. We had gone over the document just a few months before."

"I don't see the big deal," Will interjected. "You and Grandmother saw each other during social functions and at the club. She was probably calling you for a donation to her latest charity."

"Perhaps," Mr. Prestwood conceded. "But your grandmother seemed hesitant to tell me why she wanted to meet. Usually she was very forthright, set up the agenda over the phone, and came prepared with files and notes. She didn't like to waste any time."

"Which is exactly what we're doing right now," Will interjected. "This is an exercise in futility. We'll never know why Grandmother wanted to see you, and I, for one, don't really care."

The man had the manners of a pig. Or a vulture. Swooping down to tear chunks of flesh off a fresh kill, burying his nose in the blood and guts.

"Yes, well, ahem, maybe you're right." Prestwood peered over his half glasses and exchanged a look with Villari, a look I couldn't decipher. Of course I didn't understand anyone here. It seemed heartless to be reading the will before the body had spent at least one day underground.

Cassie spoke up. "I'm sure Will did not mean to sound like he doesn't care about Grandmother, because that's simply not true. The two of them were very close, and this whole situation has been devastating for both of us. But," she added with a brave little catch in her voice, "the fact of the matter is, Grandmother is gone and we must carry on."

More senseless drivel from the queen of the manor.

Prestwood pulled a sheaf of papers from his file and began reading. " 'I, Elizabeth Boyer, of El Paso County, Colorado, being of sound mind and memory and over the age of twenty-one years do hereby make, publish, and declare this to be my last will and testament . . .' "

She was dead long before I saw her floating in the filthy water, but the sense of finality, of true loss, hit me in the gut when I heard Prestwood's deep voice intoning the final words of Elizabeth Boyer. The will was written in convoluted legalese, but I could easily imagine this very grand lady sitting and strumming her fingernails against her lawyer's desk as she listed, in no uncertain terms, her final wishes. The attorney's words swirled around me like a pile of dust kicked up by a pickup traveling over a dirt road. I couldn't focus on what he was saying, although I was sure Will had a hidden tape recorder tucked in his jacket pocket, just so he could replay the exact, glorious moment when he received more money than he could spend in several lifetimes. I slumped further into my seat and stared at my feet, now clad in my favorite pair of Nike running shoes—not a great match for a funeral dress, but I thought Elizabeth would approve.

Prestwood cleared his throat again, a habit that was beginning to grate on my nerves. I looked up to see him staring at me. Will and Cassie were sitting on either side of him like a pair of bookends, both completely white and looking shell-shocked. I hurriedly scooted up in my chair.

"What?"

Will stood slowly, his hands clenched and his body radiating anger. "You conniving little slut."

I pushed my chair back and stood up. "What the hell are you talking about?"

"Like you didn't know. Like you weren't planning the whole thing with those cozy little visits from my grandmother." Will raised his arm and pointed his finger at me. "You orchestrated it all. Every last minute of it." He snarled and snapped at me like a rabid dog with spittle flying from his mouth. "You took advantage of a vulnerable old lady and twisted her mind against her own family."

My God, this was a page out of some gothic novel. I was stuck in a room with crazy people and there was no escape, not with the two live gargoyles circling and clawing at me right now.

"Look, I have no idea why you're foaming at the mouth, but I do know one thing. Your grandmother was one of the strongest women I've ever met, and if you pulled your brain out of your wallet long enough to think for a second, you'd know I was right." I turned to Cassie. "What are you crying about?" At least I *thought* she was crying. Given her amazing ability to turn tears on and off at will, it was hard to be sure.

Cassie shook her head and hiccuped a couple of times. "How could Grandmother turn her estate over to someone like you?" she asked, before bursting out into a fresh wail.

Something bad was happening here, real bad. Will, red-faced and irate, stood next to Cassie and patted her shoulder somewhat vaguely and ineffectively while she wept up a storm. The famous Boyer upper lip was crumbling at breakneck speed and it wasn't a pretty sight. And, apparently, it was all my fault.

Not only was I totally confused, I was completely embarrassed. I hadn't heard a single word Prestwood had spoken in the last fifteen minutes and now I was really paying for that lapse. I glanced at Villari, who sat kicked back in his chair with one foot resting on the opposite knee, his hands loosely clasped in his lap and a smile threatening the edges of his lips.

"Why don't you read that last couple of sentences over again, Mr. Prestwood. I believe Ms. Kean here might have missed it."

Prestwood nodded. "Let's see. The area of controversy seems to be centered on one particular portion of the will." With his right finger, he pushed his glasses up the bridge of his nose. " 'I hereby appoint my neighbor and dear friend Margaret E. Kean as fiduciary of the ten million dollars currently deposited . . .' "

Numbness spread through my body until there was no feeling left in my legs, feet, or hands. Completely stunned, I collapsed into the chair and stared dumbly at my scraped-up tennis shoes, a Kmart bargain, while visions of dollar signs and a whole string of zeros dropped like a lead balloon. No wonder Cassie and Will were upset.

"Let me guess. You had no idea. You're just as shocked as we are," Will sneered.

"You have to admit, Maggie," his sister chimed in,

"this is a little too coincidental to be completely innocent."

I grimaced. There was some truth to what she said. It did look a little too coincidental for comfort. I wasn't even sure what a fiduciary did or how much she got paid for doing it, but judging from the volume of Cassie's sobs, it was more than pocket change. And Villari's presence was making me nervous. I was afraid to look up, afraid that the smile would have disappeared and he'd be patting his jacket for a pair of handcuffs while calling for backup on his cell phone.

"Could you explain what this means, Mr. Prestwood?"

The lawyer regarded me solemnly. "Elizabeth had great faith in you, Ms. Kean. She was very fond of you and believed you would handle her assets with care. The bulk of her estate, that part in which you have no controlling interest, will continue as is, until there are certain changes in the stock market. She has left explicit instructions on when to sell her stocks and bonds and where the proceeds will go. Most of this can easily be handled through my office if you so choose."

"If it's all that neat and tidy, why did Grandmother put her in charge?" Will demanded, his voice climbing.

"Sit down, Will," Mr. Prestwood said firmly, "so we can discuss this calmly."

Will complied reluctantly, but he didn't look any calmer.

"Your grandmother," Prestwood continued, "was concerned that you and Cassandra might use the money irresponsibly." He held up his hand before Will could launch a torrent of angry words. "I realize this isn't particularly pleasant to hear, but the fact remains, Elizabeth felt the—shall we say 'excitement' of handling large sums of money could prove to be a bit overwhelming and that your judgment might be impaired."

Will looked ready to explode. "So she wanted Maggie to watch over us?" he asked incredulously.

"Certainly this sounds a little farfetched, but the idea is actually quite sound. Elizabeth was very clear about how and where her liquid assets should be spent. Ms. Kean, as fiduciary, would essentially be acting as a safeguard for your grandmother's wishes."

"But Maggie hasn't handled more than a thousand dollars a month in her whole life," Will insisted. "What does she know about ten million dollars?"

My thoughts exactly. What *did* I know?

"Ms. Kean does not have to know anything about money. The ten million dollars is not hers. She is basically a caregiver. Should you need a sum of money, submit the figure to Ms. Kean along with an explanation of how you propose to utilize the money. If the purpose is in line with Elizabeth's guidelines, then Ms. Kean is free to release the sum to you. Ms. Kean herself will receive a small painting from Elizabeth." Prestwood looked over his shoulder and gestured toward the wall. "She will also receive a monthly fee that will continue until the entire ten million dollars has been distributed."

"And what the hell are the guidelines?"

"Simply stated, the money is to be spent on educational needs or charities or establishing a reputable business. Now"—Mr. Prestwood stood—"if you don't mind, I'd like a moment to speak with Ms. Kean. Alone. I'm sure we will be meeting again soon to go over the will in further detail, but I believe there has been more than enough emotion for one day." He leveled his gaze at

Will and Cassie, almost daring one of them to disagree.

Will grabbed Cassie's arm and dragged her out of the room. Villari pushed himself out of his chair and loomed over me from his imposing height, trying hard, I thought, to intimidate the hell out of me. But I wasn't about to give him the satisfaction of knowing that his little ploy worked. I jumped up and stood toe to toe with him.

He didn't budge. "Ms. Kean," he said, his voice laced with a light threat, "we'll be talking sooner than I expected." He sent Prestwood a brief nod and left the room, closing the door behind him.

"Ms. Kean, please sit down."

I simply stared at Prestwood. My head felt muddled and confused.

"Please."

Reaching behind me, I grabbed the arms of the chair and lowered myself into the leather seat. Prestwood sat down in the now empty chair next to me.

"Ms. Kean, I know this comes as a great shock to you . . . as it has to everybody involved," he added, a vague look of disgust clouding his face as he glanced toward the door through which Cassie and Will had recently departed. "But it is exactly what Elizabeth wanted."

"How can that be? I know nothing about money," I said, gathering steam, "certainly not in that quantity. I don't even know how to balance my own checkbook and now I'm stuck overseeing a pile of money so large I can't even imagine it." I took a deep breath and exhaled slowly. "I don't want anything to do with Elizabeth's money."

"Yes, that's exactly how Elizabeth said you would respond," Prestwood said softly.

I grabbed his forearm. "You've got to get me out of this thing! What was she thinking? Will's right, you know. I barely make enough money to pay my mortgage every month; how am I supposed to handle millions of dollars?" I glared at Prestwood. "And even worse, I'll never get rid of that slimeball and his whiny little sister now. Elizabeth must have been crazy when she came up with this idea."

"Not crazy at all, Ms. Kean. A little off the beaten path maybe, but never crazy. She wanted you in this position very badly."

"Weren't you supposed to advise her or something? Surely you can see that this will never work."

"Truth be told, I did advise her against it, quite vehemently at first. But, as usual, she didn't listen to me. And now I believe she may have been right."

"But I don't want to do this!" I stated emphatically, precariously close to yelling.

"If that is your decision, no one can force you to be the fiduciary. However, I would like to ask you to reserve judgment until after you have read Elizabeth's letter." With that, Prestwood retrieved a white envelope from his folder and handed it to me. He stood, placed the folder back in his briefcase, and snapped the locks shut.

"Give yourself a couple of days, Ms. Kean," he said quietly. "I'm sure Elizabeth would appreciate that. Call my office when you've made a decision."

Prestwood strode from the room, his bearing proud and regal, as quiet and understated as old money. I looked down and ran my fingers along the edges of the thick, heavy envelope that now lay in my lap.

Chapter Four

Dear Maggie,

If you are reading this letter, then I am most assuredly no longer part of this world. Isn't that the way most letters from the deceased begin? I imagine my will has you thrashing about in confusion and you are ready to toss this letter out the window, along with both the Boyer grandchildren. No doubt William and Cassandra have been horribly unpleasant, and I shudder to think of how they must have reacted to the changes in my will, and to you. If there is any truth to these words, please accept my apologies for them. Unfortunately, it is impossible to deny that my grandchildren are terribly spoiled and I have only myself to blame.

After my beloved son, my only child, and his wife were killed, I took their children into my home, intending to raise them as my own. My husband, however, was very unhappy with the situation. Cranford could not bear to be around either child, for they were a constant reminder of the son he had lost. He was eager to ship them off to boarding school as soon as possible. I could not let this happen. How could I send two lonely children off to a strange place just days after being orphaned? For the first time in our marriage, I stood up to my husband and refused to follow his wishes. He was furious. I won't describe the scene that followed; suffice it to say that the little respect we had for each other died that day. Any love that might have grown between us ceased to exist.

It was a loveless marriage, Maggie, arranged by my father to secure a higher social position and enough money so that I would never want for anything. But I did want. I ached with want. My son was my only joy. And when he died, I lost the one person I could love freely, as only a mother can love. But the day our grandchildren came to live with us, my husband turned away and hardly spoke to them or me until the day he died, almost ten years later. To make up for their grandfather's coldness, and to assuage my own grief, I gave my grandchildren everything they asked for; anything they wanted was theirs. I gave them everything but my heart.

I never played with them, tucked them into bed at night, or even disciplined them. Lost in my own mourning, I failed to see that they were lost, too. Then one day I woke up and saw two spoiled children who had no real friends and no real family. I tried to make up for that neglect, but by then it was too late. By that time they were stubborn, angry, rebellious teenagers, and quite honestly, I was too old to handle the problems of adolescents. I couldn't just kiss and soothe them away.

Things were better when Cranford died. I realize how awful that sounds, but the truth is not always pretty. Some of the coldness left the house and the two children and I developed a somewhat uneasy relationship that still exists today. But I am still very worried about them.

William is a failure in business. He was a mediocre student and never applied himself to any job, even the ones I secured for him. I believe this may be his biggest problem. I gave him the job. He never had to go out and struggle to make a name for himself, to find his own place.

And his sister... politely stated, she is too willing, eager even, to give herself to any man that finds her attractive. Unfortunately, much of Cassandra's attraction depends on my money and I don't want to see it fall into some man's greedy hands. Money makes a cold bedfellow.

So I come to you, Maggie, the light of my life. You are the daughter I never had. None of this should be a surprise to you, not if you look deep inside yourself. I remember pulling out of my driveway and watching you through your window. You were hunched over a square chunk of clay, wearing a long shapeless blouse, your hair pulled back into a ponytail. My heart lurched a little. You reminded me so much of the dream I gave up when I married Cranford.

Knowing you brought art back into my life. I started painting again. The landscape picture behind my desk is for you. No doubt it is very flawed, but it is my thanks to you for bringing back a world I had abandoned years ago.

Keep sculpting, Maggie. You are very talented. Use the trustee fee to buy your supplies, take lessons if you feel you need to. When you're ready for a show, call Mark Gossert at the Outlook. He's waiting for your call. Don't let anyone keep you from developing your gift.

Finally, I am asking you to watch over a large portion of my money, Maggie. It is my last chance to help William and Cassandra. They need to sweat, to struggle for something they love. Actually, they both need a good swift kick in the behind. It won't be easy, I know. They'll fight you every step of the way. That's why I put you in the will. I need someone strong, someone who is not afraid, someone who won't give up.

Elizabeth

Tears splashed on the linen pages and smeared the writing. I folded the letter and rested my head against the back of the chair and closed my eyes. She was right. I had known how she felt about me, but I was too afraid to acknowledge those feelings. After my mother died, that part of my heart shut down. At least, that's what I told myself. And Elizabeth Boyer instinctively understood this, letting me accept what I could without pushing. She just meandered her way into my life, slipping past my defenses without setting off any alarms. All she did was complain, boss me around, make a nuisance of herself, and drive me crazy. She wore on my nerves and slid into my heart at the same time.

I tucked the letter back into its envelope and grabbed my purse off the floor. The room was quiet and hushed as I stood and approached her desk, wanting to touch something of hers, to bring back what had taken me too long to discover. My fingers trailed lightly over the fluted borders, pausing briefly at the burgundy chair edged in brass buttons sitting stoically behind the desk. I reached out and prodded the chair tentatively, then with more force, until it swiveled around and around in circles.

I had no choice but to sit down. The deep rich leather embraced me like a favorite flannel shirt. Suddenly I could feel her. I could smell her. The light floral scent she wore was here in this room. Elizabeth was here in this room. With me. People would think I was crazy, but I didn't care. If I reached out, I could touch her. She was next to me and behind me and in front of me. Just like she was in real life. I sank into the chair and let her ghost . . . her aura . . . certainly her spirit engulf me.

The sun spilled through the front windows and splashed over the walls and the glossy desktop. I smiled at Elizabeth's neat and orderly desk, the mahogany polished to a rich auburn. Except for the small brass lamp, a gold pen-and-pencil set lying side by side, and a leather-bound appointment book resting on top of the blotter, her desk was bare. *A place for everything and everything in its place.* I could hear her voice whispering the old adage, just as she had a million times while standing in my studio, piles of clutter threatening to overwhelm her.

I sat up and pushed the chair away from the desk, glancing once more around the room. Elizabeth was everywhere. Tears threatened again and I had to leave, to get away from here, from this place that had once housed a grand lady who had not been in my life long enough.

The moment the heavy front door clicked behind me, I flew down the driveway, thankful I had worn my oldest tennis shoes. Once outside, I turned my face to the sun and breathed in great gulps of fresh, pine-scented air. Luckily, I had somehow managed to avoid running into Will and Cassie on my way out, probably because they were busily huddled in some smoky backroom plotting an intricate strategy to mow me down. At this point it didn't much matter. All I wanted was to get away.

I hopped into the Jeep and drove it to the end of the Boyers' driveway, completed a tight U-turn, and pulled into my own driveway. My keys were already in my hand when I reached the front door and heard the phone ringing inside. Shoving the key into the lock, I pushed the door open and ran for the phone. I managed to grab the receiver on the fourth ring, one second before the answering machine turned on and repeated my rambling commentary on how I might or might not be home and it really wasn't any of your business whether I was or not, and if, by the sound of the beep you hadn't thrown down the phone in disgust, would you please leave a message?

"Hello? Maggie, is that you?" Lisa asked, concern lacing her voice. "You sound asthmatic with all that wheezing."

"That's how I breathe after running."

"Running? I thought you were going to a funeral."

"I was. I did. It's over and I had to get out."

"That bad, huh?"

"You don't know the half of it, Lisa."

"So tell me. You know I hate to be left in the dark."

"I couldn't do it justice over the phone. Why don't you come over here?"

Ten minutes later I was sitting in my oldest sweats and savoring my favorite French vanilla and Colombian blend while filling in all the blank spaces for Lisa. I leaned back and sipped the hot coffee while my best friend stared at me openmouthed.

"You're kidding, right?"

I shook my head. "Nope. The grandkids' fortune is in my hands, and they're so angry that being infected with the Ebola virus would seem like a blessing in comparison. I just wish Elizabeth was here to enjoy it."

Lisa reached across the kitchen table and covered my hand with hers. "I'm very sorry about your neighbor, Maggie. I wish there were something I could say that would help. But there isn't. The murder was shocking and there's no other way to look at it."

I rubbed my eyes to keep from crying. At least I had one person on my side. One tall and glamorous person. With five inches on me and none of the gangly awkwardness, Lisa could easily have been a model, with her rich auburn hair and large hazel eyes. In fact, I was pretty sure agents had approached her at different times in her life. But Lisa had brains, a goal, and a well-mapped-out plan. And although I never understood the harm in earning some major dollars on the side, Lisa refused to be distracted. The woman believed in straight lines and clearly defined goals—in direct contrast to the crooked lines I followed to a hazy end result.

Lisa and I were college roommates. We were best friends from the minute I walked into our dorm room and saw her sitting cross-legged in the middle of one twin bed, chewing gum and charting her strategy for the next four years of college. In between chomps, Lisa pointed out that the booklet I had tucked underneath my arm was actually last year's, out-of-date course catalog. If she hadn't taken me under her wing, I would still be in college, with a different major every year, or racing around the campus looking for classes that no longer existed. Nurturing came naturally for her, so it was no surprise that she was drawn to nursing. She received her degree four years later and was now a head OB-GYN nurse teaching childbirth classes at night.

"So what does he look like?" Among her many talents, Lisa always knew when to change subjects.

"What?"

"Detective Villari. He sounds gorgeous."

"The guy practically accuses me of killing Elizabeth Boyer and you want to know whether he's handsome or not?"

"Maggie, all he has to do is read Elizabeth's letter and he'll know you had nothing to do with the murder," she said patiently. "Now, what does this guy look like?"

I sighed. Lisa could be as stubborn as a bulldog with a raw steak clenched in its jaws. She wasn't about to let go until someone put a gun to her head.

"Fine. Have it your way. When I'm shuffling off to

the electric chair, you'll feel better knowing that the cop who brought me down was nice looking."

She frowned. "Only nice looking? I was hoping for something a little more hot-blooded, you know, a Mel Gibson look-alike. 'Nice looking' describes my father or my accountant on a good day."

"Shouldn't you be making dinner for your husband and daughter instead of drooling over a detective who would like nothing better than to throw your best friend in jail?"

Lisa shrugged. "It's a known fact that a little tension between a man and a woman can really enhance the sex. Besides, Joel's baby-sitting Mandy and stirring the chili I started. I've got at least another five minutes before Armageddon."

"I hate to disappoint you, Lisa, but the man is nothing but a walking pain in the butt. Everywhere I go, he shows up and stares at me with a smoldering look that says, 'You're guilty. I know it. You know it.' Call me silly, but romance behind the bars is not my style."

"Okay, so he's not the man of your dreams," she said begrudgingly. "Things could change."

"What is this, *The Dating Game*? I don't want things to change. I like my life the way it is—or at least the way it was. Why can't Villari just do his job and find the guy who killed Elizabeth? I don't want to be involved with him, the grandkids, or any of this."

"Sounds like you already are," she said quietly.

"What does that mean?"

Lisa got up and stuck her coffee in the microwave. "Look, Maggie, like it or not, Mrs. Boyer died and was found in your tank. Right there you're involved. Then she puts you in the will controlling a whole lot of money, money that two vindictive little pond scrapings are pitching a fit about. And last but not least, you've got a detective breathing down your neck and scaring you to death."

"I thought you said Elizabeth's letter would take me off the hook, that Villari would believe my story."

"What *is* your story?" Lisa asked, blowing on the heated coffee as she carried it back to the table.

"That's the problem. I have no story. I found Elizabeth by sheer accident. If my toilet hadn't backed up, or rather, if her body hadn't clogged up the pipes, there's no telling how long she'd have been in there. And as far as the will goes, I was more surprised than either Will or Cassie. You would have laughed if you'd been there. Before Will went nuts, I was staring down at my feet and . . ." I sat up. "Oh, my God!"

Lisa jumped and spilled half the coffee in her cup. "What? What's the matter?"

"Sorry," I said, shaking my head, "I didn't mean to scare you. I just remembered that Elizabeth willed me a picture in her office and I forgot to take it with me when I left. Now I've got to go face Will and Cassie again while they shoot verbal darts and accuse me of manipulating this whole mess."

"Look, the letter may not prove your innocence," Lisa conceded, mopping up the coffee with a handful of soggy napkins, "but it does explain a lot. Why don't you pick some neutral ground, meet with Detective Villari, and show him the letter. I'm sure he can take it from there."

I lifted my eyebrows, a little suspicious of any suggestion coming from Little Miss Matchmaker. "Neutral ground?"

"Yeah. Someplace away from the murder scene and the Boyer grandkids," Lisa said, pretending to think. "Maybe over dinner at—I don't know—Antoine's or someplace like that?"

"What a stellar idea," I responded dryly. "Maybe I should wear my satin bra and thong panties, too, just in case he wants to reread the letter in another neutral area like my bed."

"I would have suggested it if you owned something other than cotton underwear that sags in the butt," she muttered, glancing at her watch. "Look, at some point you're going to have to show the letter to the detective. What's the harm in looking nice while you hand it over?"

"I promise to give it some thought, Lisa." I waved my hand at her. "Go on home and see to your chili. Don't worry. I'll call you the moment Villari sweeps me off my feet and carries me off into the sunset and makes mad passionate love to me all night long."

Lisa rolled her eyes, got up, and rinsed her cup out in the sink.

I watched her while she shook the excess water off the cup and placed it upside down on the folded towel. She dried her fingers on the towel and was staring out the kitchen window when I saw her smiling.

"What's so funny?" I asked.

She turned and looked at me. "I think the man who's going to sweep you up in his arms just drove into the driveway. Do me a favor and put on your glasses before you open the door, because what you described as nice looking is mouthwatering handsome."

I groaned. "Villari is here?" I propped my elbows on

the table and covered my face with my hands. "The man won't give me a moment's rest."

"There's a world of women just waiting to change places with you, Maggie," Lisa said, patting my back as she went to open the front door. "In fact, if it wasn't for Joel, I'd be leading the pack."

I raised my head. "This isn't a romance novel," I snapped. "This is a murder we're talking about."

"It never hurts to be prepared." She tilted her head. "Isn't that what Elizabeth was always telling you?"

Moments later I could hear Lisa and Villari talking; their voices were muffled behind the open door, but I knew Lisa would play the perfect hostess and invite him in. I felt less than hospitable and didn't want to do anything but glare at him until he was uncomfortable enough to hit the road. But what good would it do? The man just couldn't take a hint. For all I knew, Villari was planning to stay the night, not for romance, but to further interrogate me. I imagined myself tied to a cold metal chair in the middle of some cavernous warehouse room surrounded by cement walls, shivering underneath a naked lightbulb as a steady drip of water plopped on my head. The man was determined to find me guilty of murder or force me to go stark raving mad.

"Well, I'll be leaving now," Lisa said breezily as she walked Villari to the table. "Maggie, give me a call tomorrow and we'll go to breakfast or something."

I grunted and waved halfheartedly while she floated out the front door.

"May I?"

I looked up to see Villari looking questioningly at the chair.

"Sure. Sit down. There's coffee in the pot if you want some."

"Thanks." He walked into the kitchen, grabbed a cup off the wooden mug tree, and poured himself some coffee. Lisa was right. You had to be blind not to notice the large square shoulders pulling his shirt tight against his back, or the outline of one tight little butt underneath his faded jeans.

I shook my head in disgust. Elizabeth Boyer had just been killed and I was lusting after a detective like a love-starved teenager.

Villari sat down across from me, one hand cupped around his mug.

"You look tired."

"I'm exhausted," I admitted. "I always forget how much a murder takes out of you."

His expression never wavered.

"Okay, I admit it was a lousy joke."

"Yeah, it really was," he said, taking a sip.

"Well, I'm not in top form right now . . . usually I'm much funnier. Maybe you could come back another day and I promise to have you clutching your sides with my comedic talents."

Villari narrowed his eyes. "When was the last time you ate?"

"What difference does that make?"

"Ms. Ke—"

"Maggie. Call me Maggie. If you're going to worry about my eating schedule, you might as well call me by my first name."

"Maggie, then. When was the last time you ate?"

"Like I said before, what difference could that pos-

sibly make to you? Do you normally check out the nu-
tritional habits of your prime suspects?"

Villari leveled his gaze at me. No wonder he was a
homicide detective. I bet he cracked case after case with
nothing but that piercing stare of his.

"Let's just say," he said quietly, "that I like to keep
my 'prime suspects' healthy. I wouldn't want anyone to
accuse me of coercing a confession. It wouldn't do me
any good to have you fainting from hunger at the trial.
After all," he said, a demonic smile playing at his lips,
"that might sway the jury's sympathy."

Chills tingled up and down my spine and the hairs
stood up on the back of my neck like a cat with her paw
stuck in a light socket. The man thought I was guilty.
He actually thought I had killed the dearest lady in the
world and stuffed her in my sewage tank. The more I
thought about it, the less afraid I was and the angrier I
got. The guy didn't have one shred of evidence and he
was hovering around me like a pesky horsefly. I was
getting exceedingly tired of it.

"You know, there is a real killer out there. You might
try going after him, or her, instead of wasting your time
bothering with someone you've already questioned repeatedly and gotten nowhere with."

"Do you always have trouble sticking to one topic?"
His lips started to twitch at the corners. "As much as I
appreciate you reminding me about the murder that occurred, or ended, in your front yard, the original question
was, and still is, when was the last time you ate something?"

"I give up," I said, exasperated. "Not that it matters
in the slightest, but I think I had some toast this morn-

ing." I thought back through the day. "No, that's wrong. I had toast last night."

"You haven't eaten since last night?"

"Not that I can remember. No, wait. I ate some yogurt before I went to the meeting this afternoon."

"Where's your phone?"

"What for?"

Villari sighed. "Does everything have to be difficult with you? I'm a cop, remember? We're supposed to be the good guys. The men in blue. The people you trust."

I crossed my arms across my chest. "You've obviously forgotten about Rodney King and all the other incidents where the nice guys beat people to a pulp."

"Shit," he said, running his fingers through his hair. Long, tapered fingers. "All I wanted was to order a pizza and you're discussing police brutality. Tell me where the damned phone is or I'm not going to be able to hang on to what little patience I have left."

After one look at his face, I bit back my retort and recited the number of the local pizza takeout. He looked as worn-out as I felt. Dark circles rimmed his eyes and a thick stubble covered his face, thick enough to make me believe he hadn't shaved since the day I'd found Elizabeth.

After placing the order, he hung up and leaned against the counter. "Well, Maggie, you certainly know how to stir up trouble."

"I had nothing to do with this murder, regardless of what you think," I replied tiredly. I walked into the kitchen to rinse out my cup, setting it upside down to drain before turning around just in time to see Villari slowly and methodically checking me out from head to toe.

"Is there a problem?" I asked, sarcasm dripping from my voice.

"Not really. I was just wondering why you insist on wearing such shapeless clothes. Everything you wear makes you look like a stick figure dressed in Roseanne's old clothes."

"I can't imagine why my wardrobe would be any concern of yours."

He shrugged. "You're probably right. How about this, though? How'd you get yourself in the will, Maggie?"

Chapter Five

"Can't say I didn't enjoy that little meeting we had this afternoon," Villari said around a bite of pizza. "Those two grandkids looked mad enough to tear you apart limb from limb."

The pizza sat between us on the kitchen table. I lifted my second piece from the box, put it on my plate, and immediately picked off the onions and bell peppers and piled them on Villari's plate.

"You really ought to eat your vegetables."

"You really ought to mind your own business. So far, all you've done is voice your unsolicited opinion about my clothes and my eating habits. Is there anything else you'd like to expound on?"

"Uh-huh. The will."

"Oh, yeah. Getting in the will was a breeze. I just roped the dotty old lady in, little by little. Elizabeth really was quite senile, you know. She'd wander over here in a daze and I'd sit her down in front of small clump of clay . . . humor her, make her feel important. Every once in a while, I'd give her a pad of paper and pencil and she'd try her hand at sketching. Then I started working on her paranoia, persuading her that everyone was out to get her money . . ."

Villari simply lifted his brow and kept eating.

"I had her convinced that Will and Cassie were plotting to put her in a nursing home and take over the house and all of her money. The only way to stop them was to put me in charge of their inheritance. She fell for it like a ton of bricks."

"You've got a smart mouth, don't you?"

"No, it's true," I insisted between bites. "I've always wanted to be intricately linked with Will and Cassie, I just love those two . . . I mean what's not to love? It was the perfect solution. Now we're one big happy family."

"Maggie . . ."

I leaned over and whispered conspiratorially, "So one day I called up Prestwood and pretended to be Elizabeth, using my best old-lady voice with a slight tremor, and asked him to draw up the necessary papers. Then I snuck over to her mailbox every day to check for the will. When it arrived, I slipped the last page on top of her sketches and asked her to sign her drawings. Well, the lady was blind as a bat, and not too bright to boot, so without further ado," I said, flourishing my slice of pizza, "I was in the will, signed, sealed, and delivered."

"Funny, real funny," Villari said, wiping his hands on a paper napkin. "You're a real comedian. Now let's try this one more time and see if you can answer a straight question with a straight answer. You might be surprised at how efficient a straight line is compared to the convoluted route you seem to prefer."

I threw down my pizza. "I'm so sick of this. If you knew Elizabeth at all, you'd know how ridiculous this is. That lady had more brains, more stamina . . . more sheer *willpower* than anyone I know and she was in her seventies. She was on the board of I don't know how many charities and she went to all sorts of functions and dinners. After all that, she still had time left over to point out areas I needed to work on to improve as an artist. The idea that I bamboozled her, or tricked her into putting me in as trustee, is so absurd it's laughable."

Villari leaned his elbows on the table and steepled his fingertips. "So you weren't surprised that she included you?"

"Are you kidding? I was shocked. But the fact is, she did include me, and I'm not going to start casting doubt on her sanity. Her letter pretty much explains the whole thing."

"What letter?"

"Elizabeth wrote me before she died. That's why Prestwood wanted to see me after everyone had left."

"Where's the letter now?"

I hesitated at first because I couldn't remember where I had put the letter after showing it to Lisa.

"It's in a nice safe place," I said, once I realized where it was.

Villari's eyes narrowed.

"Under the pizza box."

Muttering curses, he reached out, grabbed the box, and lifted it off the table. The letter was tucked in its envelope, now sporting a small grease stain in the corner.

Villari stared at me in shock. "A lady dies. No, she doesn't just die, she's murdered, and she isn't your average, everyday sweet old lady with white hair, but a very rich lady with money to burn." He stopped, too stunned to continue.

For once in my life, I didn't say anything.

"And you leave her personal letter to you under the pizza box like it was no more than a coupon from a box of Froot Loops?" He shook his head. "You're already on shaky ground in this investigation, Maggie. You have a stronger motive than anyone else to kill Elizabeth Boyer, especially now that we know you're in control of a large portion of her estate."

"What difference does that make? I don't get to keep the damned money. I just get to baby-sit the stuff to keep those two parasites from pitching it down a black hole."

"Either you're a better actress than I thought or you really don't get it," Villari said, exasperated. "You'll make somewhere around one percent annually with this little job. Minus the taxes, that works out to be something in the neighborhood of a hundred thousand a year. It won't make you one of the rich and famous, but as long as you decide to keep Elizabeth Boyer's money intact without handing anything to the grandkids, you'll have a nice steady income for as long as you want."

I glared at Villari. "You're starting to sound like Will, as though I rigged this whole thing. I did not plan to be in her will and I certainly did not murder Elizabeth," I said emphatically. Much to my dismay, though, my voice cracked slightly and I could feel the heat on my cheeks, my precrying routine. I jumped up, ran to the kitchen, and rummaged in the refrigerator just to have something to do. I grabbed a soda and slammed the door shut. Tears burned behind my eyes, but I could no longer tell whether they were tears of sorrow or anger.

Villari turned around so he was facing me and straddled his chair. "I haven't accused you of anything, Maggie. I just don't understand why you would treat a letter from a murder victim so carelessly. This could be entered as evidence in a courtroom and you're using it as a place mat for a pizza box."

"Evidence for what?" I asked, my hands on my hips.

"Nothing yet."

" 'Yet'?"

"Be realistic. Those two grandkids want that money and they want it right now. Chances are very good that they're going to file a suit asserting, in very nice legal terms, that Mrs. Boyer was off her rocker. This letter could help your case as long as you don't use it to line the bottom of the birdcage."

"I don't have a bird," I said, unsuccessfully trying to smile. "But that's not your biggest worry, is it? You're really worried that I may be the murderer."

"I can't overlook anything, Maggie. Every little piece fits in somehow, somewhere. Part of my job is to figure out where you fit in."

"But I'm just an innocent bystander with a plugged toilet," I insisted. I walked to the table and dropped into my chair, sagging against the back. "Next time I'm sticking with the plunger."

Villari chuckled as he swiveled around in his seat to look at me. "Try to look at this objectively. A lady is murdered and you find her in your yard. Is there a reason she's in *your* septic tank? Was it deliberate or just the nearest drop-off site?"

"What does the letter have to do with where her body was found?"

"I don't know. That's why you should take care of it and why I'd like to read it."

"No."

Villari scowled. "And why not?"

"Because it's private. It's mine. And frankly, I'm tired of everyone jumping on my butt acting as though I did something wrong. Until I'm formally charged, the letter stays in my possession. You're looking in the wrong place, Detective. Maybe you could use a little help."

"Help from whom?" he asked, staring me down. I thought about telling him how handsome he was when he was angry, but I didn't think he'd take it too well.

"Me. I know the neighborhood. Like I said at the funeral, people around here will be more willing to talk to someone they know, especially someone who knew and cared about Elizabeth, than a strange cop with a surly attitude."

"Stop right there and listen up."

"No, you stop. Elizabeth was more than my neighbor. She was an important person in my life . . . maybe I'm just beginning to realize how important. She helped me out over the years, and if I can help find out who killed her, then that's exactly what I'm going to do."

"That's exactly what you will *not* do. What you will do is stay out of this investigation, and I mean completely out. This is not a game we're playing, and the last thing I need to worry about is where you are and what mess you've waltzed yourself into."

I gritted my teeth. "Do you have any idea how chauvinistic you sound?"

"I couldn't care less how I sound. This is not a man–woman thing. This is about knowing what the hell you're doing . . . which you most definitely do not."

"But—"

"But when this is all over, we can discuss my surly attitude," he said as he reached over the table and cupped my chin. "And that discussion will very definitely be a man–woman thing."

After Villari left, I wandered around, turning on lamps scattered throughout the house. Built over fifty years ago as the caretaker's cottage for the estate in which Elizabeth spent her married years, the house had no ceiling lights, except in the kitchen, and I'd grown accustomed to the soft shadows flung against the walls by these shaded lightbulbs. Listless, I roamed aimlessly from one room to the next, stopping briefly to trail my fingers across the ratty couch in the front room. It was covered with an old and much-loved afghan my grandmother knitted for my mother on her birthday, two years before she died. The bold splashes of purple and white were supposedly nothing more than a cheery color choice, but I had a hunch my grandmother was a secret fan of the Minnesota Vikings.

Standing in my studio, a quiet calm washed over me. The thick mounds of muted brown clay scattered around the room in different positions and different stages of completion added depth to the stark white room. It seemed alive in some sort of symbiotic way, a place where life was still evolving, like one of those photograph series that show an unborn child changing from month to month. I always breathed easier in this room, where I was still discovering who I was and what I wanted, as though I wasn't yet cast in stone and still had room to maneuver. It's probably why I've always had trouble casting my figures in bronze or some other solid material . . . I can't bear for the work to be done, for the movement to stop. What good was a static picture of some great runner? It was the tempo, the motion, the rhythm that captured the imagination.

I slid onto a stool set in front of a clump of clay that was still reticent, still hesitant to tell its story. Each day I sat on this seat, locked my feet behind the footrest, and ran my fingers over the clay, pushing, prodding, pulling, and kneading, coaxing its secret into the light. It's like trying to get a wild animal to trust you enough to eat food from your hands. In the beginning, you have to remain at a safe distance and stand completely still until the animal makes the first move.

Stroking the clay, I traced the deep fissures, my fingertips listening and searching as I stared out at the forest through the large window in front of my worktable. I could see the beginning of the trail I followed on my daily treks. At the bend, the trees obscured the rest of the path and I longed for the quiet peace of the woods, the respite from life. But now I was no longer brave enough to walk to my mailbox at night, much less hike through the trees with nothing but pinpricks of moonlight to illuminate the forest floor. Like Elizabeth, there would be no witnesses to see my murder, no one to hear my screams.

I shuddered. Things that went bump in the night weren't childhood fears any longer—they were real criminals to bolt the door against. Questions flooded my brain. Did Elizabeth know her killer? Did she know she was about to die? Was it a crime of revenge, a crime of hate?

I couldn't sit around and wonder anymore, relegated to the sidelines. No matter what Villari thought or said to me, I had to do something. There had to be notes, clues, something left behind to explain why someone would take the life of a seventy-year-old woman.

Her house. A picture of that majestic house with its stone columns flashed in my brain and I knew what I had to do. Elizabeth's life was in her house. I had to get in there and look around, coax the secrets from its silent walls. In other words, I desperately needed to snoop.

And suddenly it was all so simple. Not only could I get into her house, but I could walk right up to the front door, ring the bell, and be invited in. Elizabeth herself had paved the way. Her picture, the one she had willed me, was my ticket.

I slid off the stool and rewrapped the plastic sheet around the clay. I ran down the hallway and grabbed my car keys, purse, and a light jacket to protect me from the ever-present evening chill. Mercifully, my temperamental Jeep immediately roared to life without the usual pedal pumping or clutch popping down the short incline of my driveway. Pulling up in front of Elizabeth's house, I jumped out and jogged up the front steps, silently debating whether to use the large brass knocker or the doorbell. Finally, I pushed the doorbell and waited.

"Yes, who is it?"

The deep, impatient voice crackling over the intercom startled me. Benton, Elizabeth's longtime butler and close friend all rolled in one, normally answered the door.

I pressed the talk button.

"It's me, Will. Maggie."

The intercom remained silent for several seconds. "Why are you here?"

I took a deep breath. "I came to get Elizabeth's picture. The one she left me in the will."

"You couldn't wait until tomorrow to get the damn thing?" His words seemed to jump in explosive bursts of static. "You are a greedy little bitch."

"Glad to see your mood has improved. Now could you please answer the door and let me in?"

Several long minutes went by, long enough to make me wonder if he was going to let me stand outside until I gave up and went home. Suddenly the door swung open and Will stood in front of me, his feet apart, the hall light silhouetting his rigid body as shadows accentuated the sharp planes of his face.

My heart sank when I recognized the barely controlled anger. I was not in the mood to deal with another tantrum. I was here on a mission and I needed time alone. Judging by the look on his face, though, he was going to hound my every footstep.

"Well, if it isn't the little gold digger," he sneered.

I sighed. "I just came for the picture, Will. I'm not here to engage in a verbal fistfight with you or Cassie or anyone else. Now . . . may I come in, please?"

Will moved imperceptibly, and I took the movement as a sign that I was being allowed in, admittedly without the proverbial red carpet or even a lousy welcome mat. I slipped past him and waited in the hallway until he shut the door and turned around.

"The picture's in Grandmother's office. I'm surprised you didn't take it this afternoon."

"I wasn't thinking very clearly. Some of us were more overcome by sadness than others," I said pointedly.

His face darkened. "You've accused me of not caring about Grandmother for the last time," he warned. "You have no right to speak to me that way. My feelings are my own business and I see no reason to debate the issue with someone who clearly took advantage of her advanced age and loneliness."

"Don't bother with the lies, Will. I don't believe anything that comes out of your mouth. Save the grieving-grandson routine for someone who is gullible," I said, starting down the hallway. "Right now I'm going to Elizabeth's office. Don't feel obligated to show me the way. I was here this afternoon when you got the bad news, remember?"

The flush started at his collar and worked its way up his face. When it passed his forehead, I half expected the top of his head to blow off like a cartoon character.

"Don't think for one minute that you'll see a dime of our money, Maggie. Cassandra and I are already working with another attorney to get the will invalidated."

"What do you expect to find?" I asked, spinning around to face him. "That I tampered with the will? Do you think I deleted your name and typed in my own?"

His chin jutted out like the pouty little boy he still was. "Grandmother would never forget me. She told me the money was Cassandra's and mine, not some stray oddball she picked up next door."

If I hadn't been so intent on getting to Elizabeth's office, I would have popped him right then and there. A broken nose would have been an improvement. Will's face was mottled with anger and the skin underneath his chin was beginning to sag although he was only in his late twenties, somewhere close to my age. But despite the softness, Will was still skinny, with sharp elbows, a pointy chin, and big elephant ears. He peered myopically through his black horn-rimmed glasses, still looking like Poindexter with a bad attitude, and still giving me the creeps.

"Why did you take me out to dinner if you thought I was odd?"

"It was Grandmother's idea. She thought we'd make a cute couple."

I grimaced at the picture we made that night—me in my standard bag dress and Will nervously sweating in his coat and tie, one hand fidgeting with the keys in his pocket.

"You didn't have to agree to go at all, you know. You're a big boy. I'm sure Elizabeth would have gotten over the disappointment. I'm hardly your type. You could have saved us both a fairly long evening, to put it politely."

"You know how persistent Grandmother can... could be. She thought it was a good idea and she kept pushing until it happened. She was a stubborn old lady."

I detected a faint note of wistfulness underneath his obnoxious exterior. Every once in a while a glimmer of something rose to the surface that actually made him seem human. Will tried to squelch this side of himself as often as he could, and unfortunately, he was quite successful at doing so. So Will remained Will, obnoxious and rude on the outside . . . and obnoxious and rude on the inside.

"You know, Will. Stubbornness and persistence are usually not adjectives we use to describe weak, lonely old ladies. You might want to spend time with a thesaurus looking up some new words to describe Elizabeth if you want to convince the judge that she was a crazy old lady with cotton for brains."

"You little—" he began, but I cut him off.

"Yeah, I drive men crazy that way," I said, sauntering off down the hall, praying he wouldn't follow. A door slammed behind me and I was fairly sure Will had stomped into the library to sulk.

The library. Elizabeth always began her fancy dinners with champagne cocktails and martinis in the library. In my mind, I saw her standing in my studio, staring out the window and regaling me with stories about her evening while I worked on my latest sculpture.

"Ah, Maggie, you should have seen Marianne floating into the room, wearing some little slip of a thing that was three sizes too small, with a décolletage that dipped down to her navel, the whole ensemble precariously held up by two thin spaghetti straps. I spent the whole evening waiting for the straps to break and for her superb breasts to flop into the lobster bisque, but the damn things held up magnificently." She turned to study my work in progress and sighed deeply. "Unfortunately, nothing happened, and it was another excruciatingly mundane evening with the kind of dull, polite conversation so often associated with a good cause."

"And these are the evenings you'd like me to attend?"

"Ah, yes!" she said, clapping her hands together. "We would have such a delightful time together. It would be wonderful to share them with someone who sees the world the same way I do. Who knows? If you'd been there last night, we might have found a way to snip the straps on Marianne's dress just to see everyone's expression."

I had forgotten about that mischievous sparkle that

danced in her eyes whenever she wanted to do something this side of naughty.

"Elizabeth, someday when I have nothing else to do—
and I mean *nothing* else—I'll let you drag me to one of
these dinners of yours. In the meantime, I'll just have to
be content with your stories to spice up my boring little
life."

I forced the memory aside and swiped at my eyes
with the back of my hand as I reached Elizabeth's office.
The door was open an inch or two, so I nudged it a little
and quickly stepped in. The room was dark and eerie,
her scent still permeating the air. I closed the door softly
and leaned against it. The moonlight slid noiselessly
through the windows and bounced off the back of the
same chairs we had sat in this afternoon, still arranged
in a semicircle in front of her desk. Shadows pooled on
the carpet like dark stains. Realizing I had very little
time to spare before Will became suspicious, I stopped
surveying the room and tiptoed to Elizabeth's desk. Her
leather chair swiveled as I sat down behind the desk and
began to open the drawers one by one, not sure what I
was looking for. I could only hope that if I came across
something important, it would have the sense to be
stamped and filed in an envelope marked IMPORTANT
MURDER MATERIAL.

It came as no surprise that Elizabeth's drawers were
meticulously organized. The middle one held perfectly
aligned pens and pencils, paper clips, personalized no-
tepads, and other types of stationery. The larger drawer
on the right-hand side was actually a small file cabinet
filled with twenty or thirty separate files. Each file was
neatly labeled with the names of different charities and
organizations Elizabeth contributed to in some form or

other over the years. In the last drawer on the left, there were folders stuffed with financial information. I pulled a few of these files and flipped quickly through the pages, but the numbers began to run together in my head and were nothing more than gibberish to me.

Without warning, the faint sound of footsteps disturbed the silence, growing louder and louder as they rapidly approached Elizabeth's office. With my heart pounding in my chest and my palms breaking out in a sweat, I shut the drawer, jumped up, and pushed her chair back into its original position. I took one last look around and prayed that I returned everything to where it belonged. But the moment I started to turn away, my eyes fell on the appointment book sitting on top of the desk. Without thinking, I grabbed it and threw it in my large leather bag. I raced to the wall and had both hands on the frame of Elizabeth's picture just as the door was thrown open hard enough to slam against the opposite wall. The crash seemed obscenely loud in the deep silence.

"What the hell is taking so long?" Will demanded.

I jumped back, tripped over a small painting leaning against the wall, and nearly stumbled to the floor. "My God, Will, do you have to barge into the room like you thought I was stealing the family jewels?"

"I'll enter any room in this house the way I want to. This is still my house and I want to know why you're still in it. Quite frankly, you've been in here long enough to actually steal the family jewels."

My throat closed at the thought of Will becoming suspicious enough to rummage through my purse. It would be difficult to explain Elizabeth's appointment book thrown in with my Chap Stick, checkbook, and sketchpad.

"You really do have family jewels?" I exclaimed, trying to distract him. "Tiaras and diamond necklaces and emerald chokers?"

"Of course we do, just not right out here in the open. They're in a vault—" He stopped and narrowed his eyes. "Why do you care?"

I shook my head. "I don't. Just making polite conversation." I turned back and carefully lifted the landscape from the wall. "Elizabeth was quite talented," I said so softly I might have been speaking to myself. "It's too bad she gave up painting for so many years. I think she could have been a very important artist."

"That wasn't her doing. It was that bastard she was married to."

"I never met him."

"No, he died several years ago, a true blessing. It gave Grandmother a few years to live her life the way she wanted without him trying to force her to bend to his will all the time."

"Sounds like he tried to force all of you."

Will walked over to the circle of chairs and slumped down in one of them. "Not me. He didn't bother to acknowledge me with anything more than a nod of his head as we passed in the hallway. Sometimes I used to wonder if he knew who I was or whether he thought I was just another one of the servants."

Uh-oh. I was starting to feel guilty for my small act of burglary. Maybe Will's whole loathsome, repulsive act was a poignant cry for help. Maybe this was his way of grieving, not only for Elizabeth, but for an entire loveless childhood.

"You know, Will, sometimes you say things that could actually be construed as human. Maybe you ought to try and expand that side of you a little instead of keeping it so well hidden most of the time."

He laughed. "Don't go getting all mushy and female on me, Maggie. The only thing I've ever remotely liked about you is your tough-as-nails attitude."

Great. So much for my sparkling personality.

"And the only thing that made that old man tolerable was knowing I would inherit his estate through Grandmother," he added for further clarification.

"How sentimental," I responded dryly.

"Sentiment is a waste of time. It doesn't get me, or Cassandra, any closer to the money that Grandmother assured us. The fact is, after all her promises about how I would be a wealthy man when she died, she ended up betraying me. Well, now she's dead. Grandmother is dead and she lied to me. If you expect me to be completely devastated, you'll be disappointed. The only thing on my mind is how to get rid of any obstacle that lies between me and the wealth that is rightfully mine." He took a deep breath and stared right at me, his eyes cold and flat. "And right now that obstacle is you."

My guilt flew out the window. Right then, if I could have found the family jewels, I would have gladly dumped them in my bag, too.

Chapter Six

Escaping Will was not as easy as I had hoped. He hovered right behind me, shadowing me like a police dog sniffing for drugs, down the hallway, through the front door, right to my Jeep. It wouldn't have surprised me to see him climb into the passenger seat. Terrified that he would smell my nervous perspiration, reach into my bag, and discover the evidence of the crime I'd committed, I hurriedly placed the portrait in the backseat and shut the car door in his face before peeling out of the driveway at breakneck speed.

But I made it. Safe at home, I leaned Elizabeth's picture against the wall. I tossed my purse onto the middle of the bed and took a hot shower to wash away what felt like an inch of grime from my body. Thankfully, Will hadn't smelled anything, but I was drenched in sweat and I knew I reeked. Twenty minutes later, washed, dried, and snuggled into a pair of old sweats and a soft flannel shirt I stole from my father's hunting closet, I crawled onto the bed and let out a huge sigh. After a few minutes of wallowing in my relief, I took in a deep breath, reached across the bed, and tugged my bag onto my lap. I dug around inside until my fingers closed over the appointment book. Pulling the slim volume from my purse, I studied it for a long time without moving. It was one thing to steal the book from Elizabeth's dark office with Will standing in the background ready to rip my throat out. Then, the danger was real. Self-preservation kicked in and there was a purpose to the burglary. Here in my own room, though, with the Day-Timer resting innocently in my lap, things weren't as clear. Should I have stolen the book?

I shook away the guilt. Will wasn't the only enemy. Villari was out there combing the area for information to put me behind bars, and I wasn't going to sit still while he lined all his ducks in a row. I didn't have that luxury. The longer the case dragged on, the colder the killer's trail. If the detective wanted to single me out as the guilty party, fine. But I couldn't let Elizabeth's memory be forever overshadowed by her violent murder. The only way I knew to fight back, the only way to free me from the nightmarish pictures that continually bombarded my brain, was to find the murderer myself. At least I would try.

And if Villari refused to help me, then Elizabeth would. I flipped open the appointment book and quickly riffled through the pages. Nothing immediately jumped out and cuffed me on the head, so I took a deep breath and calmed down. I told myself that what I was doing wasn't any big deal . . . a little devious perhaps, definitely a little nosy, but certainly not worth a jail term if I got caught. Surely the inmates in maximum security were guilty of bigger crimes than diary snooping. Besides, I had to start somewhere.

I went back to the beginning, back to January, and leafed through the pages one by one. There were no surprises, nothing that screamed *clue leading up to the murder,* but I refused to hurry and jump ahead. There was no rhyme or reason to my methodology; I'd never taken Intro to Criminology and didn't have the slightest idea how to go about detecting. But I figured there was nothing to lose by starting at the beginning and proceeding straight to the end.

Some of the names I read matched the ones I had seen on Elizabeth's files in her office. Some of the charity events listed were well-known gala balls and fundraisers Elizabeth organized herself. Because so many of the names were vaguely familiar in one way or another, most of the entries were easy to skim through, despite the fact that Elizabeth led a very busy life and that her calendar was stuffed with activities and appointments. By the time I reached June, the last month of her life, I was frustrated, much like I imagined a cop feels after chasing a suspect for two miles on foot only to find himself staring at a six-foot wall rimmed in barbed wire. (One day on the job and I was already thinking in police similes.) After scanning June's entries, I started to close the book when I noticed a small notation lightly penciled in at the bottom of a page marked with several small asterisks. The date was Tuesday, exactly one week before I found Elizabeth.

****1:00—*Lindsay Burns, Woodlake Meadows*
1653 Blue Spruce
*Corner of Jasmine and Ponderosa***

The address surprised me. Woodlake Meadows was a development in Peyton, a small town and suburb located on the outer rim of Colorado Springs. The land was flat and dry, blanketed in tall grass reminiscent of the fields in Kansas and Nebraska. The Meadows, as it was dubbed in the press, was hyped to be the next affordable but luxurious community development for young families. Man-made lakes and artificial waterfalls were all part of the package. An intricate irrigation system would produce rolling green hills and sustain numerous aspen trees lining the streets, an otherwise impossible task in an arid climate with extreme weather changes. Four different models of homes were advertised for immediate occupancy. The whole concept of an oasis in the middle of a desert appealed to people, a little like trying to outsmart Mother Nature.

Unfortunately, things had gone wrong right from the beginning. The water table of the development's proposed site was deeper than originally thought and the irrigation system was faulty. Investors quickly dropped out and the development died a quiet little death, leaving just two blocks of completed homes, only a few of which were actually occupied. The land was parched and the houses were tired little constructions thrown up haphazardly before the whole development went belly up. I couldn't imagine Elizabeth even visiting this neighborhood.

I put the Day-Timer in the drawer in the nightstand next to my bed, turned off the lamp, and pulled the covers up to my chin. Snapshots of Villari's dark eyes and heavily stubbled chin intermingled with drifting memories of Elizabeth working in my studio. Will's pale, clammy face wafted across my brain, dragging Cassie's pouty expression right behind. I blinked my eyes against them all and turned on my side. Tomorrow I would visit Woodlake. I couldn't do anything to change Elizabeth's death, but I could keep searching until her killer was found.

THE day dawned pale and pink, the sky swatches of diluted colors. Wearing thick cotton socks and a large sweatshirt pulled over my flannel shirt, I drank my coffee sitting on top of the bar stool at the kitchen counter. Colorado mornings and evening are always cool, even in the dead of summer, but the chill is a welcome respite from the heat of the day. It's a study of contrasts. The weather shifts from hot to cold, from sunshine to rain, and from clear skies to fog and snow in a matter of minutes. I was drawn to its volatility when I graduated from college in California, where the weather travels on cruise control.

Elizabeth's smiling face stared up at me from the newspaper. I had the paper open to the obituaries, something I did every morning. Perusing obituaries was part of my daily routine. I'd scan the page, tally the ages of the deceased, and pray that the column labeled *Over Eighty* was longer than the column marked *Under Forty*. I knew it was a morbid habit, but I couldn't shake the slight sense of relief I felt when the older folks took the lead.

It was disconcerting to see Elizabeth's picture in the obits, even though I had found her body, been to her funeral, dealt with her recalcitrant grandchildren, and stolen her appointment book. Even though I should have expected the write-up, it was one more occurrence that marked her final passing. Murder was listed simply as a cause of death, but it was obvious that the reporter had done plenty of research. The column enumerated all Elizabeth's community work and concluded with the usual family information. The funeral was described as a private memorial service for the family, and although there would be no public service due to the unusual circumstances, donations were asked to be sent to one of several specific charities in lieu of flowers. What the reporter neglected to point out was that the funeral was private because Will and Cassie couldn't wait to throw the old lady underground. They didn't give anyone a chance to arrange a regular funeral, insisting that Elizabeth would have hated it. But I knew that was a crock. She would have loved all the pomp and circumstance and everyone paying homage, as long as her spirit or ghost or whatever could sit back and watch.

I glanced at the clock and decided against calling Lindsay Burns before going to meet her. I wasn't sure how to introduce myself over the phone and I didn't want to give her the option of hanging up or refusing to see me, especially since there was a good possibility that I was off on a wild-goose chase. For all I knew, this lady could be Elizabeth's manicurist or an old friend who had fallen on hard times. Or maybe, just maybe, Lindsay Burns knew something. If she did, I wanted to be there in person.

I was out of my house in under a half hour. It never takes me long to get ready, one of the advantages of my baggy clothes uniform that Villari derided. I didn't spend time in front of the mirror wondering if something made me look fat or thin . . . everything made me look shapeless, and as far as I was concerned, this expedited the incredibly boring routine of getting dressed.

My Jeep sputtered to life after several enthusiastic pedal pumps. Out on the Interstate, I flipped on the radio to listen to the seven o'clock top-of-the-hour news as I drove south toward the Woodmen exit. I felt a little nervous about showing up uninvited at someone's house this early in the morning, but I was afraid Lindsay Burns might have a job and be out of the house before eight. Knowing my luck, we'd pass each other going in different directions, she on her way to work, me on my way to her empty house.

I turned east on Woodmen, away from the mountains. Amazingly enough, I actually flew through several green lights, so that I was out of the city and driving through farm country in no time at all. I propped a map of Colorado Springs and the surrounding areas against my steering wheel. Driving with one hand, I folded the map to the town of Peyton. It didn't take me long to find the small blue circle marked *Woodland Meadows*. I took Woodmen out to Route 83 and turned right at the light, driving south for a few miles until I saw an imposing brick structure on the left side of the road marking the entrance to a now barren community. I pulled in and drove slowly past a vacant gatehouse. Three separate roads extended out like spokes in a bicycle wheel. Blue Spruce was the first street on the right and number 1653 stood on the intersection of Blue Spruce and an un-marked street I figured was intended to be either Jasmine or Ponderosa.

I pulled a U-turn and parked at the curb. I rubbed my damp palms against my jeans as I walked past the driveway and up the front steps. Standing at the door, I took a deep breath, straightened my sweater, and rang the doorbell. I nervously shifted my weight from one foot to the other, looking like a child in dire need of a bathroom.

Suddenly the door opened just a crack. One green eye peeked out.

"Yes?"

"Hi! You must be Lindsay Burns," I chirped. My God, I sounded like a bubbly cheerleader. The kind I absolutely despise. I started over. "My name is Maggie Kean. I'm a friend of Elizabeth Boyer."

No answer. The emerald eye never even blinked.

"Mrs. Boyer died recently . . . perhaps you read about it in the newspaper?" I was desperately fishing for a way to explain my presence here, but her stare was truly disquieting. She reminded me of my second-grade teacher, Mrs. Blake. She caught me stealing Brian Simpson's crayon box and simply stared at me with her "I know what you did and we'll sit here until you decide to admit the truth" look. It worked, too. In no time at all, I broke down and confessed to the damn crime.

"Mrs. Boyer's demise was rather sudden—"

"She was murdered." Emerald Eye actually spoke.

I nodded. "That's right."

"What does that have to do with me?"

The lady could use a refresher course in social skills. "I am, or was, Mrs. Boyer's part-time secretary. I ran her office, took care of her bills, her social calendar, things like that. Since her death, I've been trying to get her affairs in order and I found your name." I was back-pedaling a mile a minute and spinning lies like crazy, but I had no other choice. I couldn't very well present myself as Elizabeth's neighbor, the one who found her body, stole her calendar, and found Lindsay Burns's name penciled in at the bottom of a page. "I was hoping to talk with you about your business with Mrs. Boyer, in case it's something I need to follow up on or complete for her."

"We didn't have any business together," she said firmly.

"Ms. Burns, would you mind if I came in? It's a little chilly out here and talking to you through a small opening isn't conducive to conversation." I held up my hand, palm out, like I was taking the Boy Scout oath. "I promise to leave as soon as we're finished talking and—"

"We're finished talking now," she said, closing the door.

Without thinking, I jammed the toe of my foot into the small gap before she had a chance to shut it completely. To my relief, I didn't hear any bones crunch, but there was something going on here and I didn't want to leave without knowing what it was.

"What do you think you're doing? Get out of the way or I'll call the cops."

She tried to shut the door, but my foot was now wedged in tightly and it was too late to turn back now. "Ms. Burns, I'm not here to start any trouble. I just want to find out where you fit in Elizabeth Boyer's life so I can finish what needs to be finished and close her office. Obviously, you're afraid of something. Maybe I can help you."

Lindsay Burns opened the door a few inches wider and stepped into the doorway. Her hair hung limply to her shoulders and her roots were in big trouble. She had a dark streak running down the middle of her head.

Lindsay Burns wasn't much older than I was—in fact, she may have been younger—but her skin was pale and translucent like someone over eighty who lived alone in a dark house with the shades drawn. One eye sported a fading but suspicious-looking bruise and her lips were chapped and cracked, especially the bottom one, which she was gnawing on at the moment. Her dress was right off an old ladies' rack, one of those square sacks my mother used to call a housedress. I didn't know what this girl's problem was, but something bad went on in this house.

Behind her, the living room was neat and tidy. Two well-worn beige couches faced each other with a small oval rug between them. There was the usual coffee table, two end tables, a lamp, and a vase filled with dried flowers, all blending together to create a space as plain and dreary as a bowl of blanched vegetables. Everything was the color of oatmeal, grits, unburied dog bones, dingy curtains, peeled potatoes, or day-old snow. And Lindsay Burns, with her yellowed dress and lousy dye job, faded naturally into this nondescript background. All pale and washed-out, except for the emerald eyes. Except for the watercolors hanging on the wall. Except for the yellow and orange and red and blue plastic toys strewn around the floor.

"Look, I'll tell you the same thing I told that woman who came knocking at my door last week. Take my advice and get out of here and throw my name in the fire before somebody gets hurt. Don't ever come back here again or I'll forget the cops and turn my dog on you for trespassing." Lindsay Burns took a step backward and slammed the door.

Thank God I moved my foot.

By the time I drove home and let myself into the house, it was still early, just a little past eight-thirty. I had stopped at Bruennegger's on the way and bought myself a garlic bagel slathered with garlic and dill cream cheese and a large cup of hot coffee. I managed to eat a few bites before throwing the rest in the trash can underneath the sink. I took my coffee into the studio. I was still shaking an hour later, but it wasn't from the caffeine. Lindsay Burns had gotten to me. Hiding behind a half-opened door when a stranger comes calling isn't surprising these days. In fact, it makes sense. But she wasn't hiding from me because I was a stranger. She was hiding because she was afraid.

That wasn't all. I'm not sure what I expected, but Lindsay Burns was not Elizabeth's usual cup of tea. Of course, neither was I, but there was a difference. My clothes didn't come from exclusive boutiques, and God knows, I'm not listed in the Social Register, but I did have a life inside and outside my home. I had the distinct feeling that the girl I met today was a recluse. The pallor she wore was the result of holing up somewhere in the dark.

I removed the plastic sheet from my latest block of "nothing yet" and ran my fingers lightly over the clay. I walked around the table and examined the clay from all angles, running my fingers down the side and across the top as every thought fled from my brain, leaving it open for what some people erroneously call inspiration. But that's not really what happens when I sculpt . . . not if I'm lucky. It's nothing I do, or think, or envision, that begins the process. It's something this brown mass of earth does all by itself. Somehow, in all the touching and probing, the clay sends a message. Without realizing or even understanding what's happening, my hands begin to shape and mold. Sometimes I simply rest my fingertips against the cool clay and my hands start to move on their own, pulling me along behind. It's a crazy, heady feeling like being on a boat and riding the waves while the captain mans the sails.

It doesn't always happen that way, though. More often than not, I have to take the long way around and sort of prod the subconscious message along. On a slow day, I usually leave the clay, drag my stool up next to the window or directly underneath the skylight, and start sketching, usually human figures. Drawing isn't my strongest skill; I'd go broke inside a month if I had to rely on my pictures for income, but it's a good foundation for sculpting.

"Are you any good?"

I jumped at least six inches off the stool and went crashing onto the floor. My sketchbook went flying and I narrowly missed landing on my charcoal pencil. I looked up to see Villari's face pressed up against the screen, chuckling at the picture I made sprawled out on the wooden floor.

"What the hell?" I sputtered.

"Are you okay?" he asked, grinning. "I didn't mean to scare you . . . well, maybe I was going for a slight startle, but I didn't expect such an explosive reaction."

I scraped myself off the ground, flustered and embarrassed by my own klutziness.

"Was the front door hard to find?" I asked sarcastically, brushing off my clothes and pushing back my hair. "How did you expect me to react when you come sneaking through the bushes and—hey, you're not stepping on my impatiens, are you?"

Villari glanced down at his feet. "Nope. I'm standing very carefully between the juniper bushes, which, by the way, need some major trimming, the wheelbarrow, and your little row of flowers. So you can stop worrying."

"Why would I worry? Now that you're stalking me at my own house, I feel perfectly comfortable."

"I'm not stalking. I knocked on the door and no one answered. I figured you were either in the bedroom or working in the studio."

I frowned. "Were you planning on peeking in my bedroom window if you didn't find me here?"

"I would have knocked on the window before peeking. It's not my policy to barge in uninvited."

"I'm so happy to hear you have such scruples," I said dryly. "I would have guessed you were the type to barge in exactly where you *weren't* invited."

Villari grinned. "See how wrong first impressions can be?"

"Enough of the chitchat, Detective. Tell me what you want, then get the hell out of here."

"Fair enough. But I'm tired of talking to you through a screen. I feel like a fly with compound eyes. Would you mind opening the front door?"

"I'll let you in, but I'm not offering you coffee or making you breakfast, so don't get any ideas. There's a neighborhood doughnut shop a couple of miles away where you can meet some of your cronies and feel right at home."

"You're downright prickly this morning."

"I was prickly before you arrived. Now I'm downright irritated," I said, my rubber-soled shoes squeaking on the wooden floor as I turned and stomped out of the room.

Villari was slouched against the doorjamb when I opened the door. At first glance, his face appeared devoid of expression, but upon closer inspection, it was impossible to miss the twinkle of amusement that flashed in his eyes. He stepped forward, forcing me backward as he closed the door behind him.

"So who pissed in your cereal this morning?"

"Lovely expression," I murmured, turning my back on him and walking into the kitchen.

"Not really, but it seems apropos. Something's happened to make you more hostile than usual."

"If something did, it's my business," I replied, pulling a mug off the wooden stand. I poured myself a cup of coffee, which at this time of the morning tasted lousy, burned and bitter, but mercifully hot. I laced my fingers around the cup before turning around, watching the steam float into the air as I blew across the top.

"Normally, it would be, but these aren't normal times," Villari said, eyeing my coffee with something akin to lust. "Want to tell me where you went this morning?"

I went completely still. How did he know I'd been anywhere? Unless . . . "You low-down, sneaky . . ." I stammered. "You're spying on me?" I slammed the mug on the counter, ignoring the coffee that spilled over the rim. "Since you obviously followed me, then you know exactly where I was. The problem is, you don't know why I was there, do you?"

Villari's eyes glittered dangerously. "For your information, we've got a cop circling the block every half hour. We want to avoid a repeat of Elizabeth Boyer. It's not much protection, but it's the best I could get. When the patrol shift changed, I happened to be at my desk finishing up some paperwork. Joe walked in and mentioned to the cop taking over the job that your car was missing from the driveway when he drove by around seven."

"So my car was missing. That's a crime now?"

"No, that's not a crime, Maggie," Villari said in a menacingly soft whisper as he walked toward me, "but I've been a cop long enough to know when someone is hiding something. Do you want to tell me what's going on?"

I wondered how much he knew and whether I could trust him. It's not that I had anything concrete to show for my little trip down to Woodlake Meadows, but when I took that book from Elizabeth's desk, I crossed a line. I knew what I wanted, what I had to do if I ever wanted to put Elizabeth to rest peacefully. But this man seemed intent on proving me guilty, whether it was true or not.

Standing in the middle of my kitchen, both hands propped on his lean hips, he saw me hesitate. "Spill it, Maggie. Whatever it is you know or think you know."

His voice snapped me from my thoughts. I turned, picked up the sponge from the sink, and mopped the counter, feeling his eyes on my back as he patiently waited for my answer. I swung around and faced him. "Look, you're very good at this intimidation routine, and if I had anything to confess, I would have done so a long time ago. But I haven't done anything wrong except go about my daily life and I don't feel obligated to tell you about every little move I make." I skirted past him and started toward the breakfast room. Of course, he followed me. Close behind.

"I don't suppose you did very well in Tailing Suspects 101? Didn't they tell you to put a little distance between you and the person you're following?"

Villari reached out and took hold of my arm to stop me. Gathering my courage for a full-blown argument, I turned and looked up to see him quietly studying my face, his coal-black eyes gentle and calm.

"I doubt you did much better in Trust 101."

And with that unexpected bombshell of sensitivity, my heart went pitter-patter and my stomach flip-flopped and my knees wobbled. I wasn't ready for understanding or simple sweetness, not with Elizabeth just barely in her grave and not with the pain so new. And I especially did not want anything from someone who looked like he stepped out of *People*'s "Sexiest Man Alive" issue while I could easily be the editor of *RagTag Weekly*.

The man was standing too damned close for comfort. His breath, warm and sweet, fanned my face, and to my complete disgust, a funny feeling kept fluttering around inside. I put both hands on his chest and pushed.

He didn't budge.

With one hand, he covered mine and held them to his chest. With his free hand, he cupped my chin and tilted it upward. "I have the feeling I may regret this, Maggie, but apparently I left my senses out there on the doorstep."

"Stop manhandling me, you overgrown dim-witted sack of muscles," I protested weakly.

"Hold still, Maggie," he said, trailing his thumb down the side of my cheek as he held my chin in his palm. "Trust me, we'll get to manhandling later. But right now we're just testing a theory."

Then he kissed me.

Chapter Seven

Don't get me wrong. I've been kissed before. Just not that way. Not with that soft, sweet nibbling at my bottom lip, nuzzling against my mouth until my knees buckled. And not with a tongue lazily skimming along the top of my teeth. Villari's lips took possession and all I could do was grab onto his shirt and hang on. He smelled faintly of coffee and minty toothpaste, and before I could stop myself, I was kissing him back.

I flushed, trembled like an aspen leaf, and was getting genuinely hot and bothered when Villari suddenly lifted his head and gazed at me with those dark liquid eyes.

"You're a lovely woman, Maggie, although God knows you do your best to hide that fact."

Heat suffused my face. "I bet you say that to all the girls."

Villari grinned. "Nope. Just you. I have a real thing for women swimming in extra-large T-shirts."

"Happy to oblige."

Chuckling, he released my chin and kissed the corner of my mouth, behind my ears, trailing his lips down to the hollow of my throat, where I could feel his moist breath on my neck. Still holding my hands close to his chest, his slid his other arm around my waist and pulled me even closer.

"I think we ought to slow down here a little, Villari," I managed to say, after coming up for air a second time.

"You're probably right," he said, his voice muffled against my skin. "I'll probably get my butt kicked for this."

"Maybe we should pick this up a little later."

"It would certainly be the smart thing to do."

I wanted to pull back, but the whispery kisses fanning the base of my throat weakened my resolve. The man was excruciatingly thorough, taking his time with each kiss, the heat of his fingertips burning my skin until I had no strength to fight him off. I hung there like a limp doll, too helpless against the sensations that radiated from every part of my body to be bothered with questions of whether or not this was the right thing to do.

As usual, life intervened. The phone rang.

Villari lifted his head and stared at me in a daze. I wasn't doing much better. I blinked my eyes several times to force my brain out of its sex-induced fog.

"I'd better get that," I said, squirming out of his embrace.

"This doesn't end here, Maggie. You know that." He dropped my hands and took a step back.

I snaked by without answering him and grabbed the cordless phone.

"Hello?"

"Maggie, it's me. I've got an hour before Joel has to

leave for work. Want to get some breakfast? I'm starving."

"Um, thanks, Lisa, but I've eaten already."

"Which means you drank two or three cups of coffee, right? If you're not hungry, come sit with me and keep me company. We can talk about that gorgeous hunk of detective that keeps sniffing around."

I glanced over at Villari, who had poured himself some coffee and was now sitting on a bar stool pulling the sports section from the newspaper. The scene was entirely too domestic for my taste. He looked up, grinned at what I thought was my very best scowl, toasted me with his cup, and mouthed, "Lousy coffee."

"Yeah, well, he's sniffing around in my kitchen as we speak," I said to Lisa.

"Detective Villari is right there?"

"Yep. He's made himself right at home and it's starting to irritate me."

"I love it. Have him stick around until you're really angry. Nothing's better than sex after a nasty fight."

I sighed. "Try to expand your horizons past the Boy Meets Girl scenario. This is the new millennium, Lisa. Women don't wear petticoats and men don't wear loincloths. I'm not the fair maiden here and—" I stopped abruptly when I realized that Villari had put down the newspaper and was staring at me with one eyebrow lifted and a very amused look on his face.

"Look, I've got to go, Lisa. I'll call you later." I hung up the receiver. "Don't say a word, Villari. I'm in a lousy mood."

"Loincloths?"

"Forget it. Lisa has her own screwy view of the world and it's rarely compatible with what's happening in the real one." I grabbed my coffee, which had cooled considerably while Villari decided to get amorous, and stuck it in the microwave to reheat. I set the timer for forty-five seconds before turning around. "By the way, are you leaving soon?"

"You've got a great way with people, Maggie. Keep it up and I may nominate you for Hostess of the Year. You'd be a shoo-in."

"I'm not trying to win a popularity contest, Detective. I'm trying to get my life back to normal and you seem intent on impeding that process."

"We're back to 'Detective,' I see."

The microwave *ping*ed. I pulled my coffee out and shut the door. "That is your job, isn't it? You *are* supposed to be finding Elizabeth's Boyer's murderer, aren't you?"

Villari leaned back in his chair and crossed his arms in front of his chest. "You get downright bristly when you're kissed, don't you?"

"Could we stick to one subject, please? The kiss was an aberration. I will admit it was nice, but it doesn't change anything. I still have rent to pay and Elizabeth is still dead."

"Okay, Maggie, we'll do it your way . . . for a little while. Let's go back to question number one. Where were you this morning?"

While I sputtered into my coffee, life interfered for the second time, this time in the form of a ringing telephone. I snatched up the hand set and prayed for a long-winded telemarketer making a pitch for a new phone service or a new credit card with a preapproved credit limit and an astronomical interest rate. Anything to keep me on the phone and away from Villari's piercing eyes and questions I didn't want to answer.

"Hello?" No one answered. I tried again. "Hello?"

"Elizabeth Boyer was killed because she asked too many questions. Don't make the same mistake." *Click*.

I felt the blood drain from my face. I never heard the phone hit the floor, but Villari was up in two seconds flat, grabbing my arms and turning me to face him.

"Who the hell was that?" He shook me. "Maggie, talk to me."

I couldn't answer him. The walls bulged in and out like they were breathing and the room began to stretch and bend like a funhouse mirror. My stomach started to pitch and turn and sweat broke out on my forehead. Before I knew it, Villari had lifted me in his arms and carried me to the kitchen table. With one foot, he pulled out a chair and sat me down.

"Put your head between your legs. I don't want you fainting on me."

I did as I was told mostly because I didn't have the strength to do otherwise. After a few minutes the rolling stopped and the world straightened out, and I felt a little better.

"Breathe slowly and evenly. Take your time."

My stomach eased up bit by bit and I managed to pull myself upright without throwing up three cups of coffee. Villari brought me a towel he had dampened with cool water from the sink. I accepted it gratefully and wiped the sheen of sweat off my face.

Villari dragged one of the kitchen chairs across the floor and sat down next to me. "What happened, Maggie? Who was on the phone?"

I shook my head. "I don't know."

"Okay, Maggie," Villari said patiently. "Just tell me what the caller said to you. Don't leave out any details."

Details? It was pretty short and sweet, if you ask me. A threat, pure and simple. No need to dress it up with fancy words. Villari waited quietly while I calmed down enough to repeat the caller's warning.

"Do you have any idea who it might have been? Did you recognize the voice?"

I shuddered. "No. It sounded like a male, but the voice was so low and whispery I could be wrong about that. It was this creepy voice, just like the ones you hear in horror movies, talking through the phone and asking if you know where your children are."

Villari laid his hand on my shoulder. "You're doing fine, Maggie. I just need to ask you a couple more questions. Have you talked to anyone about Elizabeth's death?"

"Not really. School's out, so most people are gone . . . off on vacation and things like that." I hesitated a moment. "Besides, Lisa's the only one of my friends who has even met Elizabeth." I looked up into his eyes and answered his unasked question. "Don't even go down that road, Villari. I would trust her with my life."

He was quiet for a few minutes.

"Elizabeth's funeral was yesterday, Villari. Even if I wanted to, I haven't had time to talk to anyone, even in passing. The only people who know anything are the ones who read the obits this morning, and the newspaper said very little about the actual cause of death."

"Yeah, I know." Villari scratched the stubble on his chin. "The press has been cooperative so far, but I'm not sure how long we can keep it that way. We've insisted that public knowledge would impede the investigation, but that won't work too much longer. Once the details are out, especially about your involvement, the media will circle this place like ravenous sharks."

"What about Will or Cassie?" I didn't have any difficulty seeing them huddled around the phone talking through a handkerchief and laughing with glee at my distress.

"I don't know, Maggie. So far neither one of them has hidden their animosity toward you. They've already made a big stink about the will, the investigation, and anything else that has stood in the way of them getting their hands on their inheritance. I don't see them sneaking around threatening you over the phone, not when they're already doing it in public. Of course, that's only my first hunch. It won't keep me from questioning them further."

"If it's not them, who would do this?"

"I don't know, Maggie. I'm going to get a tap put on your phone and try and beef up security around here. If we're lucky, maybe the culprit will call back and give us a chance to trace the call."

"Yeah, if we're lucky," I muttered dryly as Villari walked over and hung up the phone. Nothing sparks up my day more than a death threat. My hands were still trembling, so I clamped them together like I was praying. Which I was. I've never been a devout churchgoer; in fact, I'm a lapsed Catholic despite the years I spent doing the Big C's: Communion, Confession, and Confirmation. But at a time like this, a prayer seemed like a good idea, even though the only one I could remember at the moment was the grace before meals. I fervently hoped that whoever was looking down from the heavens had a good sense of humor, because I wasn't sure I could even recite the alphabet.

"Maggie?"

I never heard him. With my head bowed and my eyes squeezed shut, I mumbled grace over and over like a mantra, blocking out everything but my own voice.

He sat down next to me and gently touched my shoulder.

I opened my eyes, feeling a little foolish, but a little calmer.

"Will they call again?"

Villari's eyes bored into mine. "There's no way to know. Most likely this guy is just trying to scare you."

I felt the sweat break out on my palms. "He's doing an admirable job."

"And that's probably all he wants to do." Villari leaned back in his chair and crossed his arms. "Maggie, could this call have anything to do with your little trip this morning?"

As soon as the words were out of his mouth, Lindsay Burns's pinched face and burning green eyes flashed across my mind. I wasn't sure if she was part of this, but the timing did seem awfully coincidental. Only, I couldn't tell Villari. One word to him and he'd have me tied to my chair with Officer Godzilla guarding me until the murderer was found, assuming the blame wasn't pinned on me. There was no way I was going to let Villari hog-tie me and keep me from running my own investigation, not when it was my neck on the line . . . or in jail. Besides, there was no graceful way to admit that I had found Lindsay Burns's name in the book I stole off of Elizabeth's desk last night. I had the distinct feeling that learning about my nocturnal escapade would send Villari's temper up a notch or two.

So I tried evading the question. "What makes you ask that?"

"I ask because you never answered the question the first time around, which is apparently SOP for you. Then, suddenly, you get a phone call from a guy threatening to stuff you in a body bag. Call me cynical, paranoid, or whatever you want, but answer the damn question."

As a second tactic, I tried dodging the question. "The two had nothing to do with each other. And don't bother asking me where I was again because I'm not going to tell you. What I do on my own time is my own business. I don't need you hovering over my shoulder counting each hair on my head every time I turn around."

His eyes narrowed down to slits. I could almost hear his teeth grinding while veins throbbed at his temple.

"Start talking," he hissed through clenched teeth, "or you'll be very sorry you ever met me. Mess with me right now and I'll introduce you to a nice, piss-stained cell just large enough for you and a couple hundred cockroaches. I can, and will, trump up enough charges to keep you from seeing the light of day until your next birthday, starting with obstructing an investigation." He took a deep breath. "Is any of this sinking in, Maggie?"

Okay, the guy was beginning to scare me. It didn't take a rocket scientist to understand what he was saying, but I had a bone-deep fear that all the coincidences were going to mount up and bury me, starting with the fact that Elizabeth was found in my tank, not somebody else's. I couldn't afford to cower in a corner or crumble beneath Villari's threats, not while misleading information was still stacked against me. Cockroaches or not, I couldn't quit now.

"You really think I killed her, don't you?"

He paused a moment and then sighed heavily. "No, Maggie, I don't. Granted, there's a lot of circumstantial evidence that points to you, but that's all there is. This has 'reasonable doubt' stamped all over it. There's not enough solid evidence to even begin proceedings."

"Then why all the threats?"

"Because I can't remove you from the list of suspects until the case is officially closed. But more importantly, you're the type that dives without looking, straight into shallow water. I don't want you hurt and you're naive enough to stumble into a dangerous situation without realizing it until you're staring down a gun barrel."

"Gee, I sure do appreciate your faith in my intelligence."

"This has nothing to do with your IQ. It has to do with impulsiveness. Case in point: you've already made someone nervous enough to threaten your life. What I'm asking is simple. Where were you this morning?"

I wanted to answer, but I'd made a commitment to Elizabeth and to myself. The phone call didn't change anything.

I had no choice. I lied through my teeth. "I went to church."

Villari looked dubious. "Are you telling the truth this time, or hauling me down another dark alley in your zest for circumventing the truth?"

"Look, I said I went to church. You'll just have to trust me on this because there's no way of proving or disproving it. It's not like they hand out prayer receipts for tax purposes or charge admission for dipping into the holy water."

Villari ignored my sarcasm. "There's a church on every corner. Why the hell did you have to go downtown?"

Stalking. The man couldn't know where I'd been unless he had followed me and he'd already said he hadn't. I threw the question back in his lap.

"Who said I went downtown?"

Villari dug his fingers through his hair, creating deep furrows across the top of his head. It was a nervous habit I'd noticed before, one that seemed to worsen whenever he was deep in thought or especially irritated, frequently at something I'd said. My instincts said that irritation had long since fallen by the wayside and heavy exasperation had settled in its place.

"Okay, Maggie, let's say I believe you actually took a little trip to church. Can you answer a few questions for me?"

I shrugged.

"What time did you leave home?"

"Somewhere around seven. I didn't look at the clock." Best to stick as close to the truth as possible.

"What was the name of the church?"

"St. Peters. It's on Jefferson Street." Ms. Cooperative.

"I know where it is, Maggie. My mother, my Italian, *Catholic* mother, doesn't live far from here, just on the other side of the freeway, as a matter of fact."

My stomach fell like a lead balloon.

"She attends mass every morning from seven to eight. Maybe you saw her?"

"I doubt it," I began. "I sat in the back and left early."

"Right after the priest washed his hands, right?"

I managed a weak smile. When I was growing up, if you had any expectations of walking through the Pearly Gates, weekly mass was not a choice. It was mandatory. God didn't care whether you were nursing a hangover or had a new guy in your bed who was feeling his oats again. Skip a Sunday and you could march yourself straight on down to hell. Visions of raging fires and red Devils and endless pits of screaming bodies filled my head every time I missed church. For years, just to avoid the rather gruesome previews of my eternal life poofing up in smoke, I dragged myself to mass every week, but not without cutting every corner I could. The scorching heat, simmering sauna baths, bubbling wading pools, and perpetual sunburns described with alarming regularity were enough to keep me in church, but I was willing to be badgered only so far. I agreed to fulfill the minimum Heaven requirement, which meant that I was willing to climb the lowest rung on the ladder just high enough to keep the flames from licking my feet, but that was all.

It wasn't too tricky. It meant going to mass, but leaving at the end of Communion when the priest locked the chalice and the golden plate away in a gilded safe, much like clearing the dinner dishes. After a couple of quick kneelings, he would complete the ritual by washing his hands and drying them on a small cotton cloth. The moment he dried his hands, I shot out of the pew and slipped out the back, avoiding the endless announcements and the last song, inevitably eight verses long. Believe me, I wasn't the only Catholic with abbreviated church plans. More often than not, I was hit in the solar plexus or jabbed in the ribs by the throngs of people elbowing me out of the way as they headed out the door.

"Before that," I admitted. "I wasn't really listening, just looking for a quiet place where I could gather my thoughts and try to impose some kind of order or gain some perspective on everything that's happened." Okay, maybe I was pushing the drama a bit.

Villari leaned back, his dark eyes never wavering. "Is this something you do on regular basis, Maggie, or did the dark clouds open up and heavenly inspiration flash across the sky?"

"You know, Detective," I said, drawing out the syllables in his title, "some of us regular folks aren't immune to death like you. Some of us get pretty damned upset when we look out the window and see plastic yellow tape circling the yard marking the area where a close neighbor was recently found dead. Nothing about this is normal, and if I want to go to church and collect my thoughts, I don't have to ask your permission."

The man uncrossed his legs and stood up, never taking his eyes off me. "As far as I can see, you have a limited repertoire of two responses—anger or dodging the bullet. Frankly, I'm getting a little tired of both." He put both hands on the arms of my chair and pushed forward until his face was just inches from mine. "My mother hasn't missed mass a day in her life unless she was giving birth. She's just nosy enough to notice who comes to church and who doesn't. I can't help but think she would have noticed a newcomer with curly hair and baggy sweats." He sat back. "I'll give you ten-to-one odds that she's never seen your face. And if my guess is right, plan on spending the night in your new accommodations. Don't bother packing."

"Look, Villari, I'm getting sick of the threats. I've been cooperative—" I stopped at the look of disbelief that slid over his face. "Okay, maybe I was a little reluctant at first, but since then, I've been a model investigation helper. Now, all I did was leave my house for an hour and I get nothing but relentless harassment. You can arrest me if you want, but no court is going to lock me up based on whether your mother saw me at church one morning and can pick me out of a lineup. Lousy grounds for arrest, Detective."

"You've got guts. I'll say that for you." He stood up and shook his head. "I'm going to go visit Will and Cassie and see if they can meander around the truth half as well as you can. Then I'm going over to my mother's and ask if she saw you this morning. The court may not accept her word as concrete evidence, but I do."

"Why? Because she makes great lasagna?" I asked sardonically.

Villari sighed. "Trust me, Maggie. You don't want to make fun of my mother. She's a live conduit to the Man Upstairs and she's not afraid to wield a little power."

"Don't bother trying to scare me, Villari. I've had experience with overbearing Italian mothers and they don't frighten me anymore. As far as I'm concerned, they're good for one thing and one thing only."

"And that would be?"

"Fawning over the eldest son and making daughter-in-laws miserable."

He raised an eyebrow.

I shook my head. "Don't even ask. It's a long-drawn-out, ultimately uninteresting story."

"Tell you what, Maggie. Why don't I pick you up tonight and take you over to my mother's. She can try to identify you. My hunch is that you haven't stepped foot in a church for over a decade, and she'll never recognize you. But she can feed you and just possibly temper your feelings a little about Italian mothers."

"I thought I was heading for a night behind bars if Mamacita didn't recognize me."

Villari grimaced. "Call her Mamacita to her face and you'll wish I'd thrown you in jail. My mother sees herself as a modern woman and doesn't appreciate any comments to the contrary."

"Can't wait to meet the woman," I muttered.

"You'll come, then?"

"Well, let's examine my choices. On one hand, I can bunk with a swarm of nasty insects for the night, or, on the other hand, I can fill up on pasta while your mother hauls out your baby pictures and gets all misty-eyed while she recounts your childhood." I paused. "Actually, jail is looking better by the minute."

Villari's lips twitched at the corners. "I promise to keep all photos hidden." He scratched his head. "You do have a way of standing your ground even when the going gets bad and everything starts to unravel. It's an admirable quality. Annoying as hell, but admirable."

"Thanks, I guess. That's definitely the most back-handed compliment I've ever received, but I'll accept it. Besides," I said casually, "it could have been a lot worse."

"I'm afraid to hear how."

"I could have pulled out my self-defense skills," I said proudly. "Somebody might have gotten hurt."

"Self-defense?" he asked skeptically.

I nodded. "Yeah. Lisa and I took a class in college when there was a big rape scare on campus."

"So you're saying I should watch the, uh . . . 'boys' a little more closely when you're around?"

"Only if you value their health and well-being," I responded nonchalantly.

He grinned. "And why didn't I hear about this talent of yours before?"

I lifted my shoulders an inch. "Maybe because Lisa and I only managed to complete one class before getting thrown out."

"Are you going to expound on that a little?"

"Nope." I stood up. "Let's just say there was a little unresolved personality conflict."

"Somehow that doesn't surprise me."

"It wasn't our fault, although I'm sure you wouldn't believe me." I turned and started walking toward the front door. "Now, if you don't mind, I've got to get back to my studio. I'm sure you're in a hurry to follow up on a whole bunch of important leads . . . like learning whether or not I prayed this morning."

"Don't push me, Maggie," he warned quietly.

I held up my hands in surrender. "Sorry, it just slipped out. It's a bad habit of mine. Think a thought and toss it right on out."

"I'm aware of that. But listen to me. This isn't a game we're playing. The coroner says Elizabeth Boyer was killed by a sharp blow to the back of her head with a heavy object. Apparently she was dead before being thrown in your tank. Best estimation is that she was murdered between twelve and twenty-four hours before you found her. But it may have been longer. We don't know for sure."

My stomach lurched. "She was in the sewer for . . ." The words stuck in my throat. The idea of Elizabeth floating around in liquid waste for days was too horrible to contemplate. Even now, I hadn't begun to come to terms with the murder.

Villari put his hands on my shoulders. "They can't be more exact because of the harsh chemicals in the septic system. They're designed to break down and dissolve organic matter. The coroner had to take the bloating and wrinkled skin into consideration, which gave him one time element, and compare it to the disintegration caused by the chemicals, which gave him another. It wasn't an easy call."

I couldn't say anything.

"Maggie, listen to me. This was a terrible crime. And apparently, there's some unfinished business out there, because someone is calling and threatening you. I don't want a second murder on my hands." He shook me a little. "Do you understand what I'm saying?"

I nodded, but no words escaped my lips. The detective was right. Not only had Elizabeth been murdered, but somebody was coming after me as well.

Chapter Eight

Villari closed the front door quietly. The call had really disturbed me and I found myself staring anxiously at the phone, a phone that now seemed to shoot off sparks of venom and hate. Pacing nervously around the room, I felt the walls closing in on me. Staying in my house was becoming a claustrophobic nightmare and I desperately needed to escape and find the murderer, not only to avenge Elizabeth's death but so I could feel safe again. Will or Cassie seemed the obvious suspects to me, and I was almost out the door before I remembered that Villari was already there questioning them. The last thing I needed was another run-in with the detective and I was pretty sure Will wouldn't be too keen on seeing me again, not after chasing me down the hallway last night and having the car door slammed in his face. The only other possibility was Lindsay Burns.

I frowned when I thought of her. Something was definitely off with that whole situation. I couldn't pinpoint exactly what was wrong, only that things were glaringly *not right*. There was nothing unusual about Elizabeth helping someone in need; in fact, it was perfectly normal. And judging by the faint black-and-blue shadows under her eyes, I'd say that Lindsay Burns was a perfect candidate for the Center for Domestic Violence, or CDV, one of Elizabeth's favorite charities. She was always attending one fund-raiser after another for the center; it was one of the few projects Elizabeth actually called by name, as though she had a personal interest in this particular program. I knew her life with her husband had been long and hard and that she, more than most people, knew that abuse didn't necessarily come in the shape of fists.

Given our earlier confrontation, I was fairly certain Ms. Burns would not be eager to strike up another conversation with me. My only choice was to fall back on the detecting procedures I'd seen on television. Once the idea took hold, I smiled. A stakeout might be fun.

Of course, there were a couple of obstacles. First, it was not going to be easy to hide out in Ms. Burns's neighborhood, not with the area going to seed. There wasn't a tree, rock, or bush large enough to cover my body, not even if I crouched or sucked in my gut, much less conceal my Jeep. There was no way I could park anywhere within the development without sticking out like an unsightly wart. The only option I had was the ostentatious brick structure that stood at the entrance. I'd have to double-check the map, though, to make sure the structure marked the only entrance and exit route. I didn't want Lindsay slipping out the back way.

Despite the grave circumstances that led to my stakeout, I found myself excited about the idea. I started preparing immediately. My outfit would be black, of course—black sweats, black sneakers, and a black wool cap. I needed a thermos of hot coffee, several sandwiches, a blanket, CDs and a Discman, a pad of paper for notes and sketches, and, of course, a camera. I didn't have anything but the basic point-and-shoot model, but it would do.

I went to the hall closet and dug out a navy-blue vinyl gym bag with a large white *Swoosh!* painted on the side, and started stuffing my gear. In the kitchen, I pulled open the refrigerator. Judging by the smell and the suspicious-looking green fuzz, I figured the lunch meat was one day short of inedible. Perfect. I made three sandwiches, piled high with semimoldy meat, cheese, and pickles, and lathered on a thick coating of mayo. Since there was no telling how long this little excursion would take, I decided to stop at the local bakery for a dozen doughnuts, just in case it lasted all night. The only foreseeable problem was Villari. With the police cruising my neighborhood, Villari would know within an hour that I was gone and he would be livid. Apparently, my whereabouts were a major concern.

Seeing no way out of the dilemma, I shrugged into my "what the hell" attitude. Until I was arrested and forced into jail or until the police slapped an ankle monitor on me, I was not going to stay housebound just because The Detective had an explosive temper. Let him explode. If I wanted to spy on someone, that was my business.

The gym bag was bulging with food and clothes. Since there was a slight possibility of running into a cop on my way out to the car or while driving through my neighborhood, I decided to wait and change my clothes once I arrived at Woodlake Meadows. My everyday baggy shorts seemed to irritate Villari enough; I could just imagine what my black costume would do.

I cracked open my front door an inch and let out a sigh of relief. With the way my luck had been going lately, I half expected to see Villari lounging on my porch smoking a cigarette. Pulling on the door a little more, I stuck my head out like a periscope and scanned the area in both directions. Nothing. The coast was clear. Without thinking, I shut the door behind me and ran down the gravel driveway with the gym bag bouncing off my thigh. I jumped into the Jeep and ducked below the windshield. Breathing hard, I stuck the key in the ignition, prayed to the Divine Mechanic in Heaven, and cheered (quietly) when the engine turned over. With one last look in the rearview mirror, I pulled slowly out of the driveway into my street and drove past my house.

By the time I'd crossed Mitchell and driven a couple of miles, though, I found myself getting a little angry. Here I was, a grown woman, an innocent woman, and I was skulking out of my own house, like a teenager sneaking to a bar to get drunk while her parents were sleeping. This was ridiculous. By the time I reached the freeway and merged into traffic, I was madder than hell. There was a real killer out there and I seemed to be the only one doing anything productive while Villari twiddled his thumbs and kissed me . . . something I pushed firmly to the back of my mind until I was strong enough to deal with the whole mess. Romance was out of the question right now, and would be as long as a noose was being slung around my neck.

I cruised down the freeway, got off at Woodmen, and followed the now familiar streets until I reached the barricade. Built in the form of an S, it was a simple matter to park the car within the lower arch, my back fender flush against the wall, the front lights facing the barren community. Perfect. From this unobstructed vantage point, I could watch cars coming and going, while staying completely hidden within the wide curves of brick and mortar.

Within five minutes I was ready for action. I had pulled on my sweats and cap, grabbed my sunglasses from the visor, and scooted down into my seat. Twenty minutes later I was sweating like a pig. In my preparations for the Great Stakeout, I had completely forgotten that June is a summer month. My black clothes were sucking in every ounce of heat and recycling it across my body. No doubt it was a hundred degrees in the car and fifteen degrees hotter under my sweats, not to mention that, if by chance I was spotted, I would look a lot less conspicuous in a T-shirt and a pair of colorful shorts than in my Black Panther outfit.

I yanked my clothes off in a frenzy, practically jumping into my cotton shorts. Feeling a little like a wet turtle, I pushed my head through my T-shirt . . . just in time. Another second and I would have missed it. I stopped dressing and stared. On the very edge of the entryway, turning into Woodlake Meadows, driving a navy-blue Saturn, was a big, fat, sweaty man. My heart started to pound and a heavy knot of surprise and fear sunk in the pit in my stomach. I knew that man. It was Vacuum Nose.

I hunched down as far as a I could without cutting off my vision. The idea that this was mere coincidence flitted around the edges of my brain and flew right out. From the relative safety of my car, I watched the Saturn pull into Lindsay's driveway. Moments later that big bumbling cop, minus the uniform, hitched up his pants, strode up the sidewalk, and pushed open the front door.

Thoughts swirled around in my head like leaves in a storm. I wasn't sure how Vacuum Nose, or whatever the hell his name was, fit into this whole scenario, but I knew that something was drastically wrong. My reflexes took over, and I started the car and rolled forward. Very slowly. There was something eerie and unsettling about a cop working a murder scene and then showing up at an address written in the victim's appointment book. I didn't know what the connection was, but I knew I had to find out. And things became even creepier when it suddenly dawned on me that this guy hadn't knocked or rung the doorbell. Vacuum Nose wasn't visiting Lindsay Burns. He lived with her.

In no time at all, I was back out on the highway, heading north to Monument, racking my brain about what to do next. This whole thing was getting stranger by the minute. Elizabeth had written Lindsay's name in her book for a reason. With her connections and personal involvement with the Center for Domestic Violence, it wasn't a giant leap to assume that VN (a.k.a. Vacuum Nose) was the cause of Lindsay's facial bruises. He was just the type, too. I could imagine him standing a little taller, walking a little straighter, and sucking in his gut while knocking Lindsay around. Nothing like punching a woman half your size to make a lumpy doughboy feel more like a man.

By the time I reached my street I was feeling a little nauseous. It didn't help matters to find Villari's car parked in my driveway and the man leaning against the porch rail.

"Let me guess," I said as I stepped out of my Jeep, "you got an urgent call from Mr. Patrolman saying that the little lady had disappeared again."

He took one last drag on his cigarette and flicked the butt off into space.

I eyed the butt lying in my yard. "Do you mind? Just because you're addicted to a filthy weed doesn't mean I need to be the recipient of your trash." I stomped over and picked up the remains of the cigarette. Stepping past Villari, I unlocked the front door. "Come on in. You can yell at me while I throw away your litter."

Villari followed me into the kitchen, walking so close behind I could feel his breath on the back of my neck.

"Looks like we're back at square one. I don't suppose you want to tell me where you were?"

I turned around so quickly he nearly bumped into me. I stared into those dark eyes, fully aware that if I stood on my toes I would be within easy kissing range. "Sure, if you want to hear."

Villari cast a wary glance at me.

"I started my period and went down to the drugstore for some feminine hygiene products."

"Cut the crap," he growled. "My patience is wearing very thin where you're concerned. Spit it out or—"

"Yeah, I know. You've been threatening me all morning with a new residence in a bad part of town with unsavory neighbors." I slid sideways and went around him. The man had a way of nosing into my space. "Not that it's any of your business," I said, trotting out my haughtiest voice, "but I went downtown for some art supplies."

One eyebrow raised up as he glanced pointedly at my empty hands, finding them both suspiciously empty of shopping bags. "Show me what you bought."

Great. One misstep and the guy was all over me. "They didn't have what I needed."

"You know, it would be an easy thing for me to check out your story." He sighed. "You wouldn't want to save me the time and try the truth out for a change, would you?"

"Look, Detective, you asked where I went and I told you. If you want to double-check everything I say, feel free to do so, but . . ."

"But what?"

I shrugged. "Why don't you have someone follow me around, or better yet, why don't you handcuff me to the refrigerator if you're so worried about where I am every single moment? With me off your back, you might have time to act like a real detective . . . you know, gathering clues, interviewing possible suspects, making phone calls, things like that." I opened my eyes as though I'd suddenly been hit by a bolt of lightning. "Hey! You might even find the murderer!"

His mouth thinned into a straight line as he glared at me.

"Obviously, humor is not your strong suit," I said, nervously trying to fill in what was rapidly becoming a deafening silence.

"I could say the same thing about you, Maggie. Your attempts at humor leave something to be desired," he countered quietly, his face so serious I had to turn away.

"Look, Villari, I'm already nervous as a cat, and humor, weak as it may be, is my way of protecting myself. You've been looking over my shoulder ever since this whole thing started and I've run out of ways to deal with your incessant snooping." I swung around, mentally pulled back my shoulders, and stood my ground. "I had nothing to do with Elizabeth's death and I resent the fact that I'm too busy looking for the murderer myself to have time to mourn."

He stared at me for several seconds, completely still except for the small muscle jumping at the base of his jaw. "What do you mean you've been looking for the murderer yourself?"

Me and my big mouth. The man stood there just waiting to pounce. I backed away. "I just meant that I . . ." The words stumbled forth. "I've been so busy defending myself against your accusations that I've had to start thinking about who could have killed Elizabeth."

"Maggie," he warned, "I told you to stay out of this."

I held up my hands to stop him. "I'm not doing anything. I've just made a couple of lists, weighed a few pros and cons. Nothing dangerous."

He ran his hand through his hair. With that habit, it was no wonder it was perennially rumpled. Without saying a word, he stepped back, turned, and walked to the kitchen table. He pulled out a chair, swiveled it around, and straddled it so he was facing me. This was beginning to feel familiar.

"Let's see the lists."

God, the man was relentless. "No." I shook my head firmly. I had to. I was lying like crazy. "They're mine."

"Like hell. If you've got information, hand it over."

"Like hell. When you put a warrant in my hand, then I'll hand it over." Trying to look intimidating, I crossed my arms in front of my chest and stared at him, determined not to flinch. "Go ahead and put me in that jail cell you keep dangling in front of me," I said boldly, hoping like hell that he couldn't see my knees trembling.

A slow grin crept across his face. "Nah, I'm going to do something a lot worse."

Like cowardly rats on a sinking ship, I felt every drop of confidence drain from my body as I managed one word. "What?"

"I'm taking you to my mother's house for dinner."

Chapter Nine

"There's no way I'm eating dinner with Mamacita tonight," I said firmly, my hands propped on my hips. "I've got enough trouble in my life without subjecting myself to a bunch of Italians."

Villari cocked his head to the side. "You've got a problem with Italians?"

I nodded. "I've got a *big* problem with the whole hand-waving, pasta-loving, testosterone-struttin' group of you."

He had the audacity to smile. "Oh, yeah. I forgot. You were married to an Italian once, weren't you?"

"Once too many."

"I guess it wouldn't help if I mentioned that we're not all alike." He stretched his long legs in front of the chair. It was impossible to miss the muscles bunching against his jeans.

"Tell you what. Just to be fair, I'll give you a quiz, like the ones you find in magazines, and if you answer no to any of the five questions I ask, I'll shut up and eat spaghetti with you tonight." I took a deep breath. "Otherwise, if you answer yes to any—and, as I suspect, every—question, you'll leave me in peace tonight. And you won't interrogate me when I leave for the fifteen minutes it will take me to buy my very American cheeseburger and fries."

He studied me closely. "I think I'm being bamboozled here."

"No, you're not. I'm just taking you to task for your statement that all Italians are not complete clones."

"Okay, shoot." He leaned back and rested against the table, his legs still extended like two perfectly sculpted examples of hard athleticism.

I paced in a circle around the kitchen as I ticked off my questions on the fingers of one hand. "Is your family Catholic? Do you have lots of siblings and scads and scads of relatives? Does your family eat pasta, in some form, whether it's cannelloni, mastaciolli, ravioli, or some other 'oli' word, at least three times a week? Is there an unspoken rule that everyone must attend every family function, occurring on a weekly basis, functions that include *all* birthdays, holidays, graduations, first Communions, baptisms, and of course, the celebration of all celebrations—Mother's Day? Do your brothers fawn over your mother while her daughters-in-law run in the other direction?" I paused long enough to take a breath. "Should I go on?"

The man sat there with a blank look on his face. I didn't know what to think until I saw the gleam in his eye and heard the soft rumble of a chuckle. He clasped his hands behind his head and the chuckle escalated into a deep, hearty laugh.

"Let me guess," I said dryly. "It was a unanimous yes all the way down the list." I leaned my elbows on the counter and waited calmly for his reply.

"Yeah, it's all true. I've got three brothers, two sisters, tons of Catholic relatives, and we get together and eat as often as possible." He sat forward, bent his legs, and stood up. "I do love my mother and I think my sisters-in-law are scared to death of her," he said quietly as he walked toward me. "But I'm still taking you to dinner tonight."

I started to straighten up, but before I could move away, he rounded the corner of the counter and put his hands on my arms, turning me toward him.

"You reneging on the bet?"

"I have to," he assured me.

"Why? What happened to police integrity? The 'you can depend on the guys in blue' spirit?"

"Because I already told my mother I invited a guest."

"So uninvite me."

He shook his head and pulled me closer. "You obviously don't know everything about Italians. They hate being stood up, especially after spending the whole day in the kitchen cooking lasagna. If I don't bring you, I'll never hear the end of it. Besides . . ." he concluded, with a mischievous smile, "you're too damned skinny. Italian men like a little meat on their women." And with that, his lips settled over mine.

He left soon afterward. But not until he had taken his finger and dragged it softly down the side of my face, following the line of my jaw, and gently pushed a strand of hair behind my ear. He grinned that ultracharming smile of his and walked away, disarming me completely, leaving me standing there like a speechless idiot. Opening the front door, he hesitated for a moment and turned toward me.

"I'll pick you up at six." He scratched his head. "One suggestion. My mother's name is Toni Villari. You might want to can the Mamacita comments. She's a stubborn, bullheaded lady who's not afraid to fight." His eyes flicked over me and he shrugged. "But then, God help us, so are you," at which point he stepped out onto the porch and shut the door behind him.

I peered through the window and watched his car pull out of the driveway. I was so restless I resumed my pacing, except this time I didn't confine myself to the kitchen. The man had a way of getting under my skin and I didn't know what the hell to do about it. I was beginning to feel schizophrenic. One moment I was being threatened with a life sentence in the penitentiary and the next moment I was being kissed so thoroughly I was left breathless and shaky. On the other hand, maybe he was the one with the problem. His temper was so volatile and unpredictable, I never knew when he was going to pick me up and toss me into a pit of rattlesnakes and when he would seduce me with that crooked smile of his. But split personality aside, the man could kiss. I could feel it right down to my toes. And, believe me, my toes hadn't curled like that in a long time.

I shuddered. My neighbor had just been killed and here I was cuddling with a cop who still considered me a suspect, even if my name was way down the list. Why was he taking me to dinner? Was he really going to check on my church story? Obviously, his mother wasn't going to recognize me; I hadn't set foot in a church since I was in high school. But she couldn't prove anything, even if she did have a reserved seat in heaven and one in the neighborhood chapel. As Villari said himself, it was all circumstantial evidence.

Before I knew it, I was in the back of the house, turning circles in my bedroom, mimicking the actions of a dog getting ready for bed, twisting around and around before scratching the carpet, plopping down and falling asleep for the night. Finally, from sheer exhaustion, I did the same thing. I flopped down on the floor, lay on my back, and threw my arms over my head. I stretched in both directions at the same time, my upper half pulling one way, the bottom half, toes pointing, pulling the opposite way. This was the beginning of an exercise routine I performed regularly to alleviate the cramps in the small of my back after long hours of sculpting or sketching while sitting on a hard stool.

Slipping smoothly into the second exercise, I slid my arms down until they extended out from both sides until I looked like the letter *T* or a crucifix, since I had religion on my mind lately. Turning my head toward the wall, I lifted my right leg, bent it at the knee, and lifted it over my straight left leg, until my right knee was resting on the floor while my torso remained flat against the ground. I groaned when I felt the pull of muscles. I stayed in this position for a long time, longer than usual, because I found myself staring at Elizabeth's picture.

It was a soft watercolor landscape, its subject a small pond dotted with snowy-white ducks and circled by high green grass that was ruffling in the wind. As I continued to look at the picture, I realized it was a study of light and darkness, that the serenity evoked by the soft pastels was deceiving. Looming in the background was a dark indigo mountain etched in charcoal. The face of the mountain, bare of pine trees, flowers, or other foliage, stood scarred with ragged lines and stones and boulders. Dark clouds hovered menacingly over the pond, twisting in the air like a child in the throes of a tantrum. Beyond the pond sat a dilapidated wooden bench, its green paint peeling, boards cracking, half-hidden in the tall thin reeds. And suddenly the picture no longer seemed peaceful or even angry, but became lonely and sad, like a person warring within himself. The landscape turned into a forlorn scene, one of sadness. Of isolation.

It was the first time I had ever seen Elizabeth's work. She had often spoken of her attempts to paint in her youth and her regret that she had given up her dreams when she married, but this was the first painting of hers I had seen, and it surprised me. Although her talent was obvious, I had somehow expected something different, something bolder and dramatic, like the scarves she wore. Where was the flair, the boldness, the pride? This picture spoke of pain and hopelessness, of resignation—the antithesis of the Elizabeth I knew.

But then, I wondered, how much do we really know of anyone? The image a person presents to the world doesn't necessarily match the person inside. More often than not, it may actually mask personal pain, depression, and sadness. I immediately switched sides and pulled my left leg over my right one and pretended to stick my finger down my throat and gag. Whenever I attempted heavy philosophical thought, I ended up sounding like talk-radio psychobabble. Soul-searching just wasn't my forte. My thoughts were as profound as two celebrities discussing inner beauty on an infomercial while peddling their own makeup line. Funny how often it's the stunningly beautiful, rail-thin woman who lectures us on the unimportance of exterior beauty.

All of this ruminating was getting me nowhere. I still had two basic problems. One: Elizabeth's murder. What was the next step? I had to find the person who committed the crime. Two: Dinner this evening. It had all the signs of being a disaster . . . a real shame considering how much I loved to eat. Leave it to an Italian to wreck my favorite part of the day.

I finished stretching and decided to hit the studio. Summer has always been a wonderful time for sculpting since there are no classes to worry about or report cards to finish, behavior problems to deal with, or parents to call. For nine months out of the year, I struggle to squeeze my art into the few hours I have left each evening after teaching and planning for the following day. When summer finally arrives, I feel drugged by the sheer freedom of blue skies and warm afternoons. In all honesty, though, after a few days of blissful immersion in clay, oil, and charcoal, my productivity lessens, imaginative ideas slow to a dribble, and I realize once again that making art is real work.

Every summer I plan full days of work in my studio, but sooner or later hours are carved out to make time to plant my flowers, experiment with new recipes, hike in the woods, and play pool with my buddies. Procrastination is the name of the game. I'm definitely not one of those Type-A personalities who find it hard to relax and waste time. I've always labeled myself a Type-R personality—"tends to recreate."

It's hard to be disciplined with the sun banging on my window and beckoning me outside to play. Before I know it, I'm idle and lazy. Happens to me every summer. And now, with the death of a dear friend, I found it harder to push myself into the studio, but I knew Elizabeth would want me to do exactly that. It made me wistful to think of her walking into my house to visit, although her walk was actually more of a march, with her upright carriage and firm steps. She always knocked briskly but then just swooped in without waiting for an answer, as though she had every right to barge into my house uninvited and start making demands. And of course, she did. Have the right, that is.

It wasn't always that way, though. I could still remember the first time I met her.

She marched over to my house, her heels clacking against the wooden porch steps, and rapped sharply on my door.

"Yes?" I asked cautiously, cracking the door open a few inches.

"You're my neighbor," she announced as though it was headline news.

"Yes, I know that. I've seen you pulling out of your driveway," I said, impatiently tapping my sock-clad foot against the wooden floor, waiting for this lady to get to her point, if indeed she had one. If this was the neighborhood welcome wagon, I wasn't too anxious for it to stay. At that moment I was afraid I had a dotty old lady standing on my porch with no intention of ever leaving or finding her way back home.

"I'd like introduce myself. My name is Elizabeth Boyer," she stated in that regal voice of hers.

She stuck out her hand, forcing me to open my door a few more inches. When I went to shake her hand, I was totally dumbstruck. All I could do was stare at the thing. Not at her hand, but the huge diamond solitaire on her fourth finger.

"Awfully large, isn't it?" she noted when she saw me gawking at her jewelry. "I know it borders on being gaudy . . . actually it is definitely gaudy, but it's a family ring, my mother's, and I just can't bear to part with it and there's no point in keeping it locked away in a vault."

"It's lovely," I stammered, blown away by a rock the size of a shooter marble.

"It's not lovely at all, dear, but it's very polite of you to say so," she said, clasping my hand firmly and giving it a quick shake. She smiled. "Now that the preliminaries are over and we are officially introduced, I'd like to invite you over for a cup of coffee one morning this week."

"That would be great," I said with a thin, phony smile, "but I work every morning."

"Do you?" she asked dubiously. "Well, then, perhaps some other time."

Elizabeth Boyer turned to go, leaving me completely free to return to my nice, peaceful, uncluttered life. But I knew she didn't believe me, and in spite of a strong intuition that this woman would raise havoc wherever she descended, I just couldn't let her leave thinking she lived next door to a dishonest recluse of a neighbor.

"I work out of the house. I'm an artist," I explained. "At least, that's what I'm working toward."

"Really?" A gleam of interest shone in her eyes. "What is your medium?"

"Clay. Bronze. I sculpt."

She nodded. "And who is your agent?"

"No one at the moment. I'm at the bottom of the learning curve with a steep hill to climb."

"Are you taking lessons?"

I shook my head. "Can't afford a teacher right now."

"Well, let me see what you've done," she stated boldly . . . and firmly. "You can't be an artist in a vacuum. You need to show your work and let people—knowledgeable people," she amended, "suggest and critique." She checked me up and down. "From what little I know of you already, and I'm a fair judge of character, you're very independent and you like to keep to yourself. The problem is, the art world doesn't promote wallflowers. You have to promote yourself. 'Nothing is more common than unsuccessful men with talent,' " she quoted, staring off into space. "I don't remember who said that, but it's true. I see it all the time."

I know I stood gaping like an idiot as she delivered this monologue. Who was this lady who seemed so intent on invading my life? And more importantly, how in the hell did I get rid of her?

As though she could read my mind, she laughed. "Don't worry, I'm not a crazy woman. In fact, I'm the perfect person for the job. I have lots of experience with art; it's a passion of mine. I'm on several boards . . ." She rattled off the names of several prominent galleries. "I realize you don't want to hear my résumé," she said, pausing in midstream, "but I do know what I'm talking about."

"I'm sure that you do, Mrs. Boyer, but—"

"Call me Elizabeth, dear. Now, I understand your hesitation; you're not used to people bulldozing their way into your life, are you?" She patted my arm. "Sometimes Fate just waltzes in and takes over and the only thing you can do is hold on tightly and enjoy the ride." She laughed at the look on my face. "Now that I've got you completely flummoxed, why don't I take a peek at your work?"

"Well, I'm not ready to show anything publicly yet," I stammered.

"Nonsense." She waved away my reticence. "Whatever you have available right now will do just fine. I've an excellent critical eye. I'm perfectly capable of weeding the good from the bad, and I'm not afraid to let you know exactly what I think."

No doubt about that.

"May I?" she asked, gesturing toward the door. I stood by dumbly while she walked past me into my house, her spine straight and proud, her designer dress worn with ease, her hair pulled back and a scarf wound around her waist like a sash. From the moment she followed me down the hallway into my studio, I understood that life as I knew it would never be the same.

It took me some time to warm up to Elizabeth. I told myself I resented her attitude and her pushiness and unsolicited opinions, but all the while I let her into my house and, more importantly, let her into my studio and listened to her advice over coffee. Sometimes I would mutter about her overbearing behavior . . . and then I'd find myself watching the clock wondering why she was late. It wasn't long before I realized that what once seemed to me to be arrogance was actually a kind of idealism—a strong belief that people could achieve whatever they wanted with a little grit and determination and elbow grease. So it was only natural that Elizabeth detested my tendency toward laziness. What can I say? Sometimes I got tired watching all that boundless energy.

"Snap out of it, Maggie. Get your butt into the studio and begin." Her voice still rang in my mind loud and clear, even now as she lay in her grave. I bent over my sketchpad and began.

Four hours later I straightened and looked up at the clock. Damn, it was five-thirty and I was sweaty and smeared with smudges of charcoal and remnants of clay. Stepping back a few feet, I studied the unfinished sculpture. Nothing clear had emerged, but I felt calmer and stronger than I had in days. I wasn't surprised to find myself taking refuge in my work. I gently wrapped the sculpture and left the room.

Jumping into the shower, I dunked my head under a stream of hot water and scoured my hands with a soft bristly brush. My body was tinged pink when I was done. I turned off the water and toweled myself down. Standing in front of my closet, I reached for a soft denim skirt that skimmed my ankles and pulled on a fitted white cotton blouse with cap sleeves, which I tucked in and cinched with a black belt and silver buckle. I ran a brush through my hair and left it alone, knowing from past experience that if I played with it too much, it would stick out like a mushroom cloud. On a lark, I swiped some mascara on my lashes, brushed on a little rouge, and painted my lips with a flesh-toned color. I studied myself in the mirror. I wasn't going to win any fashion awards, but at least I wouldn't embarrass myself.

At the brisk knock, I ran down the hallway, knowing it was Villari. He was right on time—nothing less than I expected.

"Hey," I said as I pulled open the door.

He stood perfectly still. The only thing that moved were his eyes, which swept up and down my body.

"You really should do this more often."

"Do what?" I asked, confused by his intensity.

"Dress like a girl," he responded, his eyes twinkling. "Mom is going to love that I'm bringing home a pretty lady."

I groaned and leaned against the door frame. "I should have known you would revert to a fifties' version of male chauvinism."

He leaned over and ruffled my still-damp hair. "Come on. I told my mother I'd be there around six-thirty. Besides, I'm starving and I'm fairly sure you're not going to offer me a drink and a small appetizer . . . something simple you whipped up this afternoon."

"I don't do appetizers," I said, closing and locking the door behind me, "unless it comes already prepared. I do a mean can of peanuts. Besides, I'm not feeling particularly fond of you right now, given the way you've shanghaied me into this dinner."

He dropped his arm around me and chuckled. "You're going to like my mother, you'll fall in love with my dad, and the food will be so good you'll be begging me to bring you back."

"I seriously doubt it," I muttered.

"Trust me," he said, opening the passenger door of his black Ford Bronco.

"That won't be happening anytime soon," I said under my breath, my hands fidgeting in my lap, while he walked around the car and got in. He took one look at my face and started chuckling.

"Relax. You look like I'm taking you to meet some kind of medieval Dragon Lady."

I rolled my shoulders. "Is this a date?"

Turning on the ignition, he glanced over at me.

"Well, given that you put on a dress and I changed my jeans and slapped on cologne, I'd say it constitutes a date." He paused a moment, trying to gauge my reaction. "Is that a problem?"

"Not really. I'm just surprised that a detective is allowed to date a suspect. Seems kind of odd to me . . . sort of a conflict of interest."

"I told you this afternoon you were not a suspect, Maggie," he said quietly.

"But I'm still on the official list, right?" I persisted.

"So is the Pope," he said dryly, "until the murderer is caught.

"But you've still got some unanswered questions, don't you? The septic tank is in my yard and there's still the lack of footprints you keep mentioning."

His eyes met mine. "There are a lot of ways to cover up footprints." He shifted into reverse. "There's a fairly good chance they're underneath the tire tracks made by the Waste Management truck."

"Then tell me, Villari, why do I keep bumping into you every time I turn around?"

"Because I'm trying to keep you safe."

Goose bumps raised up on my arms. "Because of the phone call?"

He nodded. "Because of the phone call, because of your close friendship with Elizabeth, because the murderer dumped her in your tank," he said bluntly. "There's a connection somewhere, Maggie."

I must have blanched, because he put his hand over mine. "Look. Despite your less than agreeable personality, you're starting to grow on me. I don't want anything to happen to you, and if I have to stick to you like a leech to keep you from going off on some wild-ass goose chase, I will."

On that note, he backed out of the driveway.

He was right about one thing. The Dragon Lady could cook. The pasta was to die for, obviously homemade. I could imagine her afternoons, flour up to her elbows, her hands hidden in a deep round ceramic bowl, kneading enough dough to feed an army while her spicy red tomato sauce, redolent with garlic, oregano, and basil bubbled in the background.

No doubt there were similarities between Villari's family and that of my ex-husband, Michael. As soon as the front door opened, I remembered the same round of rambunctious kissing and squeezing that used to suffocate me in its blanket of goodwill. I was always uncomfortable with that initial greeting and got into the habit of leaving something in the car so I'd always be rummaging in the backseat when Michael's mother teared up at her first glimpse of her son. By the time I finally climbed out and shuffled to the front door, some of the steam would be gone, and the hellos would have simmered down to a level I could handle.

Villari must have felt my discomfort because he reached for my hand as we walked up the sidewalk, less out of affection than to keep me from bolting as the clan swooped down. He held fast as they crowded around us, at one point looking like a running back, one hand curled around my waist, the other stuck straight out in front, knocking down anyone who stepped in his path.

And then, like Moses parting the Red Sea, the group of aunts, uncles, cousins, siblings, and neighbors split in two, quieted down to a whisper, and lined the sidewalk like soldiers readying for inspection. Standing at the top of the stairs was a petite lady with a strong dignified posture, gray-white hair, and warm mocha-colored eyes. I let out a small sigh of relief. There was no rush to pull my cheeks like taffy and no big bosoms.

Proceeding down the stairs as regally as a queen, she stopped in front of me. A small grin played at the edges of her lips. "So you are giving the Italians a second chance?"

A slow flush crept across my face. In disbelief, I turned to Villari. "What did you tell her?"

He shrugged. "Only that Italians were your least favorite ethnic group."

I could have sworn a collective gasp went up in the peanut gallery.

"You didn't."

"No, he didn't." Mrs. Villari reached up and gently slapped her son's cheek. "Stop teasing." She turned back to me. "Actually, he said that you had a bad experience with your first marriage." She tucked my hand into the crook of her elbow and started up the steps, glancing over her shoulder.

"Turn her loose, Samuel. I won't let her get away," she said, winking at her oldest son.

I wasn't sure whether to laugh or cry, but I didn't have any choice but to follow his mother past the lines of relatives and into the house. We walked through the living room, a small area comfortably dwarfed by a large worn leather couch the color of brandy with colorful throw pillows. Then she guided me down a hallway lined with varying framed photographs of relatives and children at different stages of growth. Without being told, I knew where we were heading. A thick, rich fragrance floated through the air, hooked my nose and tugged me into the kitchen. Along with Villari's mother. She pulled out a wooden chair and gestured for me to sit down.

"Would you like tea or coffee?"

"Whatever you have would be fine."

She turned and fixed me with a steely stare. "Let me tell you a little secret, Maggie. It is Maggie, right?"

I nodded mutely, feeling like a child set in a time-out chair waiting to be lectured.

"My Samuel does not often bring his women friends home."

I started to object to the term, but thought better of it.

"He says it's because I wouldn't approve of them, but I think it's more that he doesn't approve of them himself. Anyway, the point is, he brought you here because he likes you and he wants you to get to know us and for us to get to know you. That can't happen if you hide behind politeness. So . . ." She stuck her hands on her hips. "What would you like to drink? Tea or coffee?"

"Coffee, if it's not too much trouble, please."

She raised her eyebrow. Villari had obviously inherited his expressive eyebrow from his mother.

"Okay, okay," I said, holding my hands up in surrender. "I'd like coffee. The truth is, I hate tea, any kind of tea, especially healthy tea from the herbal family with weird names like raspberry zinger, or something soothing like chamomile or even plain green tea, which sounds like someone is boiling up a bucket of grass." I tried to stem my nervous rambling, but words spilled out as if of their own accord.

I wasn't surprised to find myself babbling—it's been the bane of my existence since I was a child. The worst part is the lousy timing. A torrent of words spews out of my mouth at the most inconvenient times—like at the end of a sad movie when the main character utters her dying words. While the rest of the audience is bawling into wadded-up tissues, I'm blathering about movie trivia. Whenever the situation calls for a respectful silence, I can guarantee that somewhere in the background my voice is providing an irritating drone. I fully expect that if I ever succumb to the lure of marriage again, a very big *if*, I'll be too busy chattering incoherently to make it through the vows.

Mrs. Villari chuckled as she placed two heavy mugs on the table and filled them with coffee. "No one can accuse you of not being honest." She slid the pot back into its holder, lifted a small pitcher shaped like a Holstein cow out of the refrigerator, and placed it on the table. "Help yourself," she said, pointing to the cream. "Sugar's in the bowl." She sat down next to me, leaned back against the chair, and closed her eyes.

"This is the first chance I've had to sit down all day," she said, cupping her hands around the mug.

"Mrs. Villari, I could come back another day if you'd rather not have company tonight."

She opened her eyes. "Are you kidding me? This is my only chance to get any rest around here."

I must have looked dubious, because she put down her coffee and laid her hand on my forearm. "Honey, the family thinks I'm in here grilling you, asking questions about whether or not you're good enough for Sammy . . . whether you're strong enough to bear healthy children," she added, the gleam in her eye twinkling like crazy. "They won't put one foot into this kitchen until I give the signal. Until then, they're in the living room interrogating Sammy and making his life a little bit miserable."

"The signal?" I repeated dumbly.

Blowing across the top of her cup, she took a sip of coffee. "As soon as I start pulling out the plates and banging the lids on the pots, everyone will come running in to help . . . and to find out whether you survived the interrogation."

I pushed my hair off my face. "Isn't this a little old-fashioned, like putting the cart before the horse?" I asked, a kernel of anger taking root in my stomach.

She looked at me questioningly.

"Well, I'm not dating your son, you know. This isn't a date," I said emphatically. "Villari has been a regular pain in the, uh . . . behind, if you really want to know the truth, practically throwing a half nelson around my neck and dragging me over here to see if you recognized me from church this morning." Another avalanche of words threatened to descend. "It's not that I don't appreciate being invited to dinner, but your son is less than subtle when he wants something. He has been a monkey on my back since the death of my neighbor, which I'm sure he told you about, scaring me to death by practically accusing me of being the murderer." I took a deep breath. "So 'grilling' me is totally ridiculous, because Villari and I can't bear to be in the same room with each other longer than five minutes."

"A good sign," Mrs. Villari said quietly. "A very good sign."

"What?" I asked incredulously.

"There's a strong fire in you and that's what Sammy

needs. He's very used to running the show, especially at work, and he brings that home with him, and before you know it, he's bossing the family around. That's bad enough, but then he never lets go of his work, he never relaxes because there's no difference between his job and his home. He needs someone that will force him to leave his work back at the stationhouse."

My mouth gaped open. Was the woman completely deaf? "I'm not the girl for him, Mrs. Villari. Don't get your hopes up."

She stood and smiled and patted my shoulder. "Mm-hmmm," she murmured. "I think the lasagna is ready. Hungry?"

As if on cue, a dark shadow filled the doorway.

"You've hidden the girl out here long enough," a booming voice proclaimed. A large, broad-shouldered man with gray hair and sparkling dark eyes stepped into the kitchen and filled it with his energy. He reminded me of Santa Claus. Large and robust, a round belly, and a laugh that warmed the room. The room seemed to shrink around him. He walked over to the stove and patted his wife's bottom as she bent over to check the lasagna in the oven. She swatted his hand away as she shut the oven door and then twisted around, stood on her toes, and kissed his cheek. Chuckling, he turned to me. "No wonder Sam brought you home. You're pretty as a picture. Let me get a look at you." Bending at the waist, he grabbed both of my hands and pulled me out of the chair.

"She's too skinny, Sammy."

Startled, I looked over my shoulder to see Villari leaning against the doorjamb. "I keep telling her that, but the woman claims she can't cook, and judging by her weight, I think she's telling the truth."

"May I say something?" I asked, defensiveness edging my voice.

"Stop her now, Dad," Villari said, coming into the room. "I've been on the end of that tone before and it's not a pleasant experience."

Papa Villari, or whatever he was called, looked knowingly into my eyes and gently squeezed my hands. "So have I, son . . . from your mama." He smiled down at me. "Don't take offense, Maggie. All this noise and bluster is just our way of telling you that we're glad you're joining us for dinner."

I had to smile. "You've been charming your way out of difficult situations for a long time, haven't you?"

He grinned back. "Pretty damn good at it, aren't I?"

"The best I've ever seen."

He chuckled again, a deep rumble in his chest. "Sammy, you'd better take her into the other room to talk with the rest of the family. If you don't leave soon, I may have to divorce your mother and marry this one."

Dinner was loud and noisy and crazy with people talking all at once and becoming miraculously quiet whenever I spoke. I was definitely being scrutinized, and Villari—or "Sammy," as they called him—seemed to love every minute of it. I tried sneaking looks at him from the corner of my eye, but the man had that damned sixth sense and caught me every time. In between bites of pasta or laughing with his relatives, he'd turn his head and send me a quick wink.

It wasn't until the tiramisù was served with coffee that the evening took a turn for the worse.

"So, do you recognize Maggie from church, Mom?" he asked, sipping his coffee.

"Sammy . . ." she warned.

He shrugged. "I'm only asking a simple question."

"Why do you have to ask?" I blurted. "You said I wasn't a suspect anymore," I added, mentally kicking Villari's big mouth. If he had to ask, why couldn't he have waited to talk to his mother alone? Now the whole family would think they'd just had dinner with a murderer. They were probably afraid I was going to pull out an automatic weapon and mow them down at the table before they had a chance to finish dessert.

"You're not a suspect. But you do have a tendency to tell half-truths," he replied, calmly taking another bite of his cake. "And that's on a good day."

"Sammy," his mother broke in sharply, "is this really necessary?"

"If you had any idea how much trouble this girl gets into," he said, pointing his fork at me, "with little or no effort, you'd see that I'm trying to protect her. She has a nasty habit of . . . uh, shall we say, circumventing the truth? She's out acting like a detective with absolutely no idea of what she's doing."

"Well, someone has to do something," I retorted. "I haven't seen you locking up any criminals lately."

Villari turned to his mother. "I rest my case."

His mother looked decidedly uncomfortable. "I don't like the position you've put me in, either one of you, but I can't help you, Sammy. I go to church to pray, I don't keep tabs on who comes and goes each day."

"But you've never seen her there before, have you?"

"I haven't seen you there either," she remarked dryly.

Villari opened his mouth to protest and then obviously thought better of it. He leaned back, shook his head, and kept quiet. Despite my irritation, I had to smile. Villari apparently knew when he was beaten. I looked up to see his father shake his head and put his hand, which looked an awful lot like a huge bear claw, on top of his wife's. Obviously no one was stupid enough to go up against the Dragon Lady.

Chapter Ten

"Well, you were a big hit with the family," Villari growled in the dark car parked outside my house.

"You don't sound too happy."

"I'd be a lot happier if you'd quit skirting the issue and tell me what's going on in that secretive little brain of yours."

I sighed. The man sounded like a broken record, and I knew that if I didn't say something, he'd never shut up. "Look. I'll agree to cave in here a little and let you in on a few things that I've discovered, but you have to agree to back off when I tell you to."

"Back off how?"

"Like the line from an old song, 'don't ask me how I know what I know'." I could feel his scowl in the car even though I couldn't see anything with his face hidden in the shadows. The porch light only illuminated a small circle in front of the door, just large enough to see through the peephole.

He ran his hands through his hair a couple of times, obviously angry with the conditions. "These are damn stupid rules you're insisting on and this does nothing to ease my mind about you taking care of yourself and staying out of the investigation. I'll agree to your terms, but don't push me too far. I'm very close to breaking your spindly little neck."

"Mmm . . . you do have a way with words, Villari."

"Don't tempt me, Maggie," he warned. "Tell me what you know or what you think you know."

"It isn't much really; at least I don't see how it all fits in. I happen to know, and this is where you're not allowed to ask questions about how I got my information"—I ignored the strangled sounds of frustration coming from Villari—"that Vacuum Nose has some kind of relationship with Lindsay Burns."

The car went quiet. I admit I didn't think he'd whoop and holler when he heard what I had to say, but I expected more of a reaction than complete silence.

Finally he spoke. "Who is Vacuum Nose and who is Lindsay Burns?" he asked quietly.

I backed up and told him the whole story—well, the whole story minus the part about stealing Elizabeth's appointment book and the stakeout. Something inside warned me that the detective wouldn't take too kindly to my spying habits.

Villari looked confused. "And you think this Lindsay Burns had something to do with Elizabeth's death?"

"I don't have any idea. I just got her name . . ." I hesitated when Villari narrowed his eyes.

"I'm supposed to believe that you just *happened* upon

her name and then just *happened* to see her with Officer Mailer?"

"Look, Detective, you were the one who was so all-fired interested in what I was doing and what I found. Well, I told you. I told you everything except a few minor details, and now you're complaining about the information. If you don't want to know or if you're going to argue about what I've discovered, then quit hounding me." I started to pull on the door handle when he reached his arm across my waist and held me still.

"Sorry, Maggie. The things you're not telling have me worried. The only way you could have gotten that information was to do something bordering on illegal, which, on one hand, I don't even want to think about. On the other hand, it might provide me with information I really need." He leaned his head back against the seat. "What you've told me, sketchy as it is, gives me reason to check out Ms. Burns and Officer Mailer, which absolutely stinks. There's nothing easy about checking up on a fellow cop. The department is filled with big ears and even bigger mouths, and once you've made inquiries, if you're not discreet enough, the cops will circle around Mailer like a wagon train to protect their own. I'll be stonewalled before you can blink."

"Even if the guy is guilty?"

Villari turned to me, his eyes as dark as chocolate. "What's he guilty of, Maggie? Of knowing a woman named Lindsay Burns who may or may not have had any contact with Elizabeth?"

"Of course she had contact. She said so herself. She called her 'the bitch.' "

"But that's a long way from killing her."

I crossed my arms in front of my chest. "I never accused her of being the murderer. But why was her name—" I shut my mouth before I ended up in jail for burglary.

"Yes, that's the rub, isn't it? I don't know where you found her name, but I'm willing to bet it wasn't right out in the open. You went digging, didn't you?"

"Villari," I warned, "I'm not giving in here. Take the information or not, it's up to you."

He ignored me. "Are you sure it was Officer Mailer you saw?"

"I'm sure. The man snorts like a bull. He'd be hard to miss."

"Great," he said, running his hand through his hair. "Now I have to investigate a cop on the basis of his large nostrils. The captain will love this."

"Can't you just put out some feelers or something? Call in some favors?" I asked, watching his hair fall forward in loose curls. "You know, your hair would look a little less rumpled if you'd quit plowing your fingers through it whenever you get frustrated."

"You notice my hair?"

"Not really," I said flippantly. It wasn't easy being nonchalant while my stomach squirmed like a fish dangling on a hook. "I can't help but notice how you dig rows through your scalp every time things don't go your way."

"You know, Maggie," he whispered, "you're not a very good liar." He reached over and pushed a strand of hair behind my ear. Again.

Heat flooded my face and headed south. How could the simple touch of his fingers grazing my cheek throw me off balance? Instinctively, I pulled back and edged toward the door, but Villari trailed his fingers down the front of my blouse, grabbed a fistful of material, and tugged me forward, right next to him. Before I could respond, he leaned toward me and fused his mouth with mine.

His kiss was soft but insistent. His tongue parted my lips and skimmed the tops of my teeth. I could taste him, hot and sweet, as he deepened the kiss. He dragged me closer and closer until I could smell a light scent of soap mixed with clean, masculine sweat, as he held me hostage with his hands and mouth. Dazed and confused by the sheer largeness and nearness of his body, I didn't know what to think or how to respond. But my body did. Boy, did it ever. And I was powerless to resist. I ran my fingers through his hair like I'd been itching to do since the moment I first saw him standing in my front yard. My other hand came up behind him and traced the strong corded muscles that ran the length of his back.

He nipped and nibbled my bottom lip. Then suddenly, without warning, he released my blouse and cupped my chin, tilting it up until he had me pinned under those liquid eyes. "If you don't get out of the car now, there's not a chance in hell that I'll be able to control what happens next."

I felt drugged, unable to respond. Even in this awkward position, my hips were arching toward his, ready to mate like a wanton slut.

"Maggie?"

His voice came low, through the heavy fog that clouded my brain.

"Maggie?"

"That's my name," I murmured.

"Let me take you in now."

"Please take me," I practically begged. "No one's stopping you."

"I meant, take you to the door," he explained.

Mortified, I dropped my hands and scooted away as quickly as possible, wrenching the door handle in one smooth movement. At least it was smoother than the crazy jerking my heart was doing at the moment.

"Maggie, wait." He caught my arm as I was climbing out.

I stopped, but I refused to face him. The last thing I needed was for him to see how turned on I'd been, ready to ditch my panties the moment he asked.

"Sit here until I can come around," he pleaded. "Please."

But I ignored him. The moment he released my arm, I jumped out and ran up on the front porch. I pulled my key out of my skirt pocket and tried to insert it in the door. My hands were shaking badly, though, and I dropped the key on the ground. I picked it up and was still fumbling with the door when he reached me, put his hands on my shoulders, and turned me around.

"Let me explain."

"There's nothing to explain," I said, unable to look at him. "I'm just a little embarrassed. I guess I misread the signals." I looked straight ahead, studiously checking out the buttons on his shirt. No way was I going to drop my gaze any lower.

"You didn't misread any signals, Maggie. There's nothing I want more than to carry you to the bedroom and make love to you all night long, but I can't."

I waited for him to continue.

Villari dropped his hands and jammed them into the back pockets of his jeans. He paced up and down the porch, passing quietly in and out of shadows without saying a word. I thought he might slip soundlessly into the darkness, unnoticed, until I heard his car pull away from the driveway.

"I've never met anyone like you before." His voice wafted in on the blackness, a dark profile standing at the edge of the railing. But now I wanted to see his face, to gauge his expression. His words were so vague, how could I know what he was really saying unless I could see the look in his eyes, the turn of his mouth?

"Irritating, annoying, argumentative," he continued.

With that lovely trio of adjectives, however, I didn't need to see his face. There weren't going to be any gooey, lovesick eyes staring back at me. I turned around and jiggled the key impatiently. I saw no need to stick around and hear a summary of all my flaws, not as long as I still had a trace of pride left.

"With a nasty habit of running away when things get uncomfortable," he added.

With my face to the door and one hand wrapped around the doorknob, I mustered my last vestige of courage. "Only an idiot hangs around while someone shoves his face in the mud."

"That's not what I'm doing, Maggie. I'm trying to explain."

I swiveled around and peered into the darkness. "Are you crazy? Reciting a list of nasty attributes hardly explains anything." I stopped. "Maybe I'm wrong. Maybe it does. Maybe it explains why you want to keep things from going any further . . . uh, physically." I choked over the last words, humiliated to be acting like a horny teenager in the throes of unrequited lust.

"Impetuous, impulsive," he proceeded calmly, "and

crazy enough to rush headlong out of an airplane without checking to make sure there's a parachute on your back." The warped, wooden slats popped and moaned under the weight of his footsteps. Seconds later he stood in front of me. He lifted one finger and skimmed the side of my jaw, a simple gesture that sent delicious tingles up and down my arms until I had to clench my fists against the onslaught.

"Stop touching me, Villari. I get the picture, so you don't need to go through this charade. You're not interested. Believe me, I can handle this." I took a deep breath and glared at him. "Despite what your ego insists on believing, being turned down sexually is hardly life-threatening. In the scheme of things, it doesn't even register as a blip on the radar screen."

His eyes drilled a hole in my face. They practically singed my skin raw and I half expected to see smoke rising off my cheeks, but I refused to look away. Forget this guy, I told myself. First he stalks me, woos me, even takes me to his mother's for dinner, and then when I finally capitulate, he wants to play Mr. Integrity. I stared right back at him, tit for tat, narrowing my eyes into a dangerous look that was, I hoped, both strong and seductive.

Obviously it didn't work, because the next thing I knew, Villari threw his head back and laughed. My smoldering provocative look dried up like stale bread and I stood there shifting back and forth, not knowing what the hell was going on.

"Maggie," he finally managed to sputter between breaths, "you have the patience of a saint and the tenacity of a bulldog all rolled up into one extraordinarily charming package."

I stuck out my chin. "If you even think about telling me how cute I am when I'm angry, you'll be minus one manly testicle as a result."

He placed both hands on my shoulders, bowed his head, and rested his lips lightly on my forehead. "Sweetheart, you're adorable when you're angry and adorable when you're not," he whispered against my skin. "If you hadn't raced to get out of the car, I would have explained what I meant when I said we needed to stop. All I was trying to say is that we should probably wait before going any further in our relationship—"

"There is no relationship," I protested hotly, pulling away.

"—until the murder is solved and it doesn't look like a conflict of interest," he continued after grabbing my arms and tugging me back.

"What kind of conflict of interest could there be if I'm not a suspect?" I demanded, my voice muffled since my nose was now smashed against his chest, a wall of steel muscles. Sort of like crashing into Superman.

"Everyone is a suspect until the murderer is found, Maggie. Absolutely everyone. But right now you're at the bottom of the list, where I fully expect you to stay. But I'm still in charge of the investigation and I don't want any comments, raised eyebrows, or even the slightest suspicion that I compromised the case because I was involved with you. Suspect or not, you are the closest link we've got."

I relaxed against him as he tightened his arms around me. "I still can't believe all of this," I confessed. "Sometimes a few minutes will go by and I'll forget about this whole sordid mess and I'll look up, half expecting to see Elizabeth standing in front of me holding a cup of coffee and lecturing me on some aspect of art or my lousy sense of style." I turned my head and laid my cheek against his shirt, sidling closer until I could hear his heart beating rhythmically. It felt strong and powerful, pulsing loudly as though to reassure me that some things were still very much alive.

He rested his chin on the top of my head and tugged on the ends of my hair with one hand. His other arm wound around me like a boa constrictor, which sounds frightening, but really wasn't. I felt safe, cocooned from a world that had recently turned very harsh. Of course, for a moment I wondered whether the boa routinely seduced its prey before squeezing the life out its body like a tube of toothpaste. I shuddered.

"I'd love to say things will get better soon, Maggie, but the truth is, they won't. Until the murderer is put behind bars, it's hard for people to get on with their lives and move forward. And when we do catch the guy who killed Elizabeth Boyer, don't be surprised if you start grieving all over again. Right now anger and fear and all sorts of emotions have probably kept you from feeling the total impact of her death."

I pulled back and managed to wiggle out from his arms. "So where does this leave us?"

He leaned down and caressed my lips with the tip of his tongue, lingering over the sweetness of the kiss, teasing my lips apart, tasting, probing until I felt the strength desert the back of my knees and I started to buckle.

"It leaves us right here, Maggie," he said, grinning mischievously.

"And exactly what does that mean?"

"It means I won't forget where we left off."

Villari reached behind me and unlocked the door. For one glorious moment I thought he might have changed his mind about keeping our relationship chaste and pure for the time being, and I had visions of being swept up into his arms and carried off. But the man seemed to be a stickler for sticking with his decisions, one of my weaker points, so that in the end all he did was walk around the house to check for intruders. When he was satisfied that no one was lurking in the shadows or behind doors, he kissed me briefly and walked out. It was just my luck to fall for Captain Virtue.

The jarring ring pierced my eardrums, repeatedly, until I had no choice but to grope around the nightstand and answer the damned phone. It was the first decent night's sleep I'd had for several days, complete with lustful dreams of charcoal eyes and strong masculine hands, and the interruption did not put me in a particularly jolly mood.

"What?" I snapped into the telephone.

"Ms. Kean, I presume?"

I recognized Mr. Prestwood's upper-crust tones right away and sat up in bed, pulling the covers to my chin as though he were in the room. Somehow modesty was important to maintain around Prestwood, even if he couldn't see you. Proper people always know when the rules of propriety are being broken.

"Yes, this is her." Or me. Or she. I can never remember the correct grammar in that situation. I know when to use *good* and when to use *well,* but it's downhill after that. Fortunately, I teach art and seldom get bogged down with the intricacies of the human language.

"This is Allen Prestwood. We met the other day with Cassandra and William Boyer to review Elizabeth Boyer's will."

"I remember, Mr. Prestwood. What can I do for you?"

"I was wondering if we might meet again soon. As you know, Elizabeth requested that you be the fiduciary of her will, and if you have agreed to fulfill these responsibilities, there are several papers that need to be signed and filed with the state."

"Do I have to decide so quickly? I really don't even understand what the job entails," I asked nervously. "Is there any real need to hurry?"

There was a long pause, as some papers were being shuffled in the background. "Ms. Kean . . ."

"Call me, Maggie."

"Maggie, then. Normally, I like to give people plenty of time to get used to the idea of being an executor or a fiduciary or any other request a decedent may have included in a will. But the fact is, in this particular matter, I think we might want to proceed as expeditiously as possible."

"Why is that?" I asked, although I had a hunch it had something to do with the grandkids.

"If you wouldn't mind, Ms. Kean, I mean Maggie, I would much prefer to continue this conversation in person. Emotions are understandably running quite high at this time, as you can well imagine. I believe it would be easier and more prudent to explain the situation face-to-face, if you are agreeable to such a meeting."

I sighed. "Mr. Prestwood, I have no problem meeting with you, although I will warn you that I haven't made up my mind about Elizabeth's request." Unbidden tears sprang to my eyes. I felt like a pregnant woman with a vat of hormones spilling through my body. Between mourning for Elizabeth and lusting after Villari, I was hanging on to a crazy seesaw of emotions, and not doing a great job of it. "But I'm more than willing to hear what you have to say, especially since I'm sure Cassie and Will have been a real pain in the ass—uh, neck, I mean."

He chuckled. "That's quite all right, Maggie. Your first word was significantly more accurate."

"So when would you like to meet?"

"Would there be a time this morning that would be convenient for you?"

"Sure. When and where? You'll have to give me the address. I've never been to your office."

"Well, actually, I'm working in Elizabeth's office right now. I'm going through her files and gathering some information. Would you mind coming here within the next hour or two? It will take me at least that long to finish."

"I don't know, Mr. Prestwood. I'm not sure I'm ready for another confrontation with the Evil Twins."

"Perfectly understandable, my dear. I felt the same way before I arrived, but Benton has assured me that the 'Evil Twins,' as you so aptly describe them, are not due back until late this afternoon."

"Okay," I said, still a little skeptical. I was not eager to run into either of the Boyer grandchildren. The way my luck was running lately, I was convinced that a great cosmic joker was wreaking havoc on my life and laughing his butt off.

"I can expect you at ten o'clock, then?"

"Sure," I agreed hesitantly. "I'll be there."

I hung up feeling surlier than I had when I first woke up. I glanced at the clock and groaned. It was a few minutes past eight o'clock and I had less than two hours before my meeting with Prestwood. I turned over, scrunched down under the covers, pulled the pillow over my head, and pretended that everything was fine. If an ostrich could bury its head in the sand, I could bury mine in bed linens.

It didn't work. Elizabeth was nagging at me, demanding that I get up and face the day. I wondered if I was the only person whose memories of the dearly departed were so ambivalent. Where were the misty, watercolor memories that Barbra Streisand sang of so eloquently? In my mind, Elizabeth stood over me with her hands on her hips barking out the same orders she did before she died. Before she was killed.

God, I missed her.

Chapter Eleven

Someone leaned heavily on the doorbell while I was in the middle of scrubbing my head. There was shampoo in my hair, soap in my eyes, and I was in a lousy mood. I had taken the phone off the hook before getting into the shower because I hate to be interrupted. If I don't, I respond like a mouse in a behavior modification experiment: phone rings, idiot girl flies out of the shower to answer it. It doesn't make any sense. I know they'll call back if it's urgent, but I can't seem to stop myself from dropping the soap and sprinting across the floor sopping wet. I can stop the phone from ringing, but how do you disconnect the doorbell?

Then the knocking started. Whoever it was wasn't going away. Rinsing quickly, I stepped onto the cotton throw rug and pulled an old threadbare terrycloth robe over my body, tying it at the waist. With a towel twisted around my hair, turban style, I threw open the door and ran down the hallway just fast enough to feel my feet slide beneath me as I rounded the corner. My legs flew up and my bottom flew down as I skidded across the wooden floor.

I screamed as I fishtailed and slammed sideways into the wall, finally coming to a stop. Gingerly, I checked my body for broken bones and blood and gore, but I was still in one piece, despite a bruised shoulder and a sore behind. I pulled myself up slowly and hobbled to the front, where someone was apparently determined to destroy a perfectly good door.

"What is your problem?" I yelled, yanking the door open. But the hand that was pounding relentlessly just kept right on hammering, now rapping my nose like a woodpecker. Before I knew it, I was down on my butt again, this time with a bloody nose and a body sprawled on top of me. Dazed, I raised myself a few inches off the ground but all I could see was that hand, looking suspiciously like Thing, the family "appendage" that lived in a box on the old *Addams Family* television show. I shoved the person unceremoniously to the side, rolled over, and pulled myself up for the second time that morning. I took one look and groaned.

"What are you doing here, Cassie?"

"What am I doing? I was knocking on your door until you plowed into me and knocked me off my feet," she snapped as she stood up and brushed imaginary dust from her skirt. "My hose are ruined and this outfit is filthy. This is a Tsunamato original and you've got me rolling in the dirt like a common mud wrestler. I knew it was a mistake to come here."

Elizabeth's lovely granddaughter stood in my doorway spewing enough venom to flood my house, and I lost my patience. "Listen, you little shit. I didn't knock you over. You lost your balance when I opened the door. Besides, I'm not the one who came waltzing over here uninvited, beating my door down like the Gestapo. It will take less than two seconds for you to dump that dress in your maid's lap to clean, so drop the act and tell me what brings Little Miss Sunshine here for a visit." Limping like a dog with a thorn in its paw, I left the door open and went to pour a cup of coffee. One cup.

With my backside in mind, I skipped the hard, wooden kitchen chairs and opted for the couch. Drawing my legs underneath me and blowing softly on my coffee, I ignored Cassie, who was still emitting dramatic huffs and puffs in the entryway. She really was more than I could handle first thing in the morning.

"I thought you and I had an agreement to stay away from each other," I called over my shoulder.

"We did, but this is simply too important to let a minor disagreement keep us from working together for everyone's benefit."

Needless to say, I was skeptical of anything Cassie deemed beneficial to anyone else besides herself, especially knowing she regarded me as little more than a bug.

"What exactly did you have in mind?" I asked, sipping from my mug.

She stared at me. "Would you mind if I had a cup of coffee?" she asked imperiously.

"Not at all," I said, waving in the direction of the kitchen. "Help yourself."

She was still standing in the doorway when I glanced over after taking a second sip. I nearly burst out laughing at the play of emotions flitting across her face. This woman had been catered to for so long she needed to be retaught simple English words like "coffeepot" and "mug." I was tempted to get up and show her how the common folk lived, but my evil streak reveled in her discomfort.

Several minutes later she was sitting on the couch opposite me, looking terribly awkward without her usual china cup and saucer. But I had to hand it to her. Even in her slightly disheveled suit and perfectly matching low-heeled pumps, she was determined to see this meeting through to the end.

I pulled the towel off my head and dragged my fingers through my hair to fluff my curls out so I wouldn't look like my mother in those old, early-morning photos with curls pinned tightly against her head.

"Why don't you start, Cassie, since I see no particular reason for you to be here."

She took a very small, very delicate sip of coffee from the mug, her left pinkie sticking straight out. She took a deep breath and let out a small shudder.

"I might owe you an apology."

I bet that hurt. Nothing she could have said would have surprised me more than those six words. Of course, she didn't come right out and say that she *definitely* owed me an apology, but the *A* word was there, and I was willing to take what I could get. I was so shocked I didn't care *why* or *what* she was sorry about, I just wanted to enjoy the moment. Which didn't last too long.

"In my terrible grief," she began, "I said some things in Mr. Prestwood's office that might have been interpreted as a bit self-centered or a little selfish . . ."

You *think*?

"And that just wasn't the case. You see, I was really thinking of Grandmother."

Then she actually dabbed at her eyes with a tissue she dug out of her jacket pocket. That one movement summed up the difference between Cassie and me. When I cry, I sob. I wail. I make lots of noise, tears stream down my face, my nose runs like crazy and swells up to twice its normal size. And I never dab daintily with a tissue. I mop. I use an industrial-strength paper towel to sop up the river flooding down my face. The genteel woman sitting across from me, however, all decked out in her tight little red skirt and matching jacket with black velvet piping, barely managed to wring out one tear per eyeball.

"I was so distressed about the situation," she said, emphasizing the last word.

What a delicate way to describe a hideous murder.

"Are you talking about your grandmother ending up in my sewer?" I asked sweetly.

Cassie reared back and brought her tissue up to her nose as though she smelled something unpleasant. This woman sitting on my couch and drinking my coffee was really irritating me. Her whole phony act made me nauseous. "Just spit it out, Cassie. And drop the grieving-granddaughter bit. I don't believe it now any more than I did the day we found Elizabeth's body and you wanted to cover up what you called the 'unfortunate incident.' "

Her eyes narrowed and her thin little nostrils flared as far as they could given the cosmetic trimming they'd undergone. "You are a nasty little thing, aren't you?"

I smiled. "Your true colors are showing, Cassie, and you still haven't told me why you're here. Until you do, calling me names may not be in your best interest." I didn't know the exact reason for her visit, but I had no doubt she wanted something from me. And right now I wasn't willing to refill her coffee cup much less grant her any real favors.

"Will thought you might be difficult, but I assured him that the two of us could handle this in a civilized manner. I hoped you would see the sense in our proposal, but I'm beginning to have my doubts," she sniffed in that snooty voice of hers. I watched her fidget and squirm on the sofa cushions—probably trying to rearrange the thong panties she had wedged up her butt.

"Anytime you want to hit the road, Cassie, feel free to do so." I checked my watch. "I have an appointment this morning, so I'm running out of time and patience with this little chat we're having."

"Yes, I know. You're meeting Mr. Prestwood at our house. That's why I'm here. We—that is, Will and I—wanted to speak to you before you met with him."

"How did you know about the meeting?"

She lifted her manicured hand and patted her expensively cut hair, artfully arranged not to look artfully arranged. "I don't think the details really matter, but suffice it to say, we do know it and therefore need to act promptly."

"Well, suffice it to say," I said, mimicking her highbrow accent, "that I'm sure you had your ear plastered to the door when Prestwood was talking to me on the phone. You were supposed to be out this morning."

"I left just moments before your telephone conversation," she said, clearly annoyed with me. "Fortunately, my wallet was in my other purse and I had just walked back in when I overheard him talking to you. You were trying to meet behind our backs, weren't you?"

"Apparently so." There was no reason to lie about our plans, since I knew she'd heard every word Prestwood had spoken.

"That's just what I was afraid of, so—"

I interrupted her. "So you called Will on the phone, and the two of you hatched this ingenious plan that will solve all our problems and make everybody happy. Am I right?"

"Is it necessary for you to put such an ugly spin on everything?"

A sharp retort came to mind, but I was weary of this whole conversation and wanted the damn thing to end. "What is it you want, Cassie?" I sighed.

"To offer you a little proposition, Maggie." She looked around the room, her nose turning up as though rotten garbage covered the floor. "We realize that it can't be easy to live on a teacher's salary these days, especially when you are essentially trying to juggle two careers, like you are, with the, um, art you are trying to make."

"I can't imagine how my struggle affects you or your brother."

"Well, I won't lie and say that it affects us directly, but I think Will and I have come up with a solution that would immediately ease your monetary difficulties and allow us to move on from this horrible episode we've had to endure."

I was rapidly reaching my limit with this meeting. "What's your idea, Cassie?"

Taking a deep breath, she leaned forward and gingerly placed the coffee mug on the edge of my heavily scratched antique coffee table. "Will and I fully understand that your role as fiduciary for Grandmother's estate has added stress to your life, stress I'm quite sure you don't need. The entire process involves all sorts of legalistic transactions and so forth and the time commitment can be quite lengthy."

"I'm touched by your concern," I said dryly.

"Of course, as fiduciary you would earn a stipend for your services," she said, ignoring my sarcasm, "but that would be parceled out over an extended period of time, and would not make up for the time lost from your teaching or your art."

"I assume you and your brother came up with a plan to solve all my problems."

Her smile did not reach her eyes. "We thought you might appreciate a large, lump sum of money up front, right now, rather than waiting for the individual payments to add up."

I waited for her to continue.

"Of course, you would be released of your responsibilities as fiduciary and the heavy burdens that are inherent in the job, even for knowledgeable people, not to mention someone a little less experienced like yourself."

Cassie laced her fingers together and sat back, the only person I know who can sit on my down-filled cushions and still maintain perfect posture. The woman looked like a 3-D version of a ninety-degree angle. When Lisa visits, in direct contrast to the stiff rod currently occupying my couch, she heaves a large sigh and sinks into the thick pillows and almost always falls asleep in the middle of our conversation. I've often accused her of using our friendship as an excuse to get to my sofa.

"That certainly is a nice offer, Cassie," I remarked cynically, "and I'm sure that you and Will have my best interests at heart, but, speaking off the top of my head, I can see a few potential problems."

Her perfectly arched eyebrows furrowed into a scowl.

"First off, I'm not in this for the money. As you mentioned, the only way you and Will could give me a big pile of money is if I relinquish my responsibility and hand over all your grandmother's entire estate to the two of you. I'm not willing to do that." I paused briefly, searching for the right words. "Your grandmother was wonderful to me. And I never got to say thanks, or even good-bye, to her. It would be my privilege to help her in any way I can. In fact, this little chat has been very enlightening."

"I'm sure Grandmother had no idea what this job entailed when she put your name in the will," she argued.

"Elizabeth knew exactly what she was doing, Cassie. If I had any doubts before, I don't now, not after witnessing this wonderful display of greed." I stood and picked up her mug off the table. "I have a meeting with Mr. Prestwood in less than an hour and I have several things I need to do before I go. I'd like you to leave my house now." Cassie started to object, but I refused to listen to her any longer. "If you have any other questions or brilliant schemes you'd like to bounce off me, you can bring them up in, say,"—I glanced at my watch—"forty-five minutes. You know the address."

I walked into the kitchen and rinsed out the cups. I didn't turn around until I heard the front door slam. "Nice going, Elizabeth," I said, laughing to myself. "She's good and ticked off now." Drying my hands on the towel hanging from the stove handle, I grabbed the phone and punched in Lisa's number.

"You've got to be kidding," she gasped when I re-counted Cassie's visit.

"Scout's honor. The woman really expected me to be fiduciary long enough to hand her and that scummy brother of hers the entire estate, disregarding all of Elizabeth's instructions."

"And even if you did exactly that, there's no guarantee you'd ever see a dime of that money she promised to give you."

"No kidding. You know, Lisa, I think she's beginning to panic a little."

"How so?"

"She's beginning to understand what Elizabeth was trying to do—make the little princess work for her money."

With that, I hung up, promising to meet her for lunch after my appointment with the lawyer.

Prestwood was scribbling something on a yellow legal pad when I arrived. He looked up at the sound of my light tapping. Every bit the gentleman, he stood and walked to the door, clasping my hand warmly and indicating one of the chairs facing Elizabeth's desk. He peeked quickly into the hallway before firmly shutting the door.

"Don't worry, I've already been attacked by the enemy."

Prestwood sat down behind the desk and put on his glasses. "I assume you are speaking of Cassandra or William—or God forbid, both of them together?"

"Just Cassie. She came barreling into my house this morning and left with her nose out of joint."

"May I ask why she was 'barreling' into your house?"

I lifted my shoulders nonchalantly. "She and Will had this idea that maybe I could hand them the money in the will and in return they'd give me a large sum of money and relieve me of my position."

Prestwood pushed his glasses up the bridge of his nose and peered at me. "It seems they are utilizing the 'divide and conquer' strategy. I had a very similar discussion with William, which is why I want to comply with Elizabeth's wishes as soon as possible." He frowned. "I do wonder about Cassandra's timing, though. She managed to learn of our meeting and to talk with you in very short order."

"She eavesdropped. She heard you talking to me and hurried over to my place like a scared rabbit."

"Lovely children, aren't they?" he murmured. Sorting papers on his desk, he pulled out a file and flipped it open. "Well, let's move on, shall we?"

Several signatures later I was the official fiduciary. Elizabeth's wish was my command. I knew less than nothing about my new duties, but there was no doubt that Elizabeth had been well aware of that fact. If she was willing to take a chance on me, then I was willing to give it a try. I stood up to leave when I noticed the picture lying against the wall behind the desk. From where I was standing, I could see bold splashes of color, a modernistic landscape. Curious, I moved around the desk and skirted past Prestwood, who was busy organizing papers for me to take home. Squatting down, I admired the sweeping brush strokes, the bright, almost neon hues. Conical-shaped trees stretched to the sky. Fields of flowers and tall grass were represented with vivid dabs of color. And right down the center, a long dirt trail wiggled through the fields, up and over a small incline, disappearing into the forest. I recognized the trail right away. It was the one I hiked behind my house. And there in the corner, written in large loopy letters, was Elizabeth's signature. This was the picture I'd stumbled over the other night. This was the picture she left me in the will.

Then whose picture was leaning against my wall at home?

I backed up and bumped into Prestwood's chair.

"Excuse me, Mr. Prestwood."

"I see you've found Elizabeth's gift to you." He sighed. "She had such a distinctive style, don't you agree?"

I did agree, but I wasn't convinced that Prestwood was referring just to her painting talent. "I should have recognized her work right away, even though it's the first piece that I've seen." I smiled. "It certainly matches her personality. Those colors, the boldness of the stroke, it practically screams 'Elizabeth'!"

"Absolutely." His eyes gently grazed my face. "You remind me of her, Maggie. You've got the same strength, the same determination. She wanted you to have the picture. Please feel free to take it with you and enjoy it."

I nodded, unable to speak. With one hand on each side, I lifted the painting and carefully carried it out of the office, down the hallway and out the front door, looking every which way in the expectation that one of the vulture grandchildren would suddenly descend. Although the painting was legally mine, I wasn't sure how to explain the fact that this was the second painting I'd taken. Of course, it was a legitimate mistake. It was dark the night I had taken the other painting and I was in a bit of a hurry. But I didn't think Will would believe my story.

As I stepped outside, I couldn't shake the feeling that something was wrong and it had nothing to do with Cassie and Will. Walking as fast as I could without breaking into a jog, I cut across the Boyer driveway and a large expanse of green grass until I reached the scrub oaks that ran the length between the two properties. I followed a narrow path through the bushes, no easy feat given how dense and intertwined the branches were, but Elizabeth had done this a million times on her way to visit me. Weaving in and out, I felt like a wide receiver sidestepping defensive players, clutching my precious parcel. Branches snagged my shirt, but a few moments later I stepped out of the maze into my yard. I was tempted to throw my arms in the air and dance a little victory jig, but I wasn't about to drop the picture now. Besides, I'd look ridiculous. I have absolutely no rhythm when it comes to that sort of thing.

I ran through the front door and down the hallway into my bedroom. The picture I had taken the other night was still leaning against the wall. Its sad, somber message resonated. I set Elizabeth's portrait on my bed and went to look at the first painting. I crouched down and studied the colors, the lines, the brush strokes, even the lack of a signature, wondering why I couldn't shake this feeling of doom.

Then it came to me.

Chapter Twelve

"What are you doing here? I told you before, I've got nothing to say to you."

The pinched face peered through the crack in the door. The stringy hair, the dark roots and the lousy manners hadn't changed, but I wasn't backing off this time.

"I need to talk to you, Ms. Burns, and I'm not leaving until I do."

Her eyes darted back and forth like a caged animal.

"Then you'll be spending the night on the front steps because I'm not letting you in." She started to push the door shut.

"You're a talented artist, Ms. Burns."

She stopped pushing and looked at me, her gaze nervous and unsteady.

"I'm sure Elizabeth told you that. Am I right?"

Lindsay Burns looked over my shoulder. She checked up and down the street. "Look, you need to leave. It isn't safe for you. Or me." I must have looked skeptical or stubborn or both, because she quickly added, "I'll meet you at Waterford Park. Go out of the complex and take a left. The park is about a mile and a half down the road on the left. There's a lake. I'll meet you there in ten minutes."

"I'm coming back if you don't show," I warned her. She nodded and shut the door. I followed her directions and found the park easily. It was set off from the road, but you could see the lake shimmering in the sunlight like a sheet of glass. I parked the car in the small parking lot, grabbed my sweatshirt from the backseat and tied it around my waist, and began strolling toward the lake. As I came closer, things began to look familiar—the grass, the water, the ducks paddling with orange feet. Then I saw the green bench, tilted and half-hidden in the tall cattails. This was the scene in the first picture I had taken from Elizabeth's office.

I turned at the sound of crunching gravel. Lindsay Burns walked toward me, her head bowed. A faded, shapeless dress hung from her thin shoulders and a pair of old, untied tennis shoes slapped against her heels like the rubber thongs I wore to the beach. She passed me without saying a word, stepping through the high grass as it clung to the hem of her dress. I followed her through the field and around the lake until she reached the bench and sat down on the far side, leaving room for me. We sat there in silence, listening to the ducks paddling and the birds flapping their wings as they flew off.

"Elizabeth was the first person to ever tell me I could paint."

"She told you the truth." I turned and glanced at her profile. It was all lines and sharp angles, from the high cheekbones to the jutting chin. Her forehead was flat and even, her nose a straight smooth plane. I imagined her face as a study of geometric designs, one figure intersecting the other, one continuous flow of interlocking corners, until you reached her mouth. Soft and full, her lips were the stuff of romantic novels. Stuck in the middle of vectors, points and perpendicular lines, her mouth seemed oddly misplaced.

Chewing on her bottom lip, she lifted her shoulders. "She was nice enough to say so, anyway."

"Elizabeth never said anything just to be nice. If she said it, she meant it."

She turned slightly. "How do you know about me or my art?"

"It wasn't hard really, it came to me in a flash." I explained about the mix-up in paintings, leaving out the stolen appointment book where I'd found her name. "When I went back to my house and studied the picture, it was obviously your work." Distrust and confusion clouded her eyes. "I probably would have realized it sooner, except I assumed the painting I had taken off Elizabeth's wall was her work. Once I saw her signature on the second picture, all the pieces came together."

"I still don't understand. I never sign my pictures. How would you know—"

I interrupted her. "The first day I was here, when you opened the door to me, I caught a glimpse of your living room. There were a bunch of plastic toys tucked in a corner and a big-wheel tricycle in the middle of the floor." I paused a moment before continuing. "And then, before you shut the door, I saw the paintings on the wall. They jumped out at me because of the distinct contrast between the bright toys and the dark colors in the paintings. It was your art I saw hanging on the walls, right?"

She didn't say anything, just looked straight ahead. A cool breeze tickled the lake, wrinkling its smooth face.

"Your style, the tone, even the mood of your pictures are your signature." We continued to look out over the water as clouds floated in front of the sun and the air became rapidly cooler. Colorado's mountain ranges bred finicky, unstable weather. I untied the sweatshirt at my waist and offered it to her, knowing the thin cotton of her dress was no match for the cold. She shook her head, clenched her hands together, and stared straight ahead.

"So what is it you want?" she asked, almost defiantly, as though I was out to get her somehow.

"Look, I'm sure it's not easy for you to trust me," I admitted. Given the clusters of faded bruises marking her face, I doubted she trusted anybody. "I lied about being Elizabeth's secretary. I was a good friend of hers. Her neighbor, actually. Her body was found in my yard."

Lindsay Burns spun around and stared at me, her eyes widened in shock. "How did she die?"

"The police told me she was hit on the back of the head with a heavy object and then carried to my septic tank and dumped."

"Oh, my God." She covered her mouth as tears sprang to her eyes. "The paper said she had been murdered, but they didn't say anything like that."

I touched her arm. "Lindsay? Is it okay if I call you by your first name?" She nodded and I went on. "The police are trying to keep back as much information as possible. I'm not sure why, probably because of copycat killers or things like that. I don't have much more information than you do, just where she was found."

Lindsay wiped her eyes on the back of her arm. Then,

abruptly, she stood. "I'm sorry about Mrs. Boyer. She was very nice to me. But she's dead now and I don't see what you expect or want to get from me." She looked away.

I put one hand over my eyebrows to block the sun as I watched her move to the edge of the lake. She stood on the bank, the water lapping against her feet. For a moment I thought my hunch had been wrong. Maybe there was nothing more to the relationship between Elizabeth and Lindsay than a common interest in art. It wouldn't be the first time I had jumped to conclusions and fired rapidly before getting all the information. But then I noticed her arms. They were wound tightly around her waist as though she hurt inside and was shielding herself from the pain. At this point I was going on instinct. I followed her.

"Why did Elizabeth come to see you?" I asked softly, now standing beside her.

She shook her head, lifting her face upward to the weakening sun. Then she turned around and faced me. "You're Maggie Kean." She smiled at the confusion on my face. "Elizabeth told me about you. I knew exactly who you were the first time you came to see me. You were exactly as she described. I tried to warn you, but you wouldn't listen."

"Warn me?"

She ignored my question and turned back to the lake. "Elizabeth described you once. She told me that I'd recognize you anywhere, even without being introduced. She said you were a perfect candidate for that TV show called *Fashion Emergency*." Lindsay bent down and grabbed a small flat pebble. She drew her arm back and snapped it forward, sending the rock skipping lightly across the water.

"Sounds like her," I murmured. "She was always complaining about my style or lack of style. Actually, her complaints weren't confined to my clothing. Elizabeth managed to zero in on a whole bunch of weaknesses she wasn't pleased with. It wasn't until after she died that I realized how much I had come to depend on her."

Lindsay didn't respond. She just stood still, staring out over the lake as though the answers she sought would rise up out of the water like a white swan and soar through the air. She was an odd combination of pride and fear, stubbornness and docility. It was easy to imagine her facing down the Loch Ness monster with one scathing look, but it was just as easy to imagine her cringing and whimpering in its shadow.

"Elizabeth never came to see me, Maggie." She said my name with a bit of a question behind it, as though wondering if I really meant for her to call me by it. And then she looked at me with a look so wistful and sad that I suddenly realized I was not looking at pride or fear or any of those things I had thought I'd seen before. I was looking at loneliness. Sheer loneliness in all its shapes and sizes.

"How did you meet her?"

"I went to see her."

"You went to see Elizabeth? Why?"

"Because of my children. Because I was desperate."

"I don't understand."

She unwrapped her arms and rubbed her palms up and down both sides of her dress. Her hipbones poked against the thin material. With her skinny arms and legs, she reminded me of the stick figures I had drawn in kindergarten. I was tempted to drag her over to Villari's parents' house and beg Mrs. Villari to put some meat on Lindsay's bones.

"Walk with me?"

I nodded and we began walking around the perimeter of the lake, staying close enough for her to pick up a rock now and then and pitch it across the water.

"My mother died ten years ago, when I was twenty. It was very painful, and I guess I lost my balance or sense of where I was going. So I dropped out of college with no real place to go or any idea of what to do next." She glanced at me, clearly expecting a negative reaction. But I wasn't going to judge anyone's response to grief. My own mother's death had taught me that much.

"My mom died when I was young," I told her. "It changed my life."

She was quiet for a few moments and then started talking. I tried not to interrupt because I wanted her to establish her own pace and I didn't want to scare her off with all my questions. "I know it sounds strange—I mean, I was on my own and I really didn't depend on my mother for anything anymore, but . . ." She trailed off for a moment before clearing her throat and continuing. "But her death completely unhinged me. I was an only child and my father . . . well, let's just say, I never knew him. As long as I can remember, it was just my mother and myself, just the two of us. And that was okay with me. We loved each other. We had enough money. We were never rich, but we weren't starving or out on the streets or anything like that. Mom and I had a lot of fun together, maybe because it was just she and I. I know it sounds odd, but I was never really curious about my father. My life was fine and I didn't see any reason to complicate it looking for a man who had never cared enough to stick around in the first place."

We made our way through the tall grass, the cool air fanning our faces.

"Anyway . . . Mom and I took care of each other and things went along fine until I turned eighteen and I graduated from high school." She bent down and picked up a long thin branch that had fallen to the ground. "Mom really wanted me to go to college. Insisted on it, actually. I didn't care one way or the other, but Mom was determined that I would have more choices in my life than she did. She wanted me to be in charge of my life and she was positive that an education would give me that chance. Of course, I really had mixed feelings about going away. I mean, the idea of complete freedom was heady, like it is for any teenager, and I *was* your typical teenager, ready to go off and drink beer and all that stuff, but I felt terrible about leaving my mother alone. For too many years, we were all each other had." She turned and smiled at me. "I guess you weren't really expecting an autobiography, were you?"

"Trust me, Lindsay. No one can draw out an answer longer than I can," I reassured her. "I don't believe in short vignettes or abridged versions of a story. Tell the whole story, with all the details, or don't bother telling the story at all. That's my motto. Believe me, compared to my rambling style, you're practically mute."

Her smiled deepened. "Elizabeth said you had a great sense of humor."

"That's nice to know considering her rather nasty comments about my lack of fashion sense," I replied dryly. "She never did appreciate the work it took to maintain this casual, nonchalant style."

"Maggie, don't take offense," she said, laughing, "but I doubt you spend more than twenty minutes putting that look together. And if you do, then something is terribly wrong."

"Fifteen minutes," I replied. And then I laughed with her. "It used to drive Elizabeth nuts. She'd come waltzing into my studio wearing Chanel's latest and stand over me, impatiently tapping her foot like a metronome, demanding to know why I insisted on looking like a starving artist."

"That sounds just like her." She pushed her hair out of her face and tilted it to the waning sun. "She reminded me of my mother. Not so much physically—Elizabeth was a more attractive woman. But emotionally. She had that same capacity to just up and love someone without weighing the consequences."

It was true. Elizabeth had an astounding capacity to love. Maybe Lindsay was right, though. Maybe Elizabeth's capacity wasn't any greater than anyone else's; maybe she just wasn't afraid to use it.

"Anyway, after a lot of tears, I made the break and went to college." She took a deep breath and sighed, looking off into the distance as the memories washed over her. "It was everything I hoped it would be. I drank beer until I threw up, stayed out until all hours, and then crammed for tests at the last minute. I even paid my roommate, who happened to be the resident genius, to write a two-page essay discussing the theme of Dylan's Thomas's poem 'Do Not Go Gently Into that Good Night' while I went to a frat party. I'm sure it wasn't exactly what Mom had in mind when she sent me off to school, but I loved every crazy moment of it until . . ." Lindsay paused almost imperceptibly before going on. "Mom died. And then my world crashed around me."

Pale orange tendrils slipped through the long wispy clouds that cloaked the sun. Grass fluttered beneath the cool breeze skating across the water, and in the background, dark gray skies threatened to swallow the lake. Once again, I silently offered my sweatshirt to Lindsay, but she shook her head. She seemed oblivious to the changing, ominous weather, wet clothes, muddy feet, or hypothermia. But I came from much more feeble stock and I definitely did not want to chance a cold, so I pulled the sweatshirt on, glad for its protection.

"I didn't know what to do, where to turn, how to survive. Mom died of breast cancer. She'd found a lump before I went to college and didn't say anything to me . . . or to a doctor. Just let it go until it killed her. I don't know if she was in denial and thought it would go away if she ignored it long enough, or whether she was simply too tired to fight her own loneliness anymore. Somehow I think it was the loneliness." Lindsay looked at me. "And there are some days when I think of doing the same thing and joining her. Of giving up."

"Is that when you met Elizabeth?"

She shook her head. "No, we didn't meet until fairly recently, actually. Not until after I had been beaten to within an inch of my life. And even then, I don't think I would have done anything if Tom hadn't slapped my son for the first time. That was when I snapped."

"What happened?" I asked softly.

A tall willow tree stood several feet from the water's edge, the leaves rippling in the breeze. Long droopy branches calmly rearranged themselves, the perfect picture of a Southern lady shaking out her hoop skirt. Lindsay pushed aside a clump of branches and sat down with her back against the trunk, her knees pulled up to her chest. I sat down next to her and waited.

"He wasn't always like this." She lifted her shoulders and smiled a very small smile, one that never quite reached her eyes. "I'm sure I sound like a typical victim, someone who can't admit the truth."

I reached out and touched the hand clenched in a death grip on her knee. "Lindsay. I'm here to listen to your story, no one else's."

"I met Tom at the store where I was bagging groceries. It was the first job I got when I quit school. Anyway, he used to come in while I was working, doing things like putting out the produce or stocking shelves or sometimes bringing in the carts from outside. It seemed like we had this eerie connection from the first time we met. I'd be busy in the store, and then suddenly I'd get this strange feeling and I'd look up and he'd be standing there. He didn't say much, just looked at me and smiled, said hello, and walked away. And it happened all the time." She gazed past me unseeingly. "I thought it was so romantic at the time. He'd stare at me with those clear blues eyes and I imagined he could see straight into my soul. And with Mom so recently gone, I desperately needed someone to care." She shuddered. "We went on like that for a few weeks and it was perfect. It felt like I was being courted. After a while, everyone in the store noticed and started teasing me, nothing bad, just kidding around about the guy who was sweet on me. It all seemed so old-fashioned and proper. And finally, he asked me out to dinner. By this time I was practically in love with a man I'd hardly spoken to."

It was hard to reconcile this picture she drew with that of Vacuum Nose, the fat bully who beat up on women and children. Maybe he had a twin, a sweetheart of a guy who dated Lindsay, fell in love with her, and then was killed by his evil twin brother who took his place on his wedding day. As farfetched as my scenario sounded, its believability quotient was a lot higher than that of this blue-eyed lothario she was describing now. But loneliness is a lousy companion, as I well knew, and sometimes anything seems better than another night wrapped in its arms.

"He brought me flowers that first night and took me to dinner at this quaint little Italian restaurant. It was up on the top of a hill, tucked back underneath the trees, overlooking the city. I thought he was so very gallant, ordering for me, tasting and approving the wine. And he was so solicitous, asking me about my life, making sure my meal was exactly what I wanted and that I wasn't too cold." She shrugged her shoulders. "What can I say? I fell head over heels within an hour. At the time my only regret was that my mother had died before she met him." Lindsay turned to me. "Five years later that's the only thing I *don't* regret."

"What happened?"

"Nothing that hasn't happened to thousands of other women. And I can't really blame him completely; it's not like he didn't warn me. If I'd been half-awake, I would have recognized all those romantic gestures for what they were . . . sheer control. Why didn't I wonder about how often he coincidentally ran into me at the store? It wasn't until I was married and trapped in Hell that it dawned on me that the man had been stalking me from the beginning. Anyway, things went downhill the night of our wedding. I won't bore you with the details, but sex was the first area in which he decided to establish his dominance and things only got worse. He punched me the night he was demoted in the Department. Claimed it was my fault that he couldn't keep his mind on his job because I put so much pressure on him to succeed. And the next time he hit me it was because he imagined I was flirting with a waiter. It got to where I didn't even listen to the reasons anymore; I just accepted my fate as his punching bag. Then he decided to get my attention by slapping Matthew. I knew it was just a matter of time before he hit the baby. So I went to see Elizabeth."

"Why Elizabeth?"

"I needed money."

Chapter Thirteen

As is so typical in Colorado, the sun parted the curtain of clouds and peeked through, chasing away the looming thunderclouds and thawing the chilly air. The breeze slowly stilled. At high altitudes, it doesn't take much sun to warm the earth, and before I knew it, my sweatshirt was sticking to my chest. Hot and impatient, I grabbed the damn thing by the hem and yanked it over my head. The thermometers in this state shoot up and down faster than bucking broncos.

A barrage of emotions threatened to overwhelm me as Lindsay told her story. I could well imagine her childhood; it was similar enough to my own that sometimes I wanted to pull back from hearing her recount the details. My mother's death had occurred earlier in my life than hers, but being alone was lousy at any age, and alone I was. Her father existed in name only, and although my father was there until I left home for college, he was merely a sad, shadowy presence after my mother died. I know people manage to continue living after a spouse dies, but this didn't happen for my father, not until he remarried long after I was gone. He never looked upon me as a reason to live; I was something to step over or skirt around like an inconvenient mud puddle. My father never said anything, but I imagine my childhood seemed equivalent to a page of long division to him, an unpleasant task to get through. It wasn't too long before I quit expecting him to care for me with any warmth, and once I gave up the dream of an ideal father, life stayed on an even keel and I muddled through just fine.

Of course, I never expected to run into Elizabeth, who, by her very vibrant, nosy nature, turned everything upside down. Even in her death, she seemed determined to play havoc with people's lives. I swear she was looking down from heaven and enjoying every minute of my discomfort.

"Money?" I asked.

Lindsay nodded.

"But why would Elizabeth give you money? You said you didn't even know her."

"I didn't, but my mother knew her husband."

"I don't understand. Was she an employee of his?"

She shook her head. "There's only one way a poor uneducated woman can know a tremendously wealthy man well enough to discreetly pull money out of his pocket. My mother was his lover."

Lindsay could have taken a sledgehammer and slammed it over my head and I still would not have been more surprised than I was at that moment. Except when, two seconds later, understanding dawned.

"You're Cranford Boyer's daughter?"

"Yep. Genuine royalty in a faded dress and ripped tennis shoes."

My mouth gaped open; my chin hit my chest.

"How? I . . . I don't understand," I stuttered. "I mean, how did this happen?"

A smile twitched at the corner of Lindsay's mouth. "Oh, I think in the usual way. Boy meets girl . . . you know the story. Then baby comes along."

I ran my hands over my face. "That's not what I meant, I know how *that* part happened, it's probably the only part of this story I understand. I mean, how did they know each other? Did Elizabeth know about the affair? And why aren't you living up at the house along with Cassie and Will instead of with . . . with . . ." My voice dropped down to a whisper because I didn't know what to call that abusive thug she was living with.

"My husband?" she said softly. "Actually, there are a lot of reasons, and most of them don't make sense unless you've experienced a relationship like this yourself. And even then, it doesn't really make sense, intellectually anyway. You find yourself making a hundred excuses or a hundred different plans about how you're finally going to pack up the kids and leave. But then he comes in and looks at you like he knows exactly what you're thinking of doing, and he either pounds the will out of you, or worse, treats you like a queen for a few hours, apologizing for every bruise and broken rib he's ever left on your body." She lifted her shoulders at the look of disbelief on my face. "I know it's hard to believe, but by that time you're so beaten down that you cling to every soft word you hear. Next thing you know, you're pregnant again or he's beating the crap out of you, and either way, fear sets in and it feels like you're

drowning in quicksand—the more you kick, the more
the bottom sucks you down."

I could feel Lindsay backing off into some remote
corner of her mind that I'm sure she fled to every time
her husband's fists were raining blows on her. But it was
hard to wear a sympathetic face when visions of kicking
her husband right in the crotch kept intruding. Of course,
diplomacy was never my strong suit.

"Several months after my mother died," she began
again, "I finally felt strong enough to go through her
things and start making decisions. When I went through
her desk, I made a list of people and companies I needed
to call about her death and a list of outstanding bills. It
was easier than I expected because Mom was so methodical and organized. But in her bottom drawer, I
found a stack of envelopes tied together with string.
They were old love letters from a man named Cranford.
Mom never talked about any man or romantic interest,
so I was really surprised, especially when I realized that
the man was my father. I can't explain all the feelings
that came over me when I read the letters from a man
who barely existed in my life. At first it was rather com-
forting to know that some man had truly loved my
mother. But toward the end, the relationship had started
to come apart and I knew why Mom never mentioned
him."

"Why?"

"Pretty simple. She became pregnant with me, and he
wanted nothing more to do with her."

"He sounds pretty much like the scum Elizabeth used
to describe. Of course, her word choice was different,
but it meant the same thing. What did your mother do

then? She could have sued for paternity, at least for financial help. The guy was loaded."

"Mom wasn't much of a fighter; she hated confrontation. But apparently they worked out a deal. He provided a nice monthly sum of money and she kept quiet about their affair."

And then it dawned on me. "You were blackmailing Elizabeth?"

"No," she answered sharply. "Cranford Boyer kept his side of the deal. We were taken care of financially. Mom never even worked more than a part-time job."

"Then what?" I asked, completely baffled.

Lindsay looked down and started fiddling nervously with a stray thread on the seam of her dress. "I asked Elizabeth to look at my artwork. I was hoping that if she knew who I was, she might be willing to help me sell it." She took a deep breath and continued in an emotionless monotone as though she was reading from a script. "My husband was having a bad time a few weeks back and he went after me. But I felt so numb, so tired of the whole thing that I just went limp and let him do what he wanted. This infuriated him, of course, so he grabbed Matthew, knowing that I couldn't ignore him then. He slapped Matthew so hard . . . I can still see the red handprint on his little face. I ran between the two of them and screamed at him to stop. Tom grabbed my hair and . . . you don't need to hear the rest. When he left for work the next day, I went to see Elizabeth."

"What did she say?"

"That she wasn't surprised. She'd known about her husband's philandering for years. She even said I had his eyes and his mouth." Lindsay turned to me. "She looked at my bruises, listened to what I had to say, and

filled in the blanks when I was too ashamed to say the
words myself. Elizabeth made a deal with me right then
and there. She offered to come to the house and look at
my paintings, and if she liked what she saw, she would
introduce me to people, people who could help me. But
I had to agree to go for counseling at the Center for
Domestic Violence. I knew then that I could have finger-
painted all my pictures and it wouldn't have mattered.
She still would have helped me. But her offer to seriously look at my pictures kept me from feeling like a
charity case."

I couldn't get any words past the emotions logjam-
med in my throat.

"So she came to my house when Tom was at work."
Lindsay chuckled at the memory. "I knew that her main
purpose was to help get me out of the house, so I wasn't
expecting an in-depth critique of my work. But she
walked in and studied each picture like it was hanging
in a museum. She kept telling me I had talent while
ripping everything apart at the same time."

"Yeah, Elizabeth had a real knack for that," I muttered.

"But she knew what she was talking about. Even as
an inexperienced painter, I knew that what she was saying was right. It made sense, and for the first time in
years I was excited about something. She mentioned a
teacher she could set me up with. We talked for a long
time, about all sorts of things, and I got so caught up in
our conversation I didn't hear the door open." Lindsay
hugged her legs even closer to her chest and started
rocking back and forth on her heels. "Tom walked in."

"Did he touch Elizabeth?"

"Oh, no. He was terribly polite. He introduced himself and even offered her something to drink. Of course, she handled herself perfectly, never letting on that she knew anything about his abuse. She chatted with him for a few minutes about silly stuff and then left, telling me to give her a call about the art classes we talked about." Lindsay stretched her legs out in front of her and rubbed her palms down the length of her legs, wiping the moisture from her clammy hands. "But things changed the minute she left. Tom had a fit when she walked out the door, demanding to know who she was and why she was there. I said it was for the art classes, but he didn't believe me. He kept questioning me and I couldn't seem to keep things straight in my head and it wasn't long before I didn't know where the lies started and where they ended. And then he twisted my arm behind my back . . . so high . . . I couldn't stand it." She covered her face with her hands and started crying. "I caved in and told him everything."

"Lindsay, you can't blame yourself for that. Anyone would have done exactly the same thing."

"You don't understand," she cried, her words muffled behind her hands. "I knew what would happen. I knew what he was capable of."

Alarm pricked the back of my neck. "What are you talking about?"

Lindsey lifted her head. "He went to see Elizabeth the next day. He was going to blackmail her, tell the world about her husband's illegitimate daughter if she didn't pay him to stay quiet."

"Elizabeth would never fall for that, especially knowing the kind of man your husband was . . . or is."

She swallowed a sob and gazed at me with wet trails

running crookedly down her face. "A week later Eliza-beth was dead."

I was pretty shook up by her story and Lindsay wasn't faring any better. The whole sordid mess sounded surreal. It had all the makings of a good trashy miniseries: money, greed, blackmail, a murder, and an abusive husband. But this was real life and I didn't know what to do with the story she'd just dumped in my lap, even if I had come looking for it. Given a choice, I would turn the clock back a few hours when Cassie was drinking my coffee with that snooty little look on her face and the only thing I had to worry about was getting to my meeting with Prestwood on time. Life was a lot simpler then.

I was clearly in over my head, and as much as it pained me to admit, I knew I had to tell Villari. He never really appreciated my detective skills, but at this point I was more than willing to hand all the information over to him—lock, stock, and barrel. I could already see his eyes narrow and his lips tighten in anger. He was going to yell and stomp his feet and tell me what I fool I'd been to place myself in possible jeopardy by seeing Lindsay, but if I was lucky, maybe he'd kiss me after he'd blown off some steam. The guy was an amazing kisser, and even if he did want to postpone the bedroom scene until after the investigation was over, it didn't mean I couldn't try to convince him otherwise. And if I couldn't change his mind, well, I'd just settle for getting him all hot and bothered and then making a dramatic exit. If he was left in an uncomfortable "blue" state, it might make up for the embarrassment he had caused me last night. Revenge could be sweet, no matter what they say.

Lindsay glanced at her watch and jumped up next to me. "I've got to go. I've already been out too long," she stammered, her voice edged in panic.

"Is Tom due home soon?" I asked, instantly recognizing the hysteria in her voice.

She nodded. "I dropped the kids off at my neighbor's house. If I hurry, I'll have enough time to pick them up and start dinner before he gets home."

I put my hand out to stop her. I couldn't let her leave without saying something. "Lindsay, I know Elizabeth would want you to carry out your part in the deal you made with her. I can't show you the art world like she could, but she left me a list of names that might help you . . . and me, for that matter. And I'm sure Elizabeth would want you to take your children and move to a safe house, even if she wasn't here to help. She's not. But I am."

She stared at me, wide-eyed, like I'd punched her in the stomach and knocked the wind out of her. "I couldn't possibly ask you to help me. That's why I called you and warned you to stay away."

"You what? *You* called me?"

"I had to. I knew you'd keep coming back otherwise."

"You're the one who called and threatened me?"

"What choice did I have? You were determined to get information. If Tom knew you were coming around asking questions, there's no telling what he would do." After taking a few steps, she swiveled around and faced me. "I couldn't let you end up the same way Elizabeth did." Before her words had a chance to sink in, she turned away and started walking rapidly around the lake.

I was so startled by her confession that I stood looking out on the water, my mind a blank slate, a common occurrence these days. It felt like the blood had drained from my brain and pooled in my feet, leaving them heavy and too clunky to move.

"You really think Tom had something to do with Elizabeth's murder?" I yelled, sprinting halfway around the lake before catching up to her. "Why didn't you go to the police if you were suspicious?" I managed to ask between some heavy pants. I really had to start some type of workout program. One short jog and my side was cramping, not to mention the oxygen deprivation I was experiencing.

Lindsay stopped and glared at me. "What do you think? Tom finds out I'm Cranford Boyer's daughter, goes to visit her, and the next thing I know she's dead? Surely you don't think it was accidental that Elizabeth ended up murdered right after she visited me."

"Look, Lindsay," I panted, "as much as it pains me to say this, your husband may not have had anything to do with her death. If you took this to trial, a defense attorney would blow your case right out of the water. The whole thing is based on circumstantial evidence."

"You're defending the man?" she asked incredulously.

I shook my head vehemently. "No, of course not." I stooped over and propped my hands on my knees, willing my breathing to become steady and even. I had to admit, an aerobics class was looking more and more appealing . . . and necessary. "Believe me. From what you've said, I think your husband is as endearing as tooth decay. I thought so the first time I met him and I would like to avoid ever running into him again—"

"What do you mean 'again'?" she asked, interrupting me.

"I mean, I've already met the man. He was the cop who interrogated me the day Elizabeth was discovered in my septic tank."

"How did you know it was Tom? How did you connect him to me?"

This was no time to bring up my aborted stakeout. Lindsay would never trust me again if I admitted to spying on her. "I recognized him as I drove away the first time I came to your house."

"But he didn't come home after you left that day."

I shrugged my shoulders. "Maybe he just drove by to check on you and went back to the station." She looked doubtful, but clearly, checking up on his wife without her knowledge wasn't too far out of character for old Tom. Lindsay started toward the cars again. I tried to keep up with her long-legged strides.

"I remember looking at his name tag," I added. "Why do you go by 'Burns' instead of 'Mailer'?"

"Because my mother's name was Burns. I didn't want to change it when we got married . . . for sentimental reasons. And Tom didn't really complain." She brushed her hair back. "In the beginning, he could be sweet when he wanted to."

I found that hard to believe. "But why didn't you go to the police with your suspicions?"

"My husband's a cop, remember? Those guys are thick as thieves down there. It's like a fraternity. If one of them is guilty, they protect each other, no matter what. If I said anything, I'd be laughed out of the station house and Tom would be furious with me. The way he treated me this last time . . . I'm sure he would have killed me."

"Lindsay," I said, still trying to keep pace with her,

"no matter what really happened to Elizabeth, whether your husband had a hand in it or not, you have to get away from him. I know that Elizabeth would be adamant about that. She belonged to a lot of organizations, but the only one that she was really passionate about was CDV." I grabbed Lindsay's hand and forced her to stop. "I knew Elizabeth for several years. I can say this with all honesty. Cranford Boyer was a very abusive man." I shook my head at her unspoken question. "No, he never hit her. But he was verbally abusive and emotionally distant. Elizabeth was alone during their entire marriage. The only time they were together was for public functions that were held in order to benefit his company. So when he died, Elizabeth finally felt free." I took both of her arms and turned her toward me. "I know that Elizabeth would feel like her death was not in vain, even vindicated, if she knew that you and your children were safe."

"How can I do that? Tom would track me down like an animal. Don't forget, he's a cop. And now, with Elizabeth's death, he'll be even more determined to find us. And when he does . . ." she added in a whisper, "I just can't take that chance. Not with two kids."

Her argument made sense. "Look, don't do anything right now, but I have a friend who can help you." I hurried on despite the skepticism clouding her face. "He's a detective on the case and I'll talk to him. He'll know what to do and how to keep you and your children safe." There was no reason to mention that Villari was already checking out her husband, albeit discreetly. It would only frighten her, and the woman was frightened enough.

"Maggie, I don't know who your friend is, but Tom

is dangerous. Please be careful. It's hard enough for me to live with the knowledge that I might have caused Elizabeth's death by telling Tom everything. I can't live with another murder on my conscience." She held my shoulders and shook me. "Listen to me. Don't come to my house again. Don't call me. Stay away. Elizabeth loved you, and the only way I can repay her kindness is to keep you safe. Go home and forget about me."

"I can't do that, Lindsay. Elizabeth won't stand for it."

She tilted her head quizzically.

"I dream of her all the time," I responded. "It's like she's looking over my shoulder. You have no idea of the lectures I'd have to endure if I let you slip away."

Lindsay loosened her grip and smiled.

"So get used to it," I added. "I'm not going away. I'll be careful, but I'm not going away."

"Elizabeth was right," she said softly, "you *are* easy to love."

Chapter Fourteen

Lindsay drove off like a woman possessed, and considering the threat of her husband's fists, she wasn't too far off the mark. Dust flew up behind her tires as she squealed out of the parking lot. I was still coughing and trying to insert my key into the car door when a black sedan pulled up next to me. I whirled around, frightened at first, sure that Vacuum Nose had gotten wind of our conversation and was here to land a few punches before heading home and finishing up with Lindsay. Then it dawned on me that cops don't drive BMWs and my heart sank when I recognized the little weasel, Will Boyer, behind the wheel.

"What the hell are you doing here?" I demanded as he jumped out and strode purposefully around the hood of the car to stand in front of me.

"That's exactly what I'd like to know, Maggie. What are *you* doing out here in the boondocks with some lady who looks like she pushes all her belongings in a shopping cart?"

Enraged by his callousness, I stuck my hands on my hips. "Look, you little rodent. I've never answered to you and I'm not about to begin now. Since when did you decide to take on the role of bodyguard and start following me?"

"Interesting choice of words, Maggie," he mused. "Now, why would you need a bodyguard?"

Apparently, the prospect of Vacuum Nose rearranging my nose with his fists had spooked me more than I'd realized. "That's just the point. I don't." Even in the sun his face had a chalky, sallow cast. When authors wrote, "All the blood drained from his face," they could have been describing Will. A vampire had more color.

Will leaned his khaki-clad butt against the car, crossed his feet at the ankles, and stared, clearly not believing a word I said. "You're such a smart-ass," he declared insolently.

"Gee, Will, is that the best you could come up with? I thought snappy repartee was your forte."

He glared. Any minute now I expected him to stick out his tongue like a pouting two-year-old.

"I didn't come here to spar with you."

"That's just the point, Will. Why are you here? I live right next door to you, remember? We're neighbors. This is a long way to drive just to swap insults."

"I'm following you."

"That much is obvious. The question is why? What possible reason would you have for trailing me out to Peyton?"

"Because I'm suspicious."

"Of what?"

"Suspicious of how you wiggled your way into Grandmother's will. Suspicious of where her body was found. And I'm suspicious of the sudden relationship you have with Detective Villari."

"What are you talking about?" I asked coolly.

"Let's not play coy." He sneered contemptuously. "I've seen his car in your driveway several times—"

"Well, that's quite an indictment of guilt. The man's investigating the scene of a crime. Would you rather he park down the street?"

"And when I drove by last night," he continued, ignoring my outburst, "I saw the two of you fogging up the windshield like a couple of teenagers on prom night."

Blood suffused my face. So much for remaining cool under fire. I was already embarrassed about Villari's rejection and the last thing I needed was a discussion about my personal life with this little twerp. "Jealous?" I taunted, throwing the ball back in his court. One thing I'd learned over the years: when your defense is crumbling and your back is up against the wall, shore up your offense and attack. Attack in full force.

"In your dreams, Maggie."

"You're never in my dreams, Will. I like to sleep peacefully at night."

"Look, you little—"

"Don't call me names and don't threaten me, Will. The detective and I are good friends, remember? He might not take too kindly to your nasty behavior. Say what you have to say and then get lost. And don't follow me again. If you do, I'll sic him on you."

"You've got a big mouth, Maggie, and nothing to back it up."

I scratched my head. "Well now, that's not exactly true, is it, Will?" I drawled in my best "down on the bayou" Southern accent. "Right now there's that little question of Grandma's pile of money, and I do believe I have a wee bit of a say over what happens to that stack of bills." I paused. "And I've got to admit, I don't really cotton to sneaky, low-down little vermin like yourself."

"Believe it or not," he said tersely, "I didn't come here to battle with you."

"So far you haven't explained why you did come. Why don't you clear up that little question?" I scowled. "Was it Cassie? Did she come crying because I turned down your terribly generous offer?"

His voice hardened. "You should have taken the offer, Maggie, although that's not the reason I'm here. Like I said, I was suspicious. But there's more."

"Well?" I drummed my fingers on the hood.

"Dr. Cole called the house today."

"Who is Dr. Cole?"

Will frowned at my interruption. "He's an oncologist."

"I don't understand."

"Grandmother had cancer, Maggie. Terminal cancer."

I knew even before I arrived home that I'd find Villari pacing up and down the driveway. The man had an uncanny knack for knowing when I was off sticking my nose someplace he didn't think it belonged. And although I would never admit it aloud, not unless someone was prying my fingernails off with a pair of rusty pliers, I was very glad to see the guy. Will's sudden revelation about Elizabeth's cancer had thrown me for a loop, and as old-fashioned as it sounded, I desperately needed a steady man and a strong shoulder to lean on.

A million thoughts collided and crashed in my head like carnival bumper cars. I didn't have the slightest clue how to slow them down or stop them completely. How could I have been so clueless? A woman walks around riddled with inoperable cancer and I don't notice a thing? Either Elizabeth was an unbelievable actress or I was a shoo-in for the "Most Self-Absorbed Neighbor" award.

"Don't say a word, Villari," I snarled the moment he yanked open the car door. "I'm not in the mood for any of your threats or macho crap. It's been a lousy day and listening to you growl is the last thing I need right now." He took one look at my face and dropped the anger like a hot potato. He lifted one of my hands off the steering wheel and threaded his fingers through mine, tugging me gently out of the car. Villari shut the door behind me and then stood and blocked my way as I headed toward the house. Holding both my hands captive, he leaned my body against the car.

"What happened?" he asked, his warm breath fanning my forehead.

Suddenly I saw Elizabeth in my mind . . . the bright scarf, the impeccable Chanel suit . . . my chest tightened and my throat closed, choking me so I couldn't speak. I shook my head.

"Talk to me, Maggie. Are you hurt?"

Yes, I was hurt. Deeply hurt. The knife slashed through my insides until I was one bloody mess of guilt and regret and sorrow.

"Maggie, say something . . . anything," he said, tilting my chin up with one hand. "If you don't start talking,

I'm taking you to the doctor right now, even if I have to drag you there. Do you understand what I'm saying?"

I lifted my eyes and gazed at his face, a warm, rugged face that stared back at me with worry etched in his eyes. My heart slowed down a beat and my throat eased. This man touched me someplace deep inside, a place I didn't even know existed.

"Elizabeth was dying of cancer, Villari. She had less than six months to live . . . if she hadn't been murdered first. I didn't even know she was sick. How could that be?"

He brushed my hair off my face. "How did you find out?"

I looked up at him. "You knew?" I asked incredulously. "And you didn't say anything?"

"It's part of the investigation, Maggie. We've tried to recreate Elizabeth's last few days as closely as possible in order to find a clue, some piece of evidence that could lead us to the killer." His face grew more serious. "I didn't see how that information would help you."

I put my hands flat on his chest and pushed him back. "She was my neighbor, my dearest friend, and you didn't think I should know that she was dying?" I demanded, my temper flaring. Without waiting for an answer, I stomped off toward the porch.

"Why would you want to know, Maggie?" he called to my retreating back. "So you could beat yourself up with guilt?"

I stopped and spun around. "I could have been there for her. I should have been."

Villari took three long steps toward me, grabbed my arms, and hauled me against his chest.

"You *were* with her, you idiot, just the way she

wanted you to be." He wrapped his arms around my back, holding me together as though I'd explode into a million fireworks, holding me so tight I wasn't sure I could breathe. "Elizabeth didn't want you to know, can't you see that? From what you've told me, she was one proud lady. That's the way she lived her life and that's the way she wanted to die."

He was right. Elizabeth would have hated being waited on, or worse, being pitied and treated like an invalid. Once her prognosis was definite, she would have wanted to live the last few months of her life in full gear and, as she grew weaker, to die in a quiet retreat by herself. I relaxed in his arms and laid my head against his chest, breathing in the smell of sheer masculinity, of fresh scentless soap, of clean sweat that only a man can wear. If I'd been brought up with horses, I would have said he smelled of the outdoors, of leather, of hay, of long hard days and cool sweet nights. But being a city girl, I was stuck with less poetic words, like freshly cut grass from a sit-down mower and white-hot beaches occupied by crowds slathered in sunblock. Still, no matter what words I used, his fragrance defined pure male.

His heart pulsed in strong, rhythmic beats, so calm and steady I couldn't resist snuggling closer, nuzzling my face into his shirt, the sound soothing me like a lullaby. I burrowed closer and let myself enjoy the safe haven of his arms, knowing the respite he offered was brief. Sooner or later he would break the spell with his insistent questions and the peace I was enjoying right now would come to an end.

"Maggie, I know it doesn't help," he said, his tone soft and gentle, "but I didn't know, of course, until just recently."

Tears flowed in thin rivulets down my cheeks. "I know," I said, my words smothered against his chest. "You were right. Elizabeth wanted it that way, and Elizabeth always managed to get her way." I tilted my head back and smiled at him. "Thanks for putting up with me. I have a tendency to cover my emotions with anger."

His mouth twitched. "Really? I hadn't noticed."

With one hand splayed against his chest, I shoved him back again. "Why do people always feel the need to gloat when someone apologizes," I said, grinning and swiping my tears away.

Villari frowned. "That was an apology? All I heard was a thanks for putting up with your very limited repertoire of responses." Scratching his head and gazing up into the clouds, he added, "Let me see if I can list them. Would they be—in alphabetical order no less—anger, anger, and maybe anger?"

"Everyone's a comedian," I groaned.

He chuckled. "Yeah, it's one of my better qualities," he said, coming forward and putting my hand in his. "Come on, Maggie. Let's go inside. I'm starving and I know nothing would tickle your fancy more than feeding a hungry man."

Amusement gleamed in his eyes and I found myself laughing as he dragged me through the front door and stopped in the middle of the kitchen.

"I'll just make myself comfortable at the table."

I propped my hands on my hips. "You're kidding, right?"

"Nope." He released my hand and slapped me lightly on my butt before walking into the breakfast nook and dropping down into the nearest chair. I didn't even want to think about the heat his hand left on my bottom. This was the new millennium. I was supposed to be outraged.

"I don't cook, Villari. Not unless you consider peanut butter and jelly a meal."

"Throw some chips on the side and I'll crown you the next Julia Child."

Ten minutes later we were munching on dry sandwiches and washing them down with tall glasses of instant iced tea . . . another knack of mine. I had popped my last bite in my mouth when Villari started in on me.

"So where were you off to today? Let me guess. Sightseeing? Shopping for your summer wardrobe?"

"You're a funny guy, Villari," I said, feeling like Mr. Ed as I chewed around the bite that had quickly deteriorated into soggy bread and thick paste. I grabbed my glass and poured the tea down my throat.

"Yeah, I'm a laugh a minute." He dropped the last of his sandwich on his plate and leaned forward, staring me down. "Let's do ourselves a favor this time, okay? Answer the question directly instead of following the circuitous route you're so familiar with. It will save a lot of time and effort and we can then enjoy each other's company for more than a few minutes this time."

I bristled at the arrogant tone, but I felt like an emotional sieve, everything draining out of me in one large shake. The morning had been exhausting, and I realized that I simply didn't have the energy for a fight. But pride was a funny thing. Even though I was willing to capitulate and answer his questions, I didn't feel the need to volunteer information. I'd always played my cards close to my chest, and this was no exception. Besides, why should I make it easy for the guy?

"What do you want to know?"

He ignored my sullen tone. "Just the simple things. I

don't have the manpower to put a tail on you, Maggie, otherwise I would have the day Elizabeth died, and definitely after the threatening phone call, but—"

"Don't worry about the call."

As I expected, his eyes narrowed and his lips thinned into two hard lines. "What do you know about the phone call?"

I couldn't help but puff my chest out a little, not that there was much to puff. "I did a little old-fashioned detective work and discovered the name of the caller."

"Stop jerking me around, Maggie, and tell me what you know before I reach across the table and do something we'll both regret."

"You do know how to romance a girl, Villari," I cooed.

"You haven't heard anything yet," he replied sharply.

"There goes our few minutes of getting along."

I held my hands up over my head in surrender and told him the story. I started with Prestwood's phone call in the morning, Cassie's visit, and my trip to see Lindsay Burns. The bulk of my time was spent retelling as closely as possible my conversation with Lindsay. Then I quickly wrapped up the whole story describing my brief encounter with Willy Weasel.

"By the time I got home, Villari, I was actually glad to see you."

"Glad I could be of service," he murmured distractedly. He was staring off into space, oblivious to my last statement. I guess I expected some type of "attaboy," some sign of approval like a hearty slap on the back for all my good work, so I was a little disappointed by his lack of response. But the man never responded the way I expected. I knew the wheels were churning in his head and I had the sneaking suspicion that he wouldn't be nearly as forthcoming with information as I had been.

"What did you find out about her husband?"

It was like he didn't hear me. "Why do you think Will told you about the cancer, Maggie?" he asked pensively.

"To hurt me."

"Probably. But it doesn't really make sense. Elizabeth is already dead. Unless," he mused, "he wasn't just telling you, but warning you."

"Warning me of what?"

"Don't know for sure, but given his mercenary character, I'd guess it's a ploy to get Elizabeth's money." Villari spoke in low tones, as though he were talking and working it out for himself. "Will and Cassie will probably try to contest the will under the grounds that Elizabeth was dying. They'll want to prove that the stress of her disease put her in a very vulnerable, shaky state of mind and that you took advantage of her vulnerability to get yourself put in the will."

"Elizabeth was about as vulnerable as a pit bull. Besides, Prestwood would never go for it."

"They may not use Prestwood. Just because Elizabeth was loyal to him doesn't mean those two will follow suit."

"God, this just never ends."

Villari reached over and squeezed my hand encouragingly. "Don't get discouraged, Maggie. It's only a guess on my part, and if that's their plan, Prestwood will take care of the legalities for you. Besides, a lawsuit would only serve to tie the will up in court for a long time, and cost them money they don't have, which means they're stuck right where they are . . . for a while, at least. If we're lucky, we may be around long enough to see Cassie get off her cute little butt and get a real job."

"You noticed her butt?"

A slow grin spread across his face. "Hey, the girl may be a spoiled little princess, but she takes care of herself."

"I'm thrilled to hear that."

"Envious?"

"Not on your life."

Villari pulled on my arm. A second later he had me in his lap, one hand on my hip, the other curved around my neck. "You know, Maggie, if you wore a pair of pants that were even remotely your size, instead of something big enough to line my garbage can, I might be able to tell whether *your* butt is cute or not."

"Did I say I cared?" I asked pointedly.

He laughed, then drew my head down until my face was inches from his. "Honey, you'll care soon enough when we end up wrestling in bed . . ." he whispered before covering my protest with his mouth. "Naked," he added.

This time there was no skimming or nibbling or nuzzling. This kiss was a straight shot of heat. His lips were hot and demanding. I held myself stiffly and tried to hold myself back. I did not want to repeat last night's embarrassment. The last thing I needed was to get all hot and bothered only to have him pull back and play Mr. Chastity. But if he could feel my resistance, he didn't say anything. He just kept on kissing me, relentlessly and tenaciously, until my body jumped ship and melted for him. Leaning into him, I felt a suspicious bulge under my thigh and I thought—quite smugly, actually—that my baggy shorts must have something going for them after all.

We broke apart at the same time and smiled at each other.

"Well."

"Yes, well."

"What happened to the 'integrity of the investigation'?" I teased.

"Who came up with that line of bull?"

I hit him in the chest. "You did and you know it. Last night, as a matter of fact."

He held both my wrists together with one hand, slipped his free one underneath my T-shirt, and traced the top of my shorts. "Did I ever tell you my idea of a fantasy woman?"

"No," I replied, enjoying the tantalizing feeling of his fingers brushing my skin as he continued his slow exploration around my waistband.

"I've always liked tall, statuesque blondes. You know, five-foot-ten, one hundred and thirty pounds, with large breasts and honey-blond hair that looks like spun gold."

"Then what are you doing toying with *my* pants?"

"Hell if I know. All these years I've been on the prowl for a long-legged, buxom blonde, and here I am groping a skinny girl with a mop of curly hair and a mind of her own. Go figure."

"Before I break one of your ribs, you'd better tell me whether that was a compliment or an insult."

"Neither. Just a statement of fact. The fact is, you're adorable and I'm completely smitten with you. I've never met a woman who exasperated me the way you do and neither have I met a woman that made me want to toss her on the bed and make love until morning comes and then start all over again." Villari took one look at my face and chuckled. "I'll be damned. I never thought I'd see the day when Maggie Kean was speechless." Then he kissed me again, so completely and thoroughly that I thought seriously of taking out an insurance policy on those lips of his. They were priceless.

"Well, Maggie, it's your call. We can do the right thing and wait until the investigation is over, or"—he slid his hand up toward my bra—"we can move to your bedroom and play doctor."

It was a choice between a bowl of brussels sprouts and a bowl of ice cream. "I make a heck of a nurse," I purred, going for a kittenish sound that sounded like something was jammed in my throat. But it seemed to work. Before I knew it, Villari had scooped me up and was carrying me down the hallway toward the bedroom. I was swooning with the sheer romance of it all, despite the fact that he had to adjust the load in his arms a couple of times. Unlike the romance books that describe half-naked men carting their women off to bed without a hitch, lifting a hundred and some odd pounds in real life is more than a sack of potatoes. Except for bouncing my head against the doorjamb a couple of times, he managed to get me to the bedroom in one piece. I was pretty impressed.

"That was awfully manly of you, Detective," I said as he sort of dropped me on the bed.

"If you thought that was manly, you ain't seen nothing yet," Villari growled as he pulled off his shirt and tossed it on the floor.

I laughed, but as I watched him, I guess the reality

of what we were about to do started to sink in, because I could feel myself getting nervous. It had been a long while since my last sexual encounter, and those relationships were nothing to write home about. I had a gut feeling that Villari didn't do anything halfway, that sex with him would be lusty, which is the only time I've ever used that word, and out of control. I wasn't sure how well I would respond to all that virility and testosterone. Beneath my shorts was a pair of plain, white, sensible cotton panties, the kind that circled my waist, not my hips. And my bra was just as modest. I didn't see how I was going to titillate this man while sporting my no-nonsense lingerie. He was already complaining about my shorts and T-shirts; I didn't know how he'd react to my underwear.

"What's going on in that brain of yours?" he asked, sensing my hesitation.

"Not much, at the moment."

He stretched out on his side and rested his head in his hand. "Maggie, something is always going on in your head and usually shooting straight out your mouth. Why don't you let me in on the secret?"

I angled my head and gazed into his dark eyes, dark as tar. "I might be a little nervous."

"Nervous and excited or nervous and dreading?"

"Probably a little of both. Not only am I not the blond bombshell of your fantasies, but I'm also not the, well . . ."

"Not the what?"

"Let's just say I'm not the neighborhood Lolita."

He cocked one eyebrow. "Now that comes as a real surprise. Here I was expecting you to hang from the chandelier and do somersaults on the bed and you're telling me you're just a regular ol' gal."

If I hadn't seen the teasing sparkle in his eyes, I would have knocked him out cold.

"Maggie, if you're not ready for this, we can stop."

"It's not that I'm not ready," I stammered.

"Then what is it?"

I really couldn't say for sure. Last night I'd been ready to tackle the guy and take him right on the front lawn, and now, when everything was perfect—the bed was large, the air was cool, and he was grinning that lazy grin that sent molten heat right down to my belly—I was backing away. Surely I wasn't the kind of girl who would lead a guy down the path toward, uh, fulfillment, just to abandon him the moment he was reaching home.

"Maggie," he urged, "tell me what's going on."

I simply didn't have the words. I wanted to be with Villari, and I mean I wanted to be with him in the very carnal sense of the word. I wanted that piercing sweetness. I wanted to experience the intimacy that comes from tussling under the sheets with a man who was hard where I was soft, I wanted that rock-and-roll rhythm that catapults you up and over until you vibrate from the sheer freedom of it all.

But this guy scared me. He scared me a lot. He had walked into my life one day under the most horrible circumstances, irritated me at every turn, and threatened me. And I don't just mean with jail. He threatened to get close to me, to break down the barriers I had carefully built around me, brick by brick. No one had broken through those walls except Elizabeth, who had slyly maneuvered herself into my life without permission and almost without my knowledge. Now she was gone. I wasn't sure I had the strength to let someone strip down my defenses again so soon, especially someone like Villari.

I had questions about him that I couldn't really articulate. The man was hardly subtle—when he went after something or someone he bulldozed everything in his path until he got what he wanted. And now that he was going after me, I felt cornered and more than a little frightened. My independence was hard-earned and a long time coming and I wasn't sure I was ready to shuck it out the window for someone who could stomp it flat without thinking twice.

Of course, all this introspection was giving me a headache. Chances are I was just riddled with insecurities about the typical womanly things. My body. It was nothing to crow about. I could pass for Olive Oyl's out-of-shape twin sister. I had stick legs and my stomach was soft like overcooked spaghetti, soft and mushy. I was the anti-muscle poster child. When the clothes came off, every rib, knob, and bony elbow would be on full display thanks to the unforgiving afternoon light. To make matters worse, lying there on top of the comforter, seconds away from testing the Big Bang theory, I watched in horror as goose bumps sprouted up and down my arms and legs. Nothing killed a mood quite like a rash of bumps.

"Cold, honey?" Villari asked.

I nodded. "Just a little."

He pulled off his socks and tossed them over his shoulder before turning back to me. He stroked and rubbed his hand over my body, trying to warm me, but just having him next to me was enough; my body heated up all on its own. He curved his arm around my waist and scooted closer, then rolled me over until I was lying underneath him.

"You okay?"

"Yeah, I'm fine. You?"

He threw me a lopsided grin. "I'm just fine. Can't you tell?"

I rolled my eyes while the heat rose up my neck.

Villari took one look at my flushed face and burst out laughing. "Take it easy, Maggie. I was just trying to get you to relax a little. Sex is supposed to be fun, remember?"

The point was, I didn't remember, but I wasn't going to tell him that. My insides were churning with all kinds of feelings—some that I understood, others that I couldn't begin to identify. I looked into Villari's eyes, into those midnight-black eyes, and sighed. A whole well of emotions sprang to the surface and started trickling down my face.

Villari brushed the hair from my forehead. "Finding out about Elizabeth's cancer shook you up a little more than you realized."

"I guess it did," I admitted, exhaling a deep breath.

"It's going to come and go, Maggie, a little at a time. You have to expect that," he said, taking the corner of the sheet and blotting my face. Propping himself on his elbows, he kissed the top of my nose and stared down at me.

"I may not be the most sensitive man on earth," he began, his eyes crinkling at the corners, "but something tells me this may not be the best time to pursue this particular area of our relationship."

Perfect. My one opportunity and I blow it because of some inexplicable crying jag. All I wanted was an energetic roll in the hay, an uncomplicated romp in the sack, and when it's staring me in the face, I turn into an overwrought, hand-wringing female. The next time we kissed, if that was even a possibility, maybe I could retain water and start my period.

Maybe I could rustle up some cramps, too.

Chapter Fifteen

"You never told me what you learned about Tom Mailer," I said. "Did you ask around?"

Villari sat on the edge of the bed, wearing nothing but a pair of jeans and one sock. With his rumpled hair hanging low over his forehead and large shoulders tapering down to his slim waist, he looked so delectable I was tempted to push him backward and beg for a second chance. I forced the idea out of my head, firmly squelching my more lascivious desires, and tried to focus on his answer, although the only response I was getting right now was the small crease between his brows.

"What's wrong? Wouldn't anybody talk to you?" I asked.

"Have you seen my other sock?"

I sighed. "Right there." I pointed to the stray sock crumpled on top of my dresser, which was clear across the room from the bed. "You've got quite an arm there."

"Among other things," he said, retrieving his sock.

I sighed. "You're cute, if extremely predictable."

Villari pulled his shirt on and tucked the tails into his pants. He glanced in the mirror and raked his hands through his hair before turning around to answer me.

"You want to know what I found out about Mailer, right?"

I nodded, a little irritated by how good he looked after an aborted roll in the hay. There was no longer any doubt in my mind that God was a man with a lousy sense of humor. How else do you explain the fact that Villari looked sexily disheveled while I looked unkempt, with a bad case of bed hair?

He reached for my hand and sat me down next to him on the bed. "I can't tell you much, Maggie, because of the confidentiality of the investigation. But even if I could, I still wouldn't, because you'd probably manage to use what I said to get yourself kidnapped or shot."

"I don't appreciate the sarcasm, Detective. I'm not an idiot."

Villari shook his head. "I never called you an idiot, but you are impetuous. Unfortunately, in my business, leading face first can get you killed."

"Just because I embarked on a little harmless amateur sleuthing doesn't make me a moron." I held up my hands when I saw the look of exasperation flit across his face. "You forced me to tell you every little detail of what happened this morning. I deserve something in return. And," I added pointedly, "before you bring it up, I don't consider jumping in the sack, or whatever you call what we did, to be that something."

"This isn't a quid pro quo situation, Maggie. As a citizen you are bound to give the police any information you have that might aid a murder investigation. As a police officer, I'm not bound to tell you a damned thing." He ran his hands over his face in frustration. "However, I'll say this much. All I've got is a handful of rumors that won't hold water."

"I still want to hear," I said determinedly.

"Yeah, I figured as much. But you have to keep the information to yourself, even if it is nothing but innuendos and conjecture. That stuff can be just as damaging to people's reputations, and the department itself, if it gets into the wrong hands."

"I'm not going to the newspapers, if that's what you're afraid of."

He took a deep breath. "There's some talk that Tom Mailer is a heavy cocaine user, but there's never been enough to pin anything on him or even enough suspicion to have him tailed. His record is clean—no write-ups, no medical referrals, and so on. But that doesn't mean he doesn't have a friend in Records who wiped his slate clean. The story going around is that Mailer, who is noted for making drug busts, has been slipping some of the evidence in his own pockets."

"Can't they arrest him for that?"

"They could if he was caught. But if you're the first man on the scene, it's not difficult to remove evidence that no one else has seen yet. Of course, I don't know if a word of this is true and I can't question the guy based on gossip."

"What about Lindsay's story? Doesn't that help?"

He shook his head in frustration. "It's pretty difficult to step into a domestic violence situation after the fact. Right now it would be her word against his, a he said she said sort of thing and those are notoriously difficult to prosecute. And I can't do a thing anyway, not unless she decides to press charges, and frankly, she doesn't sound like she's willing to go that far. All I can do at this point is notify a social worker or give her the names of shelters to go to."

"I'll give them to her," I volunteered.

"No, you won't," he said firmly. "From this point forward, you're out of the loop."

"She won't listen to you, Villari. She's already scared of her own shadow, not to mention her husband's. What are you going to do, show up at her doorstep and say, 'Maggie told me about your problems. Here are some places you can go'? She'll run in the other direction."

"And your suggestion?"

"Let me talk to her. She knows who I am and I think she trusts me."

"I thought she told you to stay away from her, to leave her alone?"

"She was trying to protect me. She's afraid of what her husband might do if he saw me with her."

"She has a good point, Maggie. Mailer will be instantly suspicious if he sees you within ten miles of his wife. He was at the crime scene, remember? It's not a difficult leap to connect Elizabeth's showing up at his house and then you showing up, too."

"Maybe you're right," I admitted reluctantly. "But there has to be a way to help Lindsay."

"Elizabeth told her about CDV, right? She can get help there, if she really wants it, Maggie."

I heard the skepticism in his voice. "She does, Villari, but since Elizabeth was killed, she's been too frightened to move, especially since she believes her own husband may be the murderer. She's got the safety of two children riding on the decisions she makes."

"Our hands are tied, Maggie. We can't force the lady to leave Mailer, and without her pressing charges, I can't move in and start investigating her husband."

Villari stood up and started pacing the floor. "The problem is that we have no proof, other than Lindsay's word, that Mailer even knew Elizabeth or ever even talked to her. Both Cassie and Will met him during the initial investigation and neither one said a word about knowing or seeing him before. I can check with the other house employees, show them Mailer's picture, but I have a hunch we'll end up with a big zero."

"Why are you so sure about that?"

"Because the guy is a cop, Maggie. If Lindsay's story is true and he was trying to blackmail Elizabeth, I can guarantee you that he would have been as discreet as possible. Extortionists do not like witnesses. Besides, I have some real questions about the whole theory of Mailer as a murderer."

"Why? The guy likes to slap people around. What's to keep him from killing someone?"

"It's a question of motive," Villari replied. "If he wanted to blackmail Elizabeth, what good would it do to kill her? How is he going to collect from a dead woman?"

"Maybe he never intended to kill her," I mused. "Let's say he went to Elizabeth and demanded a large sum of money under the threat of exposing her late husband's philandering and his illegitimate child. My guess is that Elizabeth refused to be blackmailed for several reasons, reasons which she then proceeded to list: First and foremost, she wouldn't be bullied by someone as despicable as Mailer, especially knowing the way he treated Lindsay. Second, she had resigned herself to Boyer's infidelities years ago. And third, she never much cared what people thought about her, and with only a few months to live, she probably cared even less. Her response probably shocked the hell out of him."

"According to your scenario, he tried to blackmail Elizabeth, she refused to pay him, so Mailer went berserk and hit her on the back of the head with a heavy object, threw her over his shoulder, and tossed her in your septic tank?"

"You don't need to get sarcastic, Villari. I'm just tossing out ideas here. According to Lindsay, Elizabeth died shortly after Mailer's visit."

"If there was one."

"There was," I insisted. "If you met Lindsay and talked to her, you'd know she was telling the truth. Anyway," I went on, "my guess is that Mailer is waiting for the investigation to slow down and be relegated to a back burner. When that happens, he'll drag Lindsay by the hair to meet Will and Cassie and introduce her as Cranford's daughter. Then he'll demand Lindsay's rightful inheritance, since he'll be working under the assumption that the money goes to bloodline descendants, and as his daughter, she would receive the money before his grandchildren."

He shook his head. "It's plausible, Maggie. You've got a devious little mind for an artist."

I stood up and executed a small curtsy. Then I sat back down on the bed and shook my head. "Some of it makes sense, but I just can't see Will and Cassie going meekly along with a blackmail scheme, especially one where they lose a large portion of their inheritance. If

Mailer showed up demanding money, the two of them would race to the police and insist on protection. Besides, even Will and Cassie, with their collective IQ of seventy-five, would be suspicious of the timing: Elizabeth is murdered and now a cop is extorting money? They would force the police to reopen the case and check Mailer out and he might not do too well under close scrutiny."

"Maybe," he conceded, "but my guess is that Mailer is looking for money and money only. He's not looking for Lindsay to claim the Boyer name or to become publicly aligned with Cassie and Will—abusers tend to want to keep their spouses in the shadows. But Cassie and Will, not knowing anything about Mailer or his background, will assume that the Boyer name is also important to him."

"But not as important as it is to those two," I noted.

"Exactly. If they go to the cops, Lindsay's name will surface, the truth of her story will come out, and their inheritance will be diluted. The Boyer name will be sullied, and I'm not sure either one of them could survive that catastrophe. So they'll offer some amount of money to keep it hushed. Mailer, wary of any publicity, will hem and haw and shuffle his feet before taking the money and running. And if by chance the cops do intervene, the man's smart enough to come up with an airtight alibi for the night of Elizabeth's death."

"But what about my job as fiduciary? Will and Cassie couldn't give him any money unless I agreed to it."

Villari grinned. "Yeah, that throws a real wrench into the whole plan. If Mailer did kill Elizabeth because she refused to be blackmailed, and he was afraid she'd go to the police and tell them about his extortion attempts,

I'm sure he was under the assumption that the will was a direct descendant type of thing. If he goes to Will and Cassie and tries to get money, everyone will be in an uproar . . . they won't be able to get money without your knowledge, and Mailer"—Villari frowned as he continued—"will probably come after you for a little friendly bit of coercion."

A sliver of fear slid up my spine. "So where do we go from here?"

Villari walked over and glared at me. "Listen very carefully. *We* don't go anywhere from here. There is no *we* in this situation. There is nothing for you to do except to go on about your daily life and let the police handle the rest."

I stood and faced Villari. "First you accuse me of being a murderer and now you're telling me that Mailer may come after me, and in both situations you tell me to sit and do nothing. Why don't I just invite the guy over, offer him a knife, and let him slit my throat?"

"Very cute," he responded impatiently. "You don't know what you're getting into. This whole discussion is nothing but wild speculation; we don't have one piece of hard evidence that proves Mailer even met Elizabeth."

"We have Lindsay's word," I stubbornly insisted.

"No, we don't even have that," Villari snapped. "We have Lindsay surmising that Mailer went to see Elizabeth. For all we know, he changed his mind and spent the afternoon in a movie theater eating popcorn."

"You don't believe that."

"It doesn't matter what I believe. If the facts aren't there, there's not a damn thing I can do."

"So you're not even going to look into it?" I asked, shocked.

"Of course I'll check it out, but you stay out of it," he demanded. "Understood?"

"I really don't respond well to people barking out orders," I hissed through clenched teeth.

"I'm not vying for the title of Mr. Popularity right now, Maggie. I'm trying to keep you from becoming another statistic." He took a deep breath and reached over to caress my cheek with the palm of his hand. "I happened to enjoy wrestling around on top of the sheets today and I'd like to think we're moving toward some heavier wrestling *under* the sheets next time, but that only works if you're around to try it again." He smiled. "And again."

I softened a little. "Okay, I won't pursue anything, but I'm still uncomfortable with Lindsay living in that house."

"One thing at a time, Maggie. Let me try to solve the murder first, okay?" He took hold of my arms and pulled me toward him. "This isn't exactly the way I imagined our first sexual encounter would end."

"I'm not sure that what we did would be characterized as a sexual encounter."

The edges of his mouth twitched a little. "Maybe. Maybe not. Either way, I was still hoping for a little affection, maybe a kiss or two, before sending me out the door."

I hooked my fingers in his belt loops and wiggled closer until our hips were touching. "You're still here, Villari. Maybe it's not too late," I murmured.

He reached around my waist and pulled me tighter. "You drive me crazy, Maggie. You're the only person I know who can tick me off and make me horny as hell at the same time."

"I'll take that as a compliment, Detective," I said as he released me and pulled me down the hall to the front door. We stepped outside and stood on the porch holding hands like real sweethearts.

"When the investigation is over, I'd like to take you on a real date, Maggie."

"Think we can make it through a whole evening together without ripping each other apart?"

"I doubt it," he said, "but we'll have a great time finding out."

I laughed and pushed him toward the front steps. "I won't even ask when I'll see you again. You have a nasty habit of showing up at odd times, any time of the day."

He tipped up my chin and kissed me hard on the lips. I stayed on the porch savoring the taste of his lips on mine, and watched silently as he got in the car and backed out of the driveway.

The phone rang while I was still standing outside and I reluctantly ran to catch it before the fourth ring, when the answering machine would automatically pick it up. Although there was no pressing reason to dash across the porch and through the house at a full sprint, I always feel guilty if the machine takes a message while I'm standing right there.

"Hello?"

"Maggie? What's wrong?"

"Nothing," I panted. "Just another sign that my body is completely and totally devoid of any muscle."

Lisa chuckled. "I've been begging you to come to my aerobics class. You'll feel wonderful afterward."

"That is such a crock. I'll feel hot, sweaty, and miserable."

"Only the first couple of weeks, then you'll be amazed at how much better you feel."

"I don't believe a word of it," I grumbled, "but I may not have a choice if I don't want to end up married to my couch and a thick layer of cellulite."

"They've got a beginner's class on Monday morning. Interested?"

"Do you have to be so damned chipper about the idea?"

"Give me a month, Maggie, and I'll have you sounding like a female Richard Simmons."

"That's not exactly motivating," I quipped.

"Maybe not," Lisa said, laughing, "but we'll go with it anyway. I'll pick you up on Monday at eight-thirty. Think of it as inspiration for your sculpting. You'll be able to see bodies in all shapes and sizes."

"Which reminds me, I've got to get to my studio. Things are finally starting to move along a little."

"Does this mean our lunch date is off?"

"Oh, God, Lisa," I exclaimed apologetically, "I completely forgot about that and ate a sandwich with Villari."

"The detective? That absolutely gorgeous detective I met the other day at your house?"

I grunted in agreement.

"Tell me everything. Don't leave out any details, no matter how small."

"Lisa, there's nothing to tell. We both ate peanut-butter sandwiches, drank iced tea, and I talked about the meeting I had with Prestwood, Elizabeth's attorney, this morning. Then he left. End of story."

"Okay, I'm coming over. You're hiding something and it's too hard to drag it out of you over the phone."

"My God, I'm not hiding anything, and besides, even if I was, I've got to get some work done. I haven't done more than a few hours of work since Elizabeth's funeral."

"Fine. Go play in the clay," Lisa said disappointedly. "But I'm coming over for a drink around five, as soon as Joel gets home to watch the baby. I'll bring the vodka; you make the orange juice."

"You're not going to give up, are you?"

"Nope. I want the whole down-and-dirty story, not this rosy picture you're handing me now."

"Okay, I'll see you around five. But you're going to be disappointed. Nothing happened."

"I don't believe you, Maggie. You've got that funny hitch in your voice you always get when you're lying."

"Next you'll be telling me that my nose is growing," I muttered, before hanging up. I poured myself another glass of tea and wandered slowly back to my studio, wondering why I hadn't told Lisa the whole story. We'd been inseparable since college, so my reluctance really surprised me. Maybe I kept it to myself because I was still unsure of how I felt. No doubt Lisa would pry the whole story out of me within fifteen minutes of her arrival, but I needed to think about it myself before I said anything.

My studio, despite its bright and airy atmosphere, smelled musty and was oddly disheartening. Unwrapping the plastic from my latest sculpture, I rocked back on my stool and studied what was essentially a rough draft of the work to come. My fingertips tingled with the anticipation that never failed to arrive the moment I stepped into the studio. Unfortunately, my heart was more reluctant, more hesitant to follow this time. I was well aware that creating was my way of handling my grief, but I had to struggle to begin. Somewhere in the back of my mind, I felt that when this piece was completed, Elizabeth would be irrevocably dead. It was absurd, of course. Elizabeth was already dead. But there it was. Somehow, this sculpture was intricately linked with the finality of her death.

Using my fingers, I began smoothing the clay. I worked slowly and methodically, and was soon lost in my own rhythm, when suddenly the memories crowded in, memories of Elizabeth so strong and vivid that I could all but feel them jockeying for position in my brain. I remembered the time, right after we first met, when she gave me unsolicited advice on my gardening.

Elizabeth had braced her hands on her hips and stood towering over me while I planted my impatiens along the border of my sidewalk. When her shadow fell over me, I looked up to see my grand neighbor standing in my yard looking irritated.

"Why are you planting your flowers like that?" she asked, shaking her head.

"Like what?" was my only reply, although I really wanted to ask what business it was of hers. But I was brought up to be polite, a fairly useless trait I'm quickly learning to slough off.

"All in a row, like little soldiers. Is that the way you see the wildflowers growing when you walk through the woods?"

She must have seen the confusion on my face because she added, "I see you walking on the trail, the one that starts at the back of your property and winds across mine by the stream. My bedroom window overlooks parts of the trail."

I nodded mutely and went back to planting.

She sighed quietly. "I've been told that I can be over-bearing at times," she admitted.

No kidding.

Without waiting for a reply, she continued on. "Apparently I have offended you with my comments about your gardening, although I certainly did not intend to do so. If that's the case, however, I hope you will accept my apology."

I sat back on my heels and examined my handiwork. "You're probably right, though," I admitted. "It is a little rigid. I think they look a little like a marching band with its straight lines and crisp corners," I said, grinning.

She smiled. "Why don't we start over, Maggie? We *are* neighbors and it is so much more pleasant to live amongst friends than enemies. Don't you agree?"

The memory faded and I opened my eyes. The clay sculpture came into focus and I studied it for several minutes without moving. As I sat there, the missing pieces of the puzzle fell softly into place.

Thanks, Elizabeth.

Chapter Sixteen

"Hello, Cassie."

I'd startled her, coming into the room without knocking. Jumping up from the chair, Cassie spun around, her eyes widened in surprise. She was a lovely girl, all blond hair and cornflower-blue eyes. She stood facing me in a black knit dress, her back to the French doors. The sun strode boldly behind her and traced her body in charcoal shadows, silhouetting a proud, feminine form. Staring at her curves was enough to convince me to invest in a little breast enhancement lingerie or at least to start stuffing tissues in my bra.

"Wasn't our little chat this morning enough for you?" she snapped, a swift shadow of anger sweeping across her face as she recognized me.

"It was more than enough until I started working this afternoon. And then, suddenly, everything began to make sense," I said, closing the door behind me. As I walked toward her, I couldn't help admiring the room, with its saffron-colored walls, plump damask sofa, and polished wood floors. There was a mini-bar in the corner with crystal glasses hanging upside down and amber-colored bottles neatly lined against a mirrored wall. Burnished beams lined the ceiling and the windows overlooked a vast carpet of green grass and tall emerald trees. How ironic that such a warm, light-filled room should hold such evil.

"Look, I don't have time for this. Benton should never have let you in without consulting me. I have a dinner to attend."

"Do you mind if I sit down?" I didn't wait for an answer and took a seat on the couch.

"Apparently not," she said, her voice heavy with sarcasm. Cassie sat down in the chair across from me and lifted a slim gold case from the coffee table. Lighting a cigarette, she inhaled deeply. She leaned back into the armchair and crossed her long slender legs, her black high-heeled sandal grazing the carpet. "So, to what do I owe the pleasure of this visit?"

"You killed Elizabeth, Cassie."

She didn't skip a beat. "Did I really?" she asked almost gaily, as though she had just won the church raffle.

Her face was a mask of disinterest. I looked closely for eye tics, narrowing pupils, chewed-off lipstick, even clenched fists but there was nothing. Her features were composed, her expression completely unfazed. All I saw was the same spoiled, haughty face I had always known. For a second I wondered if, after all, I was wrong.

"Exactly how did you come to this conclusion, Maggie? Spending a little too much time alone fiddling with your Play-Doh?"

Her little snooty act didn't sit well with me. "It almost

slipped by me, Cassie. If I hadn't been thinking about Elizabeth this afternoon, I might not have remembered. I guess I was just lucky."

She leaned forward and tapped her cigarette against the crystal ashtray. "Please don't keep me in suspense any longer. If I'm going to be a famous murderess, I need to know right away so I can work out my alibi. Maybe I'll have a new dress made just for the occasion. Something deep red, you know, like blood."

I wanted to slap the girl. She was ripping my confidence to shreds as easily as peeling a banana, while I sat puddled in sweat. But it didn't matter how I felt. This was for Elizabeth.

"It was the scarf, Cassie. . . . the scarf wrapped around her head."

"Grandmother always wore scarves."

"True. But when she wound them around her head, the bow was always placed on the right side, simply because she was right-handed. When she was killed, however, the murderer tied the bow on her left side." I watched Cassie place another cigarette between her lips with her left hand. "I would never have known if I hadn't seen you drinking coffee at my house this morning."

"You think I killed Grandmother because I'm left-handed?" she asked, mocking me. "You might as well lock me up and throw away the key."

I refused to let her condescension rattle me. "You knew exactly how Elizabeth wound a scarf around her head, Cassie, but you knotted it on the left side. But that wasn't all. It was the footprints."

"What footprints?"

"Exactly. Detective Villari said they never found any

footprints other than mine and Elizabeth's, and of course, the serviceman who found your grandmother. I didn't think much about it at the time, not until you sat down in my living room and crossed your ankles."

"I don't understand."

"Your shoes were exactly like the ones Elizabeth always wore. You wear such outrageous-looking shoes most of the time," I said, indicating the black ones she was now wearing as an example, "that your low-heeled pumps made an impression on me. The only person who could tie her scarf exactly the way she did, but on the left side, and also have access to Elizabeth's shoes to wear while carrying her dead body across my yard, is you." I continued on. "The motive was the easy part. Greed and money. I haven't figured out exactly what happened, but I'm positive you overheard something or saw something you thought would jeopardize your mighty inheritance. You have quite a talent for eavesdropping."

After I finished, the accusation dangled in the air, reverberating like a tuning fork against the paneled walls and beamed ceilings. I sat there silently, my hands clasped in my lap. I don't usually sit so quietly, or demurely, but I wanted Cassie to know that I had no doubt about her guilt, and I suspected that silence would unnerve her more than a screaming match.

It came rather quickly. The crack. It wasn't very dramatic, just a small fissure. Her lips tightened imperceptibly and her right hand shook just a little as she brought her cigarette to her lips. Nothing jumped out and screamed, but it was there, and with one glance, she knew I had seen it.

She blew out a small cloud of smoke and viciously

ground her cigarette in the ashtray before standing and towering over me, a female Goliath dressed to the nines.

"Look, you little bitch," she spit out. "I've run out of patience with you and your female Sherlock Holmes act. If you think you can prove a word of what you've said, then do it. Go tell your little detective everything you think you know. But don't forget to include everything. Will told me all about the two of you cozying up the last few days. I wonder how the captain would feel about his detectives messing around with the suspects?"

I stood and faced her, feeling more like the Cowardly Lion than a modern-day David, but I refused to back down, no matter what. "Bottom line, Cassie, you murdered Elizabeth. Nothing changes that fact." I turned and walked away from her, anxious to put some distance between the two of us. A few feet from the door leading into the hallway, I stopped and wheeled around. "As a matter of fact, I will be talking to Detective Villari, and he can do what he wants with it, I don't really care. It doesn't much matter anymore."

Her cold blues eyes met mine.

"Because, as fiduciary," I taunted, exaggerating the word as I drew it out slowly and succinctly, "I'm in control of a huge chunk of change." And then I smiled. "And darlin'," I said, borrowing Villari's hillbilly drawl, "it'll be colder than a welldigger's ass before you see a dime of it." I turned on my heel and strode purposefully toward the door, mentally patting myself on the back, anxious to tell Villari how I'd wrapped up the case.

Then I heard a sharp metal click.

"I wonder what Elizabeth was thinking," she said, her contemptuous voice drifting from behind, "when she included you in the will. You're too stupid to handle a roomful of ten-year-olds much less a large estate. Turn around, Maggie."

I hesitated a second too long. "Turn around," she repeated, her voice low and menacing, "because if you don't, I'll have no choice but to shoot you in the back. It doesn't make the slightest bit of difference to me, although I think it would be rather nice to watch the light die in your eyes. Just think of this as a little favor I'm offering you. How many people get to choose how they die?"

"You're all heart, Cassie," I said, turning to face her. She was standing between the couch and the chair, her legs braced about a foot and a half apart, elbows locked, both hands clamped around a shiny silver pistol pointed directly at my chest.

"I'd keep that smart mouth of yours in check, Maggie," she threatened. "I admire your spirit in the face of overwhelming odds, but stupid is stupid. Speaking of which, what did you think I would do when you came marching over here with your accusations? Roll over, pack my suitcases, and let you chauffeur me quietly to jail? If you were so sure I killed Grandmother, what would keep me from doing the exact same thing to you?"

Okay, she had a point. I had been so full of anger and self-righteousness that I didn't take the time to map out an exit plan. In hindsight, I couldn't have been more stupid, but this was no time for Monday-morning quarterbacking, especially since the chance of actually seeing another Monday was looking rather bleak. I didn't know any more about cops and robbers and catching the bad guys than what I saw on television. And right now, with no cavalry galloping to the rescue, the only tactic I had available to me was to keep her talking.

"Why did you kill her, Cassie?"

"Just drop the innocent act, Maggie. You know all about Lindsay Burns; Will told me about your little meeting with her out at the park. What I want to know is how you discovered her."

"Mark Gossert, from the Outlook Gallery, called me," I lied. "He said that Elizabeth had given him my name. He asked me to bring in some of my pieces, and while we were talking he mentioned Lindsay's name."

"Why would he do that?"

"For the same reason that Elizabeth gave him my name. For the art."

"Yeah, she loved grand gestures, didn't she? She couldn't wait to spend her money on other people, anyone besides her family," she fumed, her grip tightening on the gun.

"I went to see Lindsay," I continued, ignoring her outburst and the fear that was tying my stomach in knots, "because she was Elizabeth's friend. I guess I just wanted to talk to someone who knew Elizabeth the way I did, someone who had been helped along artistically," I finished lamely. The more I talked, the more frightened I became. How could I keep Cassie talking when everything about Elizabeth was bound to anger her?

"So we met at the park," I hurried on, "and talked about Elizabeth for a while and then we moved on to other things—just girl talk. Then I saw Will out in the parking lot and he admitted to following me. You know all the rest."

Cassie studied me, her eyes narrowed and furious, a slow flush crawling up her neck. "You must think I'm a real idiot if you think I'm going to fall for that line of crap. You expect me to believe that you and Lindsay were out at the park playing tea party and catching up on local gossip with a little tear or two for our sad, dearly departed, very dead grandmother?" She sneered with icy contempt.

"Cassie," I said, taking a slow step forward. I had some vague notion of rushing toward her and grabbing the gun from her hand. It was a long shot, but it was all I had right now. "We talked about a lot of things. I can't remember anything specific right now, not with that barrel staring at me, but it was mostly about art. Lindsay paints. She paints landscapes and we met at the park so she could show me the scene she was trying to capture on canvas." I felt myself rearranging everything about that afternoon, throwing in some talk about art for credibility and to keep Cassie talking. For once, my tendency to ramble seemed to be a good thing. The longer I kept Cassie talking, the longer I stayed alive.

"Back off, Maggie. Take another step forward and you'll run into a bullet."

I didn't need to be told twice. I stepped back immediately and started talking again while my mind searched frantically for another plan, some sliver of hope before I was blown to pieces.

"Will told me about Elizabeth's illness."

"Ironic, isn't it?" She giggled, her laugh high-pitched and edged with hysteria. "All that trouble to kill her, and Granny was going to die anyway."

"Cassie, put the gun away," I said gently. "We can work this out. Don't do something you might regret, something that will destroy the rest of your life."

"You've got it all wrong. No piece of white trash is

going to stop me from getting my money. I deserve that money, every last dirty dime of it. I earned it, and I'm not going to let you, Grandmother, or anyone else get in my way."

Who else was there? Earned how? "What are you talking about, Cassie?"

She eased her arms down until the gun hung loosely in one hand. When she saw me studying the distance between the two of us, she shook her head. "Give it up, Maggie. I've taken lessons. I can shoot you dead before you move two feet, toward the door or me. Either way, you'll end up in a coffin."

I believed her. I stood perfectly still, waiting for her to answer my question.

She edged backward until the arms of the chair touched the back of her thighs and she sat down slowly, watching me carefully, but looking drained and emotionally wrung out at the same time. The high color in her cheeks had faded and she suddenly seemed exhausted.

"Nobody knew, of course," she began. "It started so innocently at first, I didn't really mind. In a way, I actually enjoyed the attention. He was very gentle in the beginning. He would sit and talk to me about school, who my friends were, that kind of thing. And the first time he touched me, I hardly even noticed it; he just patted my arm, like a parent almost. For the longest time he didn't do anything more than cuddle and hold me and stroke my shoulders."

Please, God, I thought, don't let this be what I think it is. I was torn between wanting her to keep talking and wanting to cover my ears and block out her voice.

"I was starved for attention after my parents were

killed, and Grandmother, to be fair, was too far gone in her own grieving to notice that I was completely alone. When Will and I first came to live with them, Grand-father was so cold and distant, so austere"—she spoke slowly, her voice settling into a slow monotone—"that I didn't know where to turn or what to do. I went to bed hugging my pillow every night, and by morning it was soaked with tears. The first time he knocked on my door and walked in, I was very afraid. He'd hardly even glanced at me before. I wasn't sure he even knew my name."

Cassie must have seen the horror reflected on my face, but she shook her head before continuing.

"Grandmother never knew. Grandfather was very careful."

"Why didn't you say something?"

She lifted her shoulders in resignation. "Because I was too ashamed, too embarrassed."

"But you were just a young girl. A victim. No one would have blamed you."

A ghost of a grin flitted across her face. Her eyes glazed over. "Maybe. Maybe not. At any rate, by the time I realized that what we were doing was wrong, even perverse, I didn't know how to stop. He was very clever, you know, moving along at such a snail's pace. He seemed so concerned about me and my life that I wasn't really aware of the exact moment when he crossed the line. It seemed like I woke up out of a fog one night and he was on top of me . . . hurting me," she choked, "doing unspeakable things, grunting and moaning, and he was so heavy I couldn't breathe. I started crying and I tried to push him off, but he wouldn't stop. Not for a long time. After he was done, he rolled off me, cleaned himself with a small towel he'd brought with him. He was always prepared, you know. Then he walked into my bathroom, rinsed the same towel with warm water, and washed off the blood between my thighs. I just lay there, dazed and confused, barely listening as he talked about 'our little secret.' He demanded that I keep quiet, insisting that people wouldn't understand how much he loved me and how he wanted only the best for me." Cassie leveled her gaze at me. "I was betrayed. Again. Just like the day my parents died and left me alone. I knew then that nothing is ever what it seems." She shrugged dismissively. "But what could I do? He'd been coming in for weeks, who would believe me when I said I never meant for anything to happen? That I didn't even know what *could* happen?"

"But," I interrupted in frustration, "the man raped you. He would have been thrown in jail for that crime alone, not to mention pedophilia and incest. Cranford Boyer wouldn't have seen the light of day for years."

"I didn't know that then, Maggie. All I knew was that he kept coming, night after night after night, until I didn't care anymore. He came in, patted me on the arm, and I opened the covers to let him in." She stared blankly ahead. "After a while it wasn't so bad. I learned to focus on one single spot between two ceiling tiles until my mind sort of slipped away. I would stay that way until long after he'd left."

I didn't know what to say.

"And then one night he walked in as usual and I pulled the covers aside. He lay beside me and started stroking my body, but something was wrong. He kept touching me, making me touch him, but nothing happened. Before he left, he looked down at me with disgust. He told me that he would never touch me again. Then he was gone. I don't know if it was my developing body he found repulsive or whether he was afraid I was old enough to question what he was doing. Maybe he was afraid I'd report him to the police. At any rate, he never came again, and I was never sure why." Cassie straightened her gun and tightened her finger around the trigger. "You know what? In an odd way I missed him."

"Cassie," I cried, my voice filled with anguish for the hell she had lived through, "why didn't you tell Elizabeth then? Even though it was over, I know she would have believed you. She would have turned Cranford over to the police and taken you to someone you could talk to. She would have helped you."

"You're so naive," she said, casually raising the gun. She closed one eye and peered down the barrel with the other, sighting me like a bottle sitting on top of a fence post. "Elizabeth wouldn't have helped me. She's the reason Grandfather came to me."

"What are you talking about?"

"Grandmother kicked him out of her bedroom the day Will and I moved in. The man had no choice," she stated flatly.

I couldn't believe what I was hearing; she kept vacillating between hating her grandfather for his nocturnal fondling and defending him. "Surely you don't believe that. Normal grown men do not visit little girls in the middle of the night looking for consolation for a broken marriage. The man was a pervert. He should have been castrated and left with the garbage."

She laughed that same crazy-sounding laugh. "You do have an active imagination, Maggie. But it doesn't matter now. Grandmother refused him, so he went out and found other women."

"Cassie, your grandfather cheated on Elizabeth long before you ever arrived at the house. She knew all about his philandering and was willing to overlook it while your father was growing up, but she would never have allowed him to stay in the house knowing what he was doing to you."

"We'll never know if that's true or not, will we?" she said harshly, lowering the gun again. "All we know is that Grandmother let him loose to prowl, and that's exactly what he did until he created another heir."

I didn't want to argue about Elizabeth's relationship with her husband. From everything she had told me, the man was a selfish bastard, and after hearing Cassie's story, I knew even that was too high a compliment. Through some convoluted reasoning, though, Cassie blamed her grandmother for Cranford's perversity, and I didn't see how I could accomplish anything but an earlier visit to the grave by arguing Elizabeth's side.

"Another heir?" I asked tentatively.

Her lips thinned. "Don't pretend you don't know, Maggie. That lowlife came waltzing over here one night, acting as though she owned the place, and tried to extort money from Grandmother."

It was hard to picture Lindsay, complete with bruises and faded dress, trying to blackmail anyone. But as much as I wanted to defend Lindsay, I had to stick with my desperate plan. Keep Cassie talking. The longer I played innocent, the longer I could draw Cassie out. Maybe it wouldn't amount to anything in the long run, but if I did somehow manage to escape, I wanted as much information as possible.

"She blackmailed Elizabeth?" I asked, interested to hear how Cassie's version differed from Lindsay's.

"You're damn right she did. I heard it all. The door was cracked open just enough for the voices to carry and I heard your precious Lindsay spill out her little sob story about her kids and her abusive husband. Grandmother was ready to pull out her checkbook right then and make out a check for some ungodly amount of money. But I wasn't about to let her give that little tramp a single cent of my money."

"What happened?"

Cassie regarded me speculatively. "You'd like to know, wouldn't you? But then, what difference would it make, you'll never leave this room alive. Grandmother made noises about helping Ms. Burns with her art, but I saw through that whole charade. She was planning to put her in the will, to split the inheritance among between the three of us—"

"Lindsay was demanding a third of the money?"

"Not in so many words. Apparently, Grandfather had supported her mother while she was growing up, no doubt to keep her from opening her mouth about their affair. Ms. Burns said she was just asking for introductions to different art dealers, to help her escape her husband."

"But you didn't believe her?"

"It doesn't matter whether I did or not. The point was, Grandmother believed all of it, the whole tragic story," she said, her voice dripping with contempt. "She even picked up the phone and made an appointment with Prestwood—with Lindsay standing right there in the room. Grandmother was always a sucker for the lost and lonely, for the downtrodden. One good look at Lindsay's life and I knew I could kiss my money good-bye."

I was almost afraid to ask the next question. "What did you do then?"

"When the meeting was over, I hid in the hall closet while they left the office and Grandmother walked her out to her car. Then I escaped and ran upstairs to begin making plans. I knew exactly what I had to do," she said, her lips twisting into a cynical smile. "Most importantly, I had to relax and bide my time. But I didn't expect everything to happen so quickly. The next afternoon, Grandmother left the house claiming she had some errands to run. I wanted to follow her, but I knew she'd recognize my car immediately. So I waited until she returned that evening, praying she hadn't gone and given away my inheritance. I was ready to do whatever was necessary."

I took a deep breath, fairly sure of what was going to come next.

"I confronted Grandmother in her office. I demanded to know what was going on—who Lindsay Burns was and what kind of claim she had on the will. But Grandmother ignored me, as usual, and said it was none of my business. She told me not to worry, that I would be taken care of." Cassie's eyes burned in outrage. "I couldn't believe it, and no matter what I said, Grandmother continued working at her desk as though I hadn't spoken, like I was no more than a pesky mosquito she could flick away." Her voice turned low and furious. "But I wasn't going away. That money was *mine*. I deserved it. I earned it . . . night after night. But Grandmother's mind was made up. I forced myself to remain calm, to do what had to be done. I took a deep breath and smiled at Grandmother. I told her I trusted her. I went around to her side to say good night. I bent down to kiss her cheek, picked up the bronze statue off the credenza behind her desk, and slammed the back of her head." Her eyes glittered when she looked at me. "It was a sculpture you had given to her as a gift."

My hands were shaking so hard I had to clench them together, but my knees started to fold and I didn't know how long I could keep myself upright. Cassie's eyes were dead and flat now; no spark of life or even a flare of anger lit them any longer. For the first time I wanted her to stop talking, to take back the pictures of that horrible night. But her words lay bare between us.

"It was perfect. Grandmother simply slumped forward, her forehead landing on the papers she was working on. I untied the scarf she was wearing around her neck and wrapped it around her head to keep any blood spots off the floor when I picked her up. Then I took off the coat I was wearing and wrapped her in it. I lifted her into my arms and took one last glance around the room before turning off the light." She ran one hand through her hair and continued emotionlessly. "I was lucky. Other than what was on the papers and file, there was no blood to clean up. Even in death, Grandmother was very neat and tidy."

Cassie described the scene dispassionately, her voice flat. Her very lack of feeling, her impassivity nauseated me. Bile rose up in my throat, threatening to choke me. I no longer cared about listening to her rant on; all I wanted was to grab the gun and turn it on her.

"She was amazingly light. I carried her across the driveway and through the hedges between our yards, just like I'd seen her do so many times when she went to visit you. You were right. I wore a pair of her low-heeled pumps so the footprints wouldn't raise suspicion. In fact, that was really the only uncomfortable part of the whole journey—Grandmother's feet were smaller than mine."

"But why the septic tank?"

She grinned like an evil Cheshire cat toying with a doomed mouse. "Because it was perfect, don't you see? There I was driving home earlier that afternoon before meeting with Grandmother and I happened to glance over at your yard. Your repairman was climbing into his truck after working on your tank, cordoning the area off with little yellow flags. It had to be fate. One look at those cute little flags fluttering in the summer breeze and everything just fell into place."

Cassie stood then, in almost the exact same spot she was standing when I first burst through the door firing accusations. Her smile faded. "Your lights were out when I came through the hedge. My only concern was getting the cement lid off while carrying Grandmother. I needed to use both hands. I didn't want to put her down and leave an imprint of her body on the ground, so I walked over to your flower garden and put her in the wheelbarrow you have leaning against the wall. Lifting the cover wasn't easy, but even that wasn't the obstacle it could have been since your repairman had removed it the day before. I pushed it over and dumped her in. Everything went off without a hitch, perfectly choreographed. And the best part was still to come."

I couldn't imagine what she meant by that.

"The murder solved more than one problem, Maggie. It eliminated Grandmother before she had a chance to change the will and divide Will's and my inheritance with a stranger. But Lindsay still posed a threat to the money. Much to my delight, Grandmother had written her name and address in her appointment book, which saved me from having to pencil it in myself. I knew the police would eventually comb through her desk and files and discover her name. Without too much trouble, the cops would discover Lindsay's relationship to Grandmother, and with me there to point the boys in the proper direction, they would find out about Lindsay's blackmailing scheme. Lindsay Burns would be an immediate suspect with an obvious motive. Once they convicted her, Will and I would be safe. The money would be intact and it would be ours. And, of course, you were a bonus."

"I don't understand what you mean."

"With Grandmother slipping your name into the will, and with the body in your front yard, the cops started breathing down your neck pretty hard and fast, and I didn't have to do anything but sit back and watch you squirm. Of course, I knew that wouldn't last long; they wouldn't have any physical evidence to pin on you and you did an excellent job of pretending to know nothing about the will, so it was only a matter of time before the suspicion shifted from you to Ms. Burns."

"I wonder why Lindsay didn't mention the cops questioning her during our conversation," I said, knowing full well that the police had never found Elizabeth's appointment book and that I myself had given Villari Lindsay's name, and had done so just this afternoon.

Cassie frowned, a fine line furrowing her brow. "Yes, there's been a slight problem. Grandmother's date book disappeared sometime after the murder, although whether a cop took it or it was misplaced by the cleaning ladies, I don't know. Apparently, I will have to devise another way of dropping her name somewhere for the police to discover themselves—but I don't see that being too much of a problem. Now, all that being said, I'm afraid you came at a very inopportune time. I have an appointment and I do hate being late. So if you'll excuse me . . ."

She spoke in such polite tones that I was ready to step aside and let her pass. It wasn't until she raised her arms and leveled the gun at my chest that I came out of my stupor and realized she was preparing to shoot me. For real this time. My body stiffened. I stared right into the long dark tunnel of that gun barrel, my heart pounding like a bongo drum, beating so loudly I couldn't hear myself praying.

Then the glass shattered. A large rock crashed to the floor.

Cassie whirled around and fired.

I hit the ground without thinking and crossed my hands over the back of my head. The room exploded with glass as Cassie fell into a low crouch and methodically shot out the large windowpanes. I managed to crawl on my elbows and knees behind the mini-bar. The wooden counter didn't offer much protection, but I was in no position to be choosy. I curled up into a fetal position, jammed myself back into the corner, and squeezed my eyes shut. The noise was deafening, but it wasn't long before I realized that all the gunshots were being fired from the inside. Cassie was the only one shooting.

Then I heard quick footsteps.

"Don't shoot or I'll kill her!"

Burning heat stroked the side of my cheek. I opened my eyes to see Cassie standing serenely overhead, her gun barrel a few inches from my face. "Stand up, Maggie," she ordered with calm authority.

My body refused to cooperate. Believe me, I tried to do as she asked, but I'd been so tightly wound up that my muscles were cramped into stiff little knots.

"Get the fuck up before I lose my patience," she repeated. Her voice, laced with just a hint of a Southern drawl, dripped with molasses sweetness. Cassie sounded more like she was offering an assortment of delicate pastries to her guests at a tea party than getting ready to shoot me in cold blood.

"Put the gun down and no one will get hurt." I recognized Villari's voice as he yelled through the broken windows. "Police officers are surrounding the house. There's no way out."

Cassie reached down and clamped her hand around the top of my arm, her fingernails digging deep into my flesh. "Move your ass now, or I'll blow your brains out all over Grandmother's pristine floors."

I did as she said. Uncurling my body, I pushed myself up until I was standing awkwardly on two wobbly legs. She grabbed me around my waist with her right arm and yanked me against her body, pressing the barrel of the pistol firmly against my temple.

"Don't do anything stupid, Detective. I've got your little sweetheart," she taunted, her voice coming over my right shoulder. "One wrong move and sweet Maggie here will be splattered all over the wall. And then where would you sleep?"

Several seconds ticked by slowly. "Let her go," he said tightly. "Don't hurt her."

"How very touching, Maggie. The man obviously cares for you. Too bad he has such lousy timing, bursting in when we were having such a nice little chat." She took two steps back, dragging me along with her. "Tell your men to drop their guns, Detective—that is, if there really are any other cops around. I'm not completely convinced you aren't the last of the white knights, riding over here on your big white horse all by yourself. But either way, if you do exactly what I say, your girlfriend may live to see another day."

"What do you want me to do?" he asked tersely.

"Stand up and let me see you. I don't enjoy talking to a voice."

Villari stepped in front of the gaping hole where the windows had been, shards of glass hanging like icicles from splintered frames. His mouth was drawn into a taut line and a muscle flicked angrily in his jaw. His eyes bored into mine. "Are you all right?"

I tried to speak, but the words were stuck in my throat.

"She's fine," Cassie assured him, jerking me even closer, her chin now resting on the top of my shoulder, her cheek grazing mine. I tried to pull back, I couldn't stand the feel of her skin against mine, but she tightened her grip and laughed. "Aren't you, Maggie dear? Or maybe you're a little uncomfortable? Don't worry, it won't be long before you and the detective will be wrapped in each other's arms forever."

Then I snapped.

Without thinking, I snapped my arm upward and smashed the back of my clenched fist into that haughty little nose, feeling bones crunch under my knuckles. At the sound of her scream, I rapidly brought my hand forward and thrust my elbow hard into her stomach while simultaneously lifting my foot and slamming it heavily on top of her expensively clad toes. I jerked away as she released her hold and started falling to the floor. Swinging around, I grabbed her hair and rammed my knee into her face. I leaned down and picked up the gun that had dropped sometime during our fight. I slid my palm around the handle and pointed the barrel down at Cassie.

"A little uncomfortable, Cassie?" Blood gushed from her nose and mouth as she rolled from side to side, fighting the pain that flooded her body. Her screaming had subsided to odd choking noises as she tried to keep from suffocating, with blood coating her face like a rubber mask. I heard smashing glass behind me as Villari cleared an area of broken panes and climbed through to stand beside me. He quietly covered my hand with his.

"Pretty impressive, Maggie," he said, gently prying the gun from my hand.

"Martial Arts 101 . . . in college . . . with Lisa. Can't believe I remembered a thing."

"I'm glad you did. We were in a world of hurt."

"Why aren't the boys in blue racing into the room right now, Villari?"

"The patrolman mentioned he saw you heading over here." He shrugged, relief filling his eyes. "Besides, why do I need backup when I've got Jackie Chan in the room?"

"*Ms*. Chan to you."

Chapter Seventeen

"Matthew, honey, would you like a little more spaghetti?"

I glanced over at the towheaded five-year-old wearing more tomato sauce around his mouth than he had swallowed. But he was up on his knees, a large dish towel tied around his neck like a bib, his eyes as round as saucers, and his mouth turned up in a wide silly grin. His mother leaned over and tried to mop up the mess, but it was useless. The only thing that would clean up that kid was a good thorough dunking in a bathtub or running him through a complete cycle in the washing machine.

"The boy's hungry. Let him eat." Villari's father leaned over and patted Matthew on the back. "Isn't that right, Matt? You've got a lot of eating to do if you're going to grow as tall as your mama." Lindsay smiled, shook her head at the sight of her son, and resumed eating.

Matthew giggled and dug into the second mound of spaghetti that the "Dragon Lady" had piled on his plate. It was hard to believe this was the same family that had arrived on the Villari porch over a week ago. Clutching his mother's hand and hiding behind her skirt, Matthew had been so shy and quiet that I wondered if anyone would ever be able to reach him. But things were changing by the moment. Even the baby seemed to sense the difference, no longer clinging to her mother and staring out with dull listless eyes. She was sitting up in the high chair, banging her plastic cup, intermittently cooing and gnawing on the pieces of pasta Lindsay placed on her tray.

And then there was Lindsay. I thought I could see the tension in her face easing a bit at a time. Her eyes were softer, less furtive and worried, the furrows in her forehead smoothed out a little, her mouth not quite as taut. But she held herself tightly, just as she had that afternoon we spent together at the park, wrapping her arms around her middle as though she was still protecting herself from uncontrollable rage and unpredictable fists. I didn't know how long it would take for her to unwrap herself, to feel free and unafraid. Maybe it would never happen. I wasn't sure how long a person could live with a nightmare before the nightmare simply became a part of herself.

"Maggie, eat. You're still a bag of bones and that's an insult to my cooking." The Dragon Lady smiled down at me from the head of the table. I needed a new nickname for Villari's mother. Although she could instill fear in any of her grown children with one look of displeasure, she had freely opened her house and home to

Lindsay and her kids for as long as they needed, no questions asked.

Villari had gone to Lindsay's house the day after Cassie had attempted to kill me, the day after I knocked her flat with my incredible fighting skills. Villari insisted that it was the element of surprise that saved me, although I personally believe it was sheer fright. I was seconds away from death . . . a woman can do a lot of damage if she thinks her life is ending before the next commercial. But whatever it was, Cassie was going to rot in jail for a long time, maybe in that nasty cell Villari had threatened me with. The roaches will love her. Will was shell-shocked after hearing the whole story, although I know his pain will ease once he realizes that he has a good chance of going to court and claiming his sister's portion of the inheritance for himself. Large sums of money can soothe a lot of aches and pains.

Anyway, even though Cassie had confessed to her crime during our little hair-raising discussion, and the case was for all intents and purposes closed, Villari couldn't stand the idea that Lindsay was still stuck in that house with her abusive husband. Especially since Elizabeth had fully intended to help the woman. So deciding to bypass the red tape, he went to Lindsay's house one evening when he was sure that Vacuum Nose would be at home. Before I knew it, Villari was driving up to my house with a woman, two kids, and a few ratty old suitcases. He picked me up without saying a word and we headed out to his mother's.

I don't know what happened at Lindsay's house. Villari never said and Lindsay refused to speak a word about it. But I have a feeling that Villari didn't follow the rules that day.

When dinner was over and we had said our good-byes to the family, Villari drove me home. We didn't talk much, but it was a comfortable silence, and I leaned my head on his shoulder and closed my eyes until we pulled up in my driveway. Villari and I walked hand in hand to the porch, softly lit by a single yellow bulb. I unlocked the door and pushed it open, the shadows embracing the two of us like quiet lovers.

Villari shut the door and gathered me into his arms, just holding me. I laid my forehead against his chest, breathing in the fresh cotton smell of his T-shirt that always reminded me of clothes hanging out to dry on a hot summer's day. I lifted my head and searched his coal-black eyes, so dark I couldn't see the pupils. A moment passed as we simply gazed at each other. Then, lifting one hand, he held my face gently. He leaned down and brushed his lips against mine, a mere whisper of a kiss. It wasn't enough. I stood on tiptoe and curled my arm around his neck, pulling him closer and demanding more. I felt him smile against my lips. And I smiled back.

"Come here," I whispered. "There's something I want to show you." I took his hand and laced my fingers through his. We walked down the hallway and I could see the surprise in his face when I pulled him past the bedroom. I stepped into my studio with him by my side.

"There," I said, indicating the bust in the middle of the room.

I knew the moment he recognized her. His eyes widened slightly and he tightened his hold on my hand.

It was Elizabeth. In all her glory, with all her patrician haughtiness and all her kindness that overflowed like a waterfall. I had tried to capture it in my sculpture. I think she would have been proud.

Except for one thing. Her voice was as clear as a bell in my head, demanding that I quit wasting time staring at her and take that gorgeous man to bed.

So I did.